Praise for Nicci French

"Razor-sharp writing by French expertly amps the tension."

—*People*

"Reads like lightning."

—*The Guardian* (UK)

"Genuine chills and page-turning suspense."

—*Entertainment Weekly*

"Fabulous, unsettling, and riveting."

—Louise Penny

"Nicci French has become synonymous with suspense."

—*Daily News* (New York)

"Complex. . . . Intriguing. . . . Truly unique."

—Tami Hoag

"Psychological suspense at its brightest and most blazing."

—A. J. Finn

"Excellent psychological suspense . . . a book for your 'must list.'"

—Popular Culture Association

"Unforgettable. Psychological dynamite."

—Alan Bradley

"Ingenious . . . French continues to impress."

—*Publishers Weekly*

WHAT TO DO
WHEN
SOMEONE
DIES

Books by Nicci French

WHAT TO DO
WHEN
SOMEONE
DIES

A Novel

NICCI
FRENCH

wm

WILLIAM MORROW
An Imprint of HarperCollins*Publishers*

WHAT TO DO WHEN SOMEONE DIES. Copyright © 2008 by Nicci French. Excerpt from HOUSE OF CORRECTION © 2020 by Nicci French. All rights reserved. Printed in the United States of America. No part of this book may be used or reproduced in any manner whatsoever without written permission except in the case of brief quotations embodied in critical articles and reviews. For information, address HarperCollins Publishers, 195 Broadway, New York, NY 10007.

HarperCollins books may be purchased for educational, business, or sales promotional use. For information, please email the Special Markets Department at SPsales@harpercollins.com.

Originally published in the United Kingdom in 2008 by Michael Joseph, an imprint of Penguin Books.

FIRST U.S. EDITION PUBLISHED 2021.

Designed by Diahann Sturge

Library of Congress Cataloging-in-Publication Data has been applied for.

ISBN 978-0-06-287609-6

21 22 23 24 25   LSC   10 9 8 7 6 5 4 3 2 1

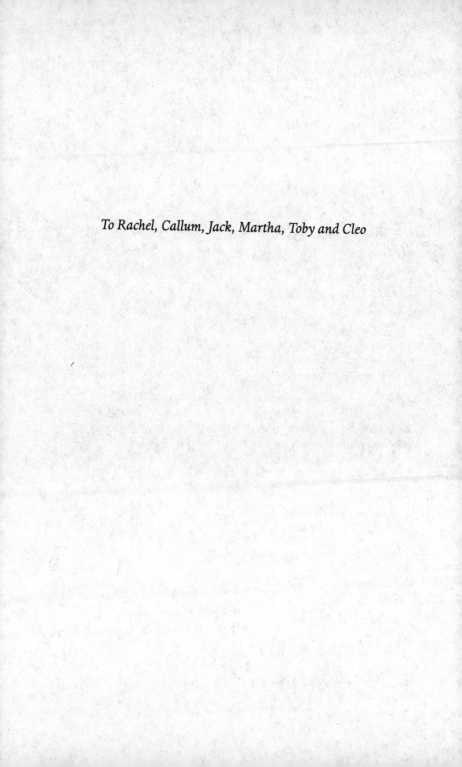

To Rachel, Callum, Jack, Martha, Toby and Cleo

Chapter One

Moments when your life changes: there will always be a before and an after, separated, perhaps, by a knock at the door. I had been interrupted. I was tidying up. I had cleared up yesterday's newspapers, old envelopes, scraps of paper, left them in the basket by the grate ready to make a fire after supper. I had just got the rice bubbling nicely. My first thought was that it was Greg and he had forgotten his keys, but then I remembered he couldn't have because he had taken the car that morning. Anyway, he probably wouldn't knock but shout through the letterbox. A friend, perhaps, or a neighbor, a Jehovah's Witness, a cold call from a desperate young man trying to sell dusters and clothes-pegs house-to-house. I turned away from the stove and went through the hall to the front door, opened it to a gust of cool air.

Not Greg, not a friend, not a neighbor, not a stranger selling religion or domesticity. Two female police officers stood in front of me. One looked like a schoolgirl, with a block fringe covering her eyebrows and jug ears; one was like her teacher, with a square jaw and graying hair cut mannishly short.

"Yes?" Had I been caught speeding? Littering? But then I saw an expression of uncertainty, even surprise, on both their faces and felt the first small prickle of foreboding in my chest.

"Mrs. Manning?"

"My name's Eleanor Falkner," I said, "but I'm married to Greg Manning, so you could say . . ." My words trailed away. "What is it?"

"Can we come in?"

I led them into the small living room.

"You're the wife of Mr. Gregory Manning?"

"Yes."

I heard everything, I noticed everything. I saw how the younger one looked up at the older one as she said the words, and I noticed she had a hole in her black tights. The older officer's mouth opened and closed but didn't seem synchronized with the words she was speaking so that I had to strain to make sense of them. The smell of risotto reached me from the kitchen, and I remembered that I hadn't turned the ring off and it would be dry and ruined. Then I remembered, with a stupid dullness, that of course it didn't matter if it was ruined: nobody would be eating it now. Behind me I heard the wind fling a few dry leaves against the bay window. It was dark outside. Dark and chilly. In a few weeks' time the clocks would go back. In a couple of months it would be Christmas.

She said, "I am very sorry, your husband has been in a fatal accident."

"I don't understand." Though I did. The words made sense. Fatal accident. My legs felt as if they didn't know how to hold me up any more.

"Can we get you something? A glass of water, perhaps?"

"You say . . ."

"Your husband's car left the road," she said slowly and patiently. Her mouth stretched and shrank.

"Dead?"

"I'm very sorry," she said. "Sorry for your loss."

"The car caught fire." It was the first time the younger woman had spoken. Her face was plump and pale; there was a faint smudge of mascara under one of her brown eyes. She wears contact lenses, I thought.

"Mrs. Falkner, do you understand what we have said?"

"Yes."

"There was a passenger in the car."

"Sorry?"

"He was with someone else. A woman. We thought . . . Well, we had thought it might be you."

I stared dumbly at her. Did she expect me to produce identification?

"Do you know who that would have been?"

"I was just cooking supper for us. He should have been home by now."

"Your husband's passenger."

"I don't know." I rubbed my face. "Didn't she have her bag with her or anything?"

"They couldn't recover much. Because of the fire."

I put a hand against my chest and felt my heart beating heavily. "Are you sure it was Greg? There might have been a mistake."

"He was driving a red Citroën Saxo," she said. She looked down at her notebook and read out the registration number. "Your husband is the owner of the vehicle?"

"Yes," I said. It was hard to speak properly. "Perhaps someone from work. He sometimes took them when he went to visit clients. Tania." I found, as I was speaking, that I couldn't bring myself to care if Tania was also dead. I knew that later this might disturb me.

"Tania?"

"Tania Lott. From his office."

"Do you have her home number?"

I thought for a moment. It would be on Greg's mobile, which was with him. I swallowed hard. "I don't think so. It might be somewhere. Do you want me to look?"

"We can find out."

"I don't want you to think me rude, but I'd like you to go now."

"Have you got someone you can call? A relative or friend?"

"What?"

"You shouldn't be alone."

"I want to be alone," I said.

"You might want to talk to someone." The younger woman pulled a leaflet out of her pocket: she must have put it there before they'd left the station together. All prepared. I wondered how many times they did this in a year. They must get used to it, standing on a doorstep in all weathers with an expression of sympathy on their faces. "There are numbers here of counselors who can help you."

"Thank you." I took the leaflet she was holding out and put it on the table.

Then she offered me a card.

"You can reach me here if you need anything."

"Thank you."

"Will you be all right?"

"Yes," I said, more loudly than I'd meant to. "Excuse me, I think the pan might have boiled dry. I should rescue it. Can you let yourselves out?"

I left the room, with the two women still standing awkwardly in it, and went into the kitchen. I took the pan off the hob and poked at the sticky mess of burnt risotto with a wooden spoon. Greg loved risotto; it was the first meal he had ever cooked me. Risotto with red wine and green salad. I had a sudden clear picture of him sitting at the kitchen table in his shabby home clothes, smiling at me and lifting his glass in greeting, and I spun around, thinking that if I was quick enough I could catch him there.

Sorry for your loss.

Fatal accident.

This is not my world. Something is wrong, askew. It is a Monday evening in October. I am Ellie Falkner, thirty-four years old and married to Greg Manning. Although two police officers have just come to my door and told me he is dead, I know that can't be true because it happens in a world meant for other people.

I sat down at the kitchen table and waited. I didn't know what I was waiting for; perhaps to feel something. People cry when a loved one dies, don't they? Howl and sob, tears running down their cheeks. There was no doubt that Greg was my loved one, my dear heart, but I had never felt less like crying. My eyes were dry and hot; my throat ached slightly, as if I was coming down with a cold. My stomach ached too, and I put my hand on my belly for a few seconds and closed my eyes. There were crumbs on the surface, from breakfast. Toast and marmalade. Coffee.

What had he said when he left? I couldn't think. It had been just another Monday morning, gray sky and puddles on the pavement. When had he last kissed me? On the cheek or on the lips? We'd had a stupid argument on the phone that afternoon, just a few hours ago, about what time he was coming home. Had those been our last words? Little bickering phrases before the great silence. For a moment I couldn't even remember his face, but then it came back to me: his curly hair and his dark eyes and the way he smiles. Smiled. His strong, capable hands, his solid warmth. It had to be a mistake.

I stood up, pulled the phone from its holster on the wall and punched in the number of his mobile. I waited to hear his voice and, after a few minutes, when I didn't, I put the phone carefully back and went to press my face to the window. There was a cat walking along the garden wall, very delicately. I could see its eyes shining. I watched until it disappeared.

I took a forkful of rice out of the pan and put it into my mouth. It had no taste. Perhaps I should pour myself a glass of whisky. That was what people did when they were in shock, and I supposed I must be in shock. But I didn't think we had any whisky in the house. I pulled open the drinks cupboard and gazed at the contents. There was a bottle of gin, a third full; a bottle of Pimm's, but that was for lazy, hot summer evenings a long way from here, from now; a small bottle of schnapps. I twisted the lid off and took an experimental sip, feeling its burning thread in my throat.

Burst into flames. Burst into flames.

I tried not to see his face on fire, his body consumed. I pressed the palms of my hands into the sockets of my eyes and the smallest sound escaped me. It was so quiet in the house. All the noises came from outside: the wind in the trees, the sound of cars passing, doors slamming, people getting on with their normal lives.

I don't know how long I stood there like that, but at last I went up the stairs, gripping the banisters and hauling my weight from step to step like an old woman. I was a widow. Who was going to set the video for me, who was going to help me fail to do the crossword on Sunday, who was going to keep me warm at night, to hold me tight and keep me safe? I thought these things, but did not feel them. I stood in our bedroom for several minutes, gazing around me, then sat heavily on the bed—on my side, careful not to disturb Greg's space. He was reading a travel book: he wanted us to go to India together. There was a bookmark a third of the way through. His dressing-gown—gray and blue stripes—hung on the hook on the door. There were slippers with their heels turned down under the old wooden chair, and on top of it a pair of jeans he'd worn yesterday with an old blue jumper. I went and picked it up, burying my face in the familiar sawdusty smell. Then I took off my own and pulled Greg's over my head. There was a bald patch in one elbow and the hem was fraying.

I wandered into the small room next door to our bedroom, which, for the time being, served as a junk room, although we had plans for it. It was full of boxes of books and stray objects we'd never got around to unpacking, though we had moved to this house well over a year ago, as well as an old-fashioned bath with claw feet and cracked brass taps that I had picked up from a reclamation center and had planned to install in our bathroom once I had done something about the taps. We had got stuck carrying it up the stairs, I remembered, unable to go backward or forward and giggling helplessly, while his mother had shouted useless instructions at us from the hallway.

His mother. I had to call his mother and father. I had to tell them that their eldest son was dead. I felt breathless and had to lean against the door jamb. How do you break that kind of news? I returned to the bedroom and sat on the bed once more, picking up the phone that was on my bedside table. For a moment, I couldn't remember their number, and when I did, I found it hard to press the buttons. My fingers weren't working properly.

I hoped she wouldn't answer, but she did. Her high voice sounded aggrieved to be called at this late hour.

"Kitty." I pressed the receiver to my ear and closed my eyes. "It's me, Ellie."

"Ellie, how—"

"I've got some bad news," I said. And then, before she could draw breath to say anything: "Greg's dead." There was complete silence from the other end, as if she had hung up. "Kitty?"

"Hello," she said. Her voice had dwindled; she sounded very far away. "I don't quite understand."

"Greg's dead," I persisted. "He died in a car crash. I've only just heard."

"Excuse me," she said. "Can you hold on a moment?"

I waited and then another voice came on the line, in a kind of gruff, no-nonsense bark. "Ellie. Paul here. What's this?"

I repeated what I'd said. The words were becoming more and more unreal.

Paul Manning gave a short, nervous cough. "Dead, you say?" In the background I could hear sobbing.

"Yes."

"But he's only thirty-eight."

"It was a road accident."

"A crash?"

"Yes."

"Where?"

"I don't know. I don't know if they told me; maybe they did. It was hard to take everything in."

He asked me more questions, detailed questions, none of which I could answer. It was as if information would give him some kind of control.

Then I dialed my parents' number. That's what you do, isn't it? Even though you may not be close to them, that's the right order. His parents, then my parents. Chief mourners. But there was no reply and I remembered that Monday was quiz night at the pub. They would stay until closing time. I depressed the button and sat for a few seconds listening to the dial tone in my ear. The alarm clock on Greg's side of the bed told me it was thirteen minutes past nine. Hours to go before morning came. What was I supposed to do until then? Should I start calling people, telling them the news in descending order of importance? That was what you did when a baby was born—but was it the same when a husband had died? And who should I tell first? Then it came to me.

I found her home number in Greg's old address book. The phone rang several times, four, five, six. It was like a terrible game. Answer the phone and you're still alive. Don't answer and you're dead. Or perhaps just out.

"Hello."

"Oh." For a moment I couldn't speak. "Is that Tania?" I asked, although I knew it was.

"Yes. Who's this?"

"It's Ellie."

"Ellie. Hi."

She waited, probably expecting an invitation. I took a deep breath and said the nonsense words again. "Greg's dead. In an accident." I cut into the expressions of horror that came down the line. "I rang you because, well, I thought you might have been with him. In the car."

"Me? What do you mean?"

"He had a passenger. A woman. And I assumed, you know, that it was someone from the office, so I thought . . ."

"Two of them died?"

"Yes."

"Christ."

"Yes."

"Ellie, how awful. God, I can't get my head around this. I'm so incredibly . . ."

"Do you know who it could have been, Tania?"

"No."

"He didn't leave with anyone?" I asked. "Or go to meet anyone?"

"No. He left about half past five. And I know he'd said earlier he was going to get home in good time for once."

"He said he was coming straight home?"

"I assumed that. But, Ellie . . ."

"What?"

"It might not mean what you're thinking."

"What am I thinking?"

"Nothing. Listen, if there's anything, anything at all, I can do, you only have to—"

"Thanks," I said, and put the phone down on her.

What was I thinking? What might it not mean? I didn't know. I only knew it was cold outside, and that time moved sluggishly on, and there was nothing I could do to make it go faster. I crept downstairs and sat on the sofa in the living room, Greg's jersey pulled down over my knees. I waited for it to be morning.

Chapter Two

The sound of the newspaper and then, a few minutes later, a bundle of post being pushed through the letterbox and hitting the mat was a reminder that the world was outside, trying to get in. Soon there would be things to do, duties to fulfill, responsibilities, observances. But first I phoned Tania again. "I'm sorry," I said. "I wanted to catch you before you went to work."

"I've been thinking about it all night," she said. "I've hardly slept. I can't believe it."

"When you get in, could you check who Greg was seeing yesterday?"

"He just spent the day at the office, then left to go home."

"He might have called in on a client on his way, dropped something off. If you could have a look at his diary . . ."

"I'll do anything, Ellie," said Tania, "but what am I looking for?"

"Ask Joe if Greg said anything to him yesterday."

"Joe wasn't in the office. He was on a visit."

"It was a woman."

"Yes, I knew that. I'll try."

I thanked her and put the phone down. It rang instantly. Greg's father had questions he wanted to ask me. He sounded formal and rehearsed, as if he had written them down before speaking to me. I wasn't able to answer any of them. I had already told him everything I knew. He told me that Kitty hadn't slept the whole night and I wondered if he was making a point about who was mourning most. When he put the phone down, I felt I had failed a test. I wasn't being an adequate wife. Widow. The word almost made me laugh. It wasn't a word for people like me. It was for old women with headscarves, pulling shopping baskets on wheels, women who had expected widowhood, had prepared for and accepted it.

I played over in my mind the exact moment when the policewoman had told me the news, that moment of transition. It was a line drawn across my life and everything after it would be different. I wasn't at all hungry or thirsty but I decided I ought to have something. I walked into the kitchen and the sight of Greg's leather jacket draped over one of the chairs hit me so that I could hardly breathe. I used to complain about that. Why couldn't he hang it on a proper hook, out of the way? Now I leaned down and tried to smell him on it. There would be a lot of moments like that. As I made myself coffee there were more of them. The coffee was Brazilian, a kind he always chose. The mug I took from the cupboard was from the gift shop of a nuclear-power station; Greg had got it as a joke. When I opened the fridge door, I was bombarded with memories, things he had bought, things I had bought for him, his preferences, his aversions.

I realized that the house was still almost as it had been when he had left it, but with every action I took, every door I opened, everything I used or moved, I was eliminating his presence, making him that little bit deader. On the other hand, how did that matter? He was dead. I took his jacket and hung it on the hook in the hall, the way I'd always nagged him to do.

My mobile was on the shelf there and I saw I had a text message—and then that it was from Greg, and for a moment I felt as though someone had taken my heart in their two hands and wrung it out like a flannel. With thick fingers, I called it up. It had been sent yesterday, shortly after I'd got upset with him for staying later at the office than he'd promised, and it wasn't very long: "Sorry sorry sorry sorry sorry. Im a stupid fool." I stared at the message, then pressed the phone against my cheek, as if there was a bit of him left behind in the message that could enter me.

I took the coffee, his address book, my address book and a notebook and started to think of who I should call. I was immediately reminded of the party we had given earlier in the year, halfway between his birthday and mine. Same address books, same table and much the same sort of decisions. Who absolutely had to be invited? Who did we want? Who didn't we want? If we invited X, we had to invite Y. If we invited A, we mustn't invite B.

I felt as if my mind wasn't working properly and that I had to write everything down, so that I didn't forget someone or ring someone twice. There were close friends I would have to try to reach before they left for work. First of all, though, I rang my parents once more, dreading the call but knowing they would both be there at that time of morning.

My father answered and immediately called my mother so they were both on the line. Then they began telling me about a friend of theirs—did I remember Tony, who had just been diagnosed with diabetes and it was all because he ate too much, wasn't that a ridiculous thing and why couldn't people exercise control over their lives? I kept trying to interrupt them and finally managed to insert a loud "Please!" between two sentences and blurted it all out.

There was a sudden outpouring of emotion and then of questions. When had it happened? Was I all right? Did I need any help? Should my mother come over right now? Should they both come over? Had I told my sister or should she do that for me? And what about Aunt Caroline—she had to know? I told them I had to go, I would speak to them later, but right now I had calls to make and things to do. When I put the phone down, I thought about that. What were the things I had to do? There were death certificates to be signed. Wills to be read. A funeral. Did I have to do all that or did it happen automatically?

I needed to speak to Joe, Greg's partner and his dear friend. But I only got through to his answering machine, and I couldn't bear to break the news like that. I imagined his face when he heard, his blazing blue eyes; he would be able to cry the tears I didn't yet seem able to. Tania would have to tell him for me. I thought she'd want to anyway; she was new to the company and adored Joe, as a schoolgirl adores a movie star.

I went through Greg's address book and mine and wrote out a list of forty-three people. It was a more select group than had been at our party. Then we had invited plenty of people we hadn't seen since the previous year's party, some neighbors, people we were gradually losing touch with. They would find out on the grapevine, or when they got in touch with me, or perhaps some would never find out. They would wonder occasionally what had happened to old Greg and Ellie and then they would think of something else.

I got the phone and started calling the people roughly in the order they had come out of my address book and then out of Greg's. The first was Gwen Abbott, one of my oldest friends, and the last was Ollie Wilkes, the one cousin Greg had stayed closely in touch with. Making that first call, I could hardly punch out the number, my hands were trembling so much. When I told Gwen and heard her cry of shock and surprise, I felt that I was experiencing it all over again, except that it was worse because the blow was struck on bruised and broken flesh. After I had put the phone down I simply sat, almost gasping for breath, as if I was in thin air at high altitude. I felt I couldn't go through with it, reliving the moment through other people over and over again.

But it got easier. I found a form of words that worked and practiced it before making the calls. "Hello, this is Ellie. I've got some bad news . . ." After a few times, I became quite calm about it. I managed to steer each conversation and bring it to a fairly quick close. I had a few set phrases. "I have things to do"; "I'm sorry, I can't really talk about him at the moment"; "That's very kind of you." It was worst with his dearest friend Fergus who had loved Greg for much longer than I had. He'd been his running companion, confidant, surrogate brother, best man. He said, "What will we do without him, Ellie?" I heard his dazed, cracked voice and thought, Thats how I'm feeling too; I just don't know it yet. I felt about grief as if it was crouching out of sight in hiding from me, waiting to spring out and ambush me when I least expected it.

Halfway through the list, there was an urgent knocking at the door and I opened it to find Joe standing there. He was in a suit and carrying the familiar slim briefcase that Greg used to tease him about, saying it was always empty and just for show. But although there were no bruises or injuries on him, he looked like a man who had been in a punch-up and come off worst, reeling, pale and glassy-eyed. Before I could speak, he stepped over the threshold and enveloped me in his embrace. All I could think of was how different he felt from Greg, taller and broader, with a different smell as well, soap and leather.

I wanted so badly to break down and cry in his arms, but somehow I couldn't. Instead Joe cried, tears coursing down his lived-in face, as he told me how wonderful my husband had been, and how lucky he was to have known me. He said I was family to him and that I must lean on him over the next few weeks. He kissed me on both cheeks and held my hands in his and told me very solemnly that I didn't have to be strong. He scoured the pan I'd burned the rice in, wiped the kitchen table and put out my rubbish bin. He even started trying to clear up some of the mess, lifting piles of paper and putting books on shelves in a frantic, utterly ineffectual way until I told him to stop. Then he left and I continued with my task.

When I had broken the news to someone, I ticked off their name on my piece of paper. Sometimes a child answered or a partner I didn't know or didn't know well enough. I didn't leave a message, I didn't even say who had called. I did less well on Greg's part of the list. By the time I got to them, people had started leaving for work. I didn't phone people's mobiles. I couldn't bear the idea of talking to people on trains, of them having to keep their voice down, getting embarrassed about their reactions in front of strangers.

I also got slowed up because by then the phone had started ringing. People I'd talked to had digested the news and thought of things they needed to say, questions they wanted to ask. Friends had rung other friends and some of those friends immediately rang me and if they couldn't get through, they rang my mobile, which I switched off. Later I discovered that if they couldn't get through to my mobile, they'd sent me an email. But a lot of them did get through, one expression of grief after another, so that they seemed to merge into a continual howl. After each call, I wrote the name at the bottom of the list so that I wouldn't call them again by mistake.

One of the calls wasn't from a friend or relative, but from WPC Darby, one of the women who had broken the news to me. She asked how I was and I didn't really know what to say. "I'm sorry to bother you," she said, "but did I say anything about identifying the body?"

"I can't remember," I said.

"I know it's a difficult time," she said, and there was a pause.

"Oh," I said. "You want me to identify the . . ." I stopped. "My husband. But you came here. You told me about it. You know already."

"It's a requirement," she said. "You could always nominate another family member. A brother or a parent."

"No," I said immediately. The idea was impossible. When

Greg had married me, he had become mine. I wasn't going to let his family reclaim him. "I'll do it. Should I do it today?"

"If you can."

"Where is he?"

I heard a paper rustle.

"He is in the mortuary of the King George V hospital. Do you know it? Is there someone who can take you?"

I PHONED GWEN and she said she would drive me to the hospital, even though I knew it meant she would have to phone in sick. I realized I was still in the clothes I had put on the previous morning. Greg had seen me put them on. Maybe he hadn't actually seen it. He was too used to me and too busy in the morning to sit and watch me but he had been bustling around when I was getting dressed. I took them all off, another bit of my life with Greg gone, and I stood in the shower under the very hot water, my head lifted into the jet and my eyes closed. I turned the water up hotter still as if it could scorch away what I was feeling. I dressed quickly, glanced in the mirror and saw that I was entirely in black. I took off my sweater and replaced it with a rust-colored one. Somber, but not like a Mediterranean widow.

Some people know instinctively how to respond to your moods. Gwen is like that. Greg and I once had a conversation about who of our friends never irritated us and she was the only name we both agreed on. She senses when to stand back and be dispassionate, even critical, when to come close, hug you, show you love and physical affection. Mary and I regularly argued, but Mary argues with most people, almost for the sake of it—you see a contrary gleam come into her eye and you know she's in one of her itchy, confrontational, emotionally volatile moods and there's nothing to be done about it except ride out the storm—or leave the room. I usually leave the room. But Gwen, with her soft mop of golden hair, her gray eyes, her quiet clothes, her calm and reflective manner, doesn't like to raise her voice. At university people who knew her called her "the diplomat," a tag that was both admiring and sometimes slightly resentful, because she seemed to hold back from intimacy. But I had always liked her reserve; it felt like a privilege to be let into her tiny circle of friends. Now, when I answered the door to her, she didn't open her arms, inviting me to step into them to cry and be comforted. Instead she looked at me with a grave tenderness, putting a hand on my shoulder but letting me decide if I wanted to break down or not. And I didn't. I wanted, needed, to hold myself together.

As she drove me toward the hospital in King's Cross, she didn't speak and allowed me to stay silent. I stared out of the window at passersby, suddenly fascinated by the idea of people who were doing today what they had planned yesterday. Didn't they realize it was temporary? It might all seem to be going smoothly, but one day, tomorrow or the day after or in fifty years' time, the charade will come to an end.

We arrived at the hospital and discovered that we had to pay to park. I got suddenly and pointlessly angry. "If we were going to the supermarket instead of to the morgue, we wouldn't have to pay."

"Don't worry," said Gwen. "I've got the change with me."

"What about people who come day after day?" I said. "People with dying relatives."

"You probably get a discount," said Gwen.

"I wouldn't bet on it," I said, and then I stopped, aware that I was behaving like those people I see shouting in the street, arguing with voices in their own head.

I experienced the hospital mainly as a succession of smells. Near the front desk there was a coffee shop of the kind you find in every shopping center and high street. I could hear the hiss of cappuccino being frothed. There was a café as well. As we walked, the aroma of frying bacon gradually gave way to the smell of floor polish, air freshener, then the sting of cleaning fluids, carbolic and bleach, with an under-smell of something nasty. I hadn't been able to take in the instructions that the receptionist had given us but Gwen led me along corridors, down in a lift to a basement and another reception, with nobody in attendance.

"There's probably a bell or something," Gwen said.

There wasn't. Gwen pulled a face. "Hello?" she called.

There was the sound of footsteps and a man emerged from an office behind the reception desk. He was wearing a green coat, like someone at the counter of a hardware shop. He was very pale, as if he spent all his time down there underground, away from the sun. His stubble stood out plainly. While shaving he had missed a patch under his jaw. I thought of Greg shaving, holding his nose as he did the area beneath his nostrils. The man looked at us inquiringly.

"My friend is here to identify a body."

He nodded in acknowledgment. "I'm Dr. Kyriacou," he said. "I'm a senior registrar. Are you a relative?"

"He's my husband," I said. I wasn't ready to use the past tense yet.

"I'm very sorry for your loss," he said, and for a moment I thought he really was sorry, as sorry as you could be when you expressed it every day, except for weekends and holidays.

"Do you need my name?" I said. "Or his?"

"The deceased's," said Dr. Kyriacou.

"His name is Gregory Manning," I said.

Dr. Kyriacou rummaged through some files piled in a metal tray on the counter until he found the one he wanted. He opened it and examined the papers inside. I tried to lean across and see but I couldn't read anything.

"Do you have any identification?" he asked. "I'm sorry. It's a regulation."

I handed him my driving licence. He took it and wrote something on his form. He frowned. "Your husband's body was badly burned," he said. "This will be distressing for you. But may I say that in my experience it's better to see the body than not."

I wanted to ask if that was really true, even after plane crashes, people hit by trains, but I couldn't speak.

"Do you want me to come with you?" Gwen asked.

Suddenly I felt possessive of the experience. I shook my head. She sat down and Dr. Kyriacou led me along the corridor and into a room that looked as if it were full of filing cabinets with drawers four deep, but with handles like old-fashioned fridges. He glanced at the clipboard he was carrying, then walked to one and turned to me. "Are you ready?" he asked.

I nodded. He pulled open the door and there was a rush of cold air into the already cold room. He drew out a tray. There was a body lying on it, covered with a sheet. Without hesitating he lifted a corner of the sheet. I couldn't stop myself gasping because now I knew, finally, decisively, that there was no mistake and that he was dead, my darling Greg, whom I'd last seen rushing out of the house, a half-eaten piece of toast between his teeth, so we hadn't even kissed.

I made myself look closely. His face was blackened by the fire, some of his hair was burned away and his scalp scorched. The only real damage was above his right eyebrow where there were signs of a terrible collision. I reached out and touched some of his hair, then leaned forward and touched it with my lips. There was a strong smell of burning. "Goodbye," I whispered to him. "My love."

"Is this Gregory Manning?" said Dr. Kyriacou.

I nodded.

"You need to say it aloud," he said.

"Yes, it is."

"Thank you," he said, and wrote on his clipboard.

Dr. Kyriacou took me back to Gwen and then a thought occurred to me. "The other person in the crash. Is she here?"

"Yes," he said.

I paused. I hardly dared ask the question. "Do you . . ." I began. "Do you know her name?"

Dr. Kyriacou rummaged through the files. "Her husband came," he said. "Yes, here we are." He looked at the front of the file. "Milena Livingstone."

Gwen looked at me. "Who is she?"

"I've never heard of her," I said.

Chapter Three

My little house filled with people. Filled with forms, with tasks, with long lists of what I had to do. Friends made me cups of tea and pushed pieces of toast at me that I tried to eat. The phone rang and rang. Gwen and Mary must have set up a rota between them, because as soon as one left it seemed that the other arrived. My parents turned up with an overcooked ginger cake in a tin I remembered from childhood, and bath salts. Joe came with whisky. He sat on the sofa, shook his head slowly from side to side in disbelief and called me "darling." Fergus arrived, his face ashen with shock; he called me "sweetheart." Everyone tried to hug me. I didn't want to be hugged. Or, at least, I didn't want to be hugged by anyone except Greg. I woke at night out of dreams in which he was holding me in his warm embrace, keeping me safe, and lay with dry, sore eyes, staring at the darkness, feeling the space in the bed beside me.

I needn't have worried about what I had to do for at every stage there were plenty of people to tell me. I had become part of a bureaucratic process and was channeled smoothly and efficiently toward the end point, the funeral. But before there could be a funeral, the death had to be registered, and for that, I discovered, there needed to be an inquest to establish the cause of death.

We used to talk about dying. Once, while drunk, we answered a questionnaire online that then provided you with your date of death (me at eighty-eight, Greg at eighty-five), because death seemed ludicrously far away, a joke and an impossibility. If we had ever thought about it seriously, we would have assumed that when it came we would be old, and one of us would be holding the other's hand. But I hadn't been holding his hand and someone else had been with him. Milena Livingstone. The name crackled in my head. Who was she? Why had he been with her?

"Why do you think?" asked my mother, grimly, and I ordered her out of the house, slamming the door so hard behind her that little bits of plaster flaked to the floor.

"Why do you think?" asked Gwen, and I laid my head on the table, on top of all the bits of paper, and said I didn't know, I had no idea. But I knew Greg. He would never . . . I didn't finish the sentence.

"Tell me about her."

"Who?" Joe looked at me with a grave, attentive expression.

"Milena. Who was she?"

"Ellie." His voice was kind. "I've already told you. I've no idea. I didn't know about her."

"She wasn't a client?"

Joe and Greg were partners in their own business. Accountants are supposed to be thin, gray men in suits and glasses, but that certainly wasn't true of those two. Joe was flamboyant and charismatic. Women always gravitated toward him, drawn by his blue eyes, his wide smile, his air of utter attention. He was rather handsome himself, but Greg and I used to say that the real secret of his charm was that he made other people feel beautiful, special. He was older than us, in his late forties, so he seemed like an uncle or a much older brother. And Greg—well, Greg was Greg. He used to say that if I'd known what he did for a living, I'd never have gone out with him. But I couldn't have known. We'd met at a party, a mutual friend of a friend's, and if I'd had to guess, I would have said he was a TV director, a writer, even an actor or a professional activist. He looked raffish and stylishly unkempt; there was a slightly dreamy, unworldly air about him. I was the one who was methodical and practical, whereas he was enthusiastic, untidy, boyish. Certainly not what I thought of as an accountant.

"No," said Joe. "I've looked through everything. Twice."

"There must be an explanation."

"Can't you think of anything?" This time his kind voice, pushing me gently to acknowledge the obvious, made me shudder.

"I would have known." I glared at him. "*You* would have known."

Joe put his hand on my shoulder. "Everyone has secrets, Ellie. Both of us know how wonderful and adorable Greg was but, after all—"

"No," I repeated, cutting him off. "It's not possible."

"WHO WAS MILENA?" I asked Fergus.

"I have no idea," he replied. "I swear he never mentioned anyone called Milena."

"Did he mention . . ." I hesitated. "Did he ever say he was . . . you know?"

"Having an affair?" Fergus finished the sentence I couldn't.

"Yes."

"He adored you."

"That's not the question."

"He never mentioned he was having an affair. Nor did I ever suspect that he might be. Not for a single second."

"And now?"

"Now?"

"Do you suspect he might have been?"

Fergus rubbed his face. "Honestly? I don't know, Ellie. What can I say? You know I was in his office with him the day he died, working on the computers. He seemed completely normal. He talked about you. He never said anything that would make me suspect. Yet he died in a car with a strange woman whom no one seems to have heard of. What's your explanation?"

THE INQUEST WAS set for ten o'clock on Tuesday, October 15, in the coroner's court off Hackney Road. I was to attend and, if I wanted, I could ask questions of the witnesses. I could bring family and friends if I wished. It was open to the public and to the press. After the inquest, Greg's death could be registered, I could collect the appropriate forms, E and F, and could set a date for the funeral.

I asked Gwen if she and Mary would come with me. "Unless it's difficult for Mary to arrange childcare," I added. Mary had a young son, nearly a year old now. Until Greg's death, the conversations between us had been dominated by nappies, first smiles, teething problems, cracked nipples, the swamping pleasures of maternity.

"Of course we'll come," said Gwen. "I'm going to cook you something."

"I'm not hungry and I'm not an invalid. Does everyone think she was another woman?"

"I don't know. It doesn't matter. What do *you* think?"

What did I think? I thought I couldn't survive without him, I thought he had abandoned me, I thought he had betrayed me. I knew, of course, that he hadn't. I thought when I woke up at night that I could hear him breathing in the bed beside me, I thought a hundred times a day of things I needed to say to him, I thought I could no longer remember his face and then it returned to me, teasing and affectionate, or scorched into its death mask. I thought he should never have left me and it was his fault because he had chosen to go with her, and I thought, too, that I would go mad with not knowing who the woman was and yet if I discovered I should very likely go mad as well. Mad with sorrow, anger, or jealousy.

"I'VE HEARD HE was having an affair."

My sister Maria's voice sounded solemnly sympathetic. I could hear her baby crying in the background.

"You've got to go." I banged the phone back into its holster.

An affair. Like death, affairs happen to other people, not me and Greg. Milena Livingstone. How old was she? What did she look like? All I knew about her was that she had a husband who had identified her body at the same morgue as Greg was in. Perhaps she'd been lying in the drawer above him. In death as in life. I shivered violently, feeling nauseous, then went upstairs to my laptop and turned it on, then Googled her name. There aren't many Milena Livingstones around.

I clicked on the first reference and the screen was filled with an advertisement for a business, though at first I couldn't make out what it was. Something about everything being taken out of your hands and no detail left unattended to. Venues. Meals. I scrolled down. It seemed to be a glorified catering and party-arranging business for people with lots of money and no time. A sample menu. Tuna sashimi, sea bass marinated in ginger and lime, chocolate fondants. And here, yes, were the people who ran it, the hostesses.

Two photographs smiled at me from the screen. The face on the left was pale and triangular, with dark blond hair cut artfully short, a straight nose and a restrained smile. She looked attractive, clever, classy. It wasn't her. No, it was the other one, with a tawny mane (dyed, I thought spitefully, and I bet she tosses it back all the time with one ringed hand; I bet she pouts), high cheekbones, white teeth, gray eyes. An older woman, then. A rich woman, by the look of it. A beautiful woman, but not the kind of beauty I'd ever expected Greg, who had fallen so heavily for me, to fall for. Milena Livingstone had a glamorous, artful look to her; her eyebrows were arched and her smile knowing. She was sure to have long, painted nails and immaculately waxed legs. A man's woman, I thought. But not my man. Surely not Greg. Bile rose in my throat and I turned off the computer without looking through any more references and went into the bedroom where I lay facedown on my side of the bed. It was almost dark outside; the nights were getting longer and the days shorter.

I don't know how long I lay there like that, but at last I got up and went to the wardrobe. Greg's clothes hung on the right-hand side. He didn't have many: one suit that we'd bought to-gether for our wedding and he'd hardly worn since, a couple of casual jackets, several shirts. What had he been wearing when he died? I screwed my eyes shut and forced myself to remember—dark trousers and a pale blue shirt; his favorite jacket over the top. That was it: his non-accountant's accoun-tant's outfit.

I started systematically to go through everything in the cupboard. I felt in each pocket, and found only a receipt for a meal we'd had in an Italian restaurant two weeks ago. I remembered: I'd been upset and he'd been patient and opti-mistic. A crumpled flyer for a jazz night that had been put under our windscreen wipers a few days ago. I pulled open the drawers where he kept T-shirts and underwear, but I didn't discover any lacy women's knickers or incriminating love let-ters. Everything was as it should have been. Nothing was as it should have been.

I stood in front of the mirror, examined myself and found myself wanting. I weighed myself and realized I was shrink-ing. I boiled myself an egg, broke open the top, then dabbed my spoon into the yellow yolk. I made myself eat half of it before I felt so sick I had to stop. I had stomach cramps, a grim, familiar backache, so I ran a bath and lowered myself into it, hearing the phone ring. I couldn't bear to answer it and heard

Mary's voice saying into the answering machine that poor little Robin was running a fever, she'd be around as soon as she could. I lay in the hot water and closed my eyes. Then I opened them and watched a curl of red blood run out of me and spread, then another.

So.

It wasn't to be, after all. Once again, as with all the other months of trying and hoping and praying, I wasn't pregnant, and Greg had died in his car with another woman and left me alone, and what on earth was I going to do now?

Chapter Four

It was drizzling. Gwen and Mary arrived early, when I was still in my dressing-gown trying to decide what to wear. The pair of them were dressed in almost identical clothes, and I could see they'd been aiming for the casual but smart, sober but not somber look I was intending for myself. Mary had brought some Danish pastries, which were warm and sticky in their paper bag, and I made us a big pot of coffee. We sat around the kitchen table, dunking the pastries, and I was reminded of when we were students together, sitting just like this in the kitchen of the house we'd shared together in our final year.

"I'm so glad the two of you could be here," I said. "It means a lot."

"What did you think?" said Mary, heatedly. Her face was flushed with excitement. "That we would let you go through this alone?"

I thought I might cry at that, but I didn't, although grief felt rather like a fishbone that was gradually working itself loose in my throat. I asked Mary how her son was and she replied in a constrained, self-conscious way, very different from the eager assumption she had made in the past that I would be interested in every belch and gurgle he made. I had crossed into a different country. No one felt able to have an ordinary conversation with me, no one was about to tell me their petty anxieties and daily fears in the way they would have done a week ago.

I went upstairs and chose my clothes: black skirt, stripy gray shirt, black woolen waistcoat, flat boots, patterned tights, hair tied back. I was so nervous that it took me three attempts to thread my earrings through the lobes of my ears; my hands trembled so that I smudged my lipstick. I felt as though I was about to be put on trial: what kind of wife were you, anyway, that your husband was with another woman? What kind of fool, that you never had the slightest idea?

WHEN WE REACHED the coroner's court, a low, modern building that looked less like a court than an old people's home, the feeling of unreality continued. At first we couldn't find the entrance, but pushed uselessly against glass doors that refused to budge until a policeman on the other side mouthed something at us and pointed, indicating we should try further on, the next entrance. We went into a corridor that led through a series of swing doors into a room where lines of chairs faced a long table. The air-conditioning hummed loudly and the fluorescent light shimmered overhead. I had been expecting something impressive, wood-paneled perhaps, with an air of formality, not this blandly cheerful room with louvered blinds. Only the crest of the lion and the unicorn, squeezed between the two windows, gave any hint that this was a court. Several people were already there, including a couple of middle-aged men wearing suits and ties, with folders on their laps, and two police officers in the second row, sitting up stiff and straight.

To one side there was a table with a piece of lined paper taped to it, reading PRESS. Behind it a bored-looking young man was reading a tabloid newspaper.

A gray-haired man in a suit was blocking our way. He had a moustache and the air of a sergeant major. "Sorry to bother you. Can I take your names, please?"

"I'm Eleanor Falkner. I'm Greg Manning's wife. These are my friends."

He introduced himself as the coroner's officer and pointed us to seats in the front row. Mary sat on one side of me, Gwen the other. A middle-aged woman in fawn slacks and a red sweater came to the front of the room and tinkered with a huge old-fashioned tape recorder. She pushed cables into sockets and fiddled with switches. She looked up at the room and smiled vaguely at us. "It'll be all right on the night," she said, and bustled out again, throwing bright, complicit smiles around the room, as if we were all in on a tremendously good joke.

Two women with identical bright blond helmets of hair positioned themselves just behind us; they were whispering to each other and occasionally giving discreet chuckles. It was like a register-office wedding, I thought. I wiped my palms down my skirt and pushed invisible strands of hair behind my ears.

Just before ten, the door opened again and a group of three entered and were directed by the coroner's officer to the front-row chairs a few places along from where we sat. A middle-aged man with corrugated graying hair and a silk tie, a slender young woman, whose pale hair rippled down her back and whose aquiline nose quivered, and a young man with untidy dark hair, untied shoelaces and a stud in his nose. I tensed and clutched Gwen's arm.

"That's them," I hissed.

"Who?"

"Her family."

I stared at the man. After a few seconds he turned and met my gaze. Again I felt it was like a wedding: the bride and bridegroom's families finding themselves in the same room, curious and suspicious. Someone near him murmured something and he turned around. It was his name. Hugo. Hugo Livingstone. The proceedings were late getting under way because the woman couldn't get her tape recorder to function. She pushed switches up and down and even banged it with her hand but nothing worked. A couple of men behind me got up and joined her. In the end, they just pushed the plug into another electrical socket and its lights came on. The woman put on some earphones and sat down behind the machine, which almost hid her from view. The court officer asked us all to rise. I had expected a judge in robes and a wig but Dr. Gerald Sams was just a man in a suit, carrying a large bundle of files. He sat down behind the table at the front and began to address us in a calm, deliberate tone. He offered his condolences to me and to Milena Livingstone's husband and two children. "*Step*-children," muttered one loudly.

He gave a brief talk about the process. He said there might be some details that family members would find upsetting, but that the inquest was often helpful to the next of kin, giving a clear account of what had happened and perhaps some sort of closure. He would call witnesses, but this was not a trial. Any interested person could question them and, indeed, ask questions at any point. He also said that he had read through the preliminary material, it seemed to be a straightforward case and we would get through it quickly. He asked if anybody had legal representation. Nobody spoke.

I took a notebook and a pen from my pocket. I opened it and wrote "Inquest" at the top of a blank page. I underlined the word, then turned the underlining into a box surrounding it. Then I turned the box into a three-dimensional box and shaded the top with crosshatching. Meanwhile a police officer had come forward to the little desk and chair at the front of the room and swore, on a tatty copy of the New Testament, to tell the truth. He was an unremarkable young PC, with reddish-brown hair combed flat against his head, but I studied him with fascination and dread. He was the man who had found my husband.

He consulted his notebook and, in a strange monotone, like an unprepared and untalented actor, he gave a halting account of how he had driven to Porton Way in response to a call from a member of the public who had reported seeing a fire.

Dr. Sams asked if the officer could describe Porton Way.

He looked puzzled. "There's not much to say, really," he said. "There used to be factories and warehouses there, but it's mainly derelict now. They're starting to redevelop it, though. There are going to be new houses and office blocks."

"Is the road busy at that time of night?" asked Dr. Sams. "With commuters and suchlike?"

"No," said the officer. "It's not a through route. There are a few construction people during the day but not at that time. Sometimes kids steal cars and drive them around there, but we didn't see anyone else."

"Tell us what you found."

"The fire had died down by the time we got there but we could see the smoke. The car had slipped down the embankment and turned over. We scrambled down and we quickly saw that there were people in it but they were clearly dead."

"Clearly?"

The officer pulled a face. "We didn't even see there were two of them at first."

"And what did you do?"

"My partner called the fire brigade and an ambulance. I walked around just checking. I couldn't really get close. It was still hot."

He was talking as if he had come across a bonfire that had got out of control. Dr. Sams was writing notes on a pad of paper. When he had finished he put the end of the pen into his mouth and chewed it thoughtfully. "Did you form an impression of what had happened?"

"It was obvious," the officer said. "The car lost control, came off the road, rolled down the embankment, hit a concrete ridge, burst into flames."

"No," said Dr. Sams. "I meant more *how* it had happened, *how* the car lost control."

The officer thought for a moment. "That's pretty obvious

as well," he said. "Porton Way goes straight and then it suddenly curves to the right. It's not very well lit. If a driver was inattentive—if he was talking to his passenger, or something like that—he could miss the turn, carry straight on and then be in big trouble."

"And you think that was what happened?"

"We checked the scene. There were no skidmarks, so it looks as if the car left the road at speed."

Dr. Sams grunted, scribbled some more notes, then asked the officer if he had anything else he wanted to add. The policeman looked at his notes. "The ambulance arrived a few minutes later. The two bodies were pronounced dead at the scene, but we knew that anyway."

"Is there any suggestion that any other vehicle was involved in the crash?"

"No," said the officer. "If he crashed because he was avoiding another vehicle, there would have been skid marks of some kind."

Dr. Sams looked toward those of us in the front row. "Does anyone have any questions arising from this statement?"

I had many, many questions buzzing around my head, but I didn't think that the answers to any would be found in that officer's little black notebook. Nobody else spoke either.

"Thank you," said Dr. Sams. "Could I ask you to stay for a few minutes, in case any questions arise?"

He nodded and made his way to his seat, a few rows behind. It occurred to me that this was probably a morning off for him, an escape from the office and having to fill in reports.

Dr. Sams then called Dr. Mackay. A woman in a trouser

suit came forward and sat in the chair. She was about fifty with dark hair that looked dyed. She didn't swear on the Bible. Instead she read a promise from a piece of paper. I agreed with that in theory, but as she said the words, they sounded thin and unconvincing. I preferred the idea that if you didn't tell the truth a bolt of lightning would strike you dead and you'd be punished in hell for all eternity.

Dr. Sams looked at us again, especially me, the grieving widow, and him, the grieving widower.

"Dr. Mackay carried out the post-mortem examination on Mr. Manning and Ms. Livingstone. It's possible that the details in her evidence will be distressing. Therefore some of you might wish to leave the court."

I felt a hand grip one of my arms. I didn't look around. I didn't want to catch anybody's eye. I simply shook my head.

"Very well," said Dr. Sams. "Dr. Mackay, will you give us a brief account of your findings?"

Dr. Mackay laid a file on the table in front of her and opened it. She scrutinized the text for a few moments, then looked up. "Despite the condition of the bodies, I was able to undertake a complete examination. The police report stated that the two people in the car were not wearing seat belts and the injuries were consistent with that: I mean, consistent with the head of each person being thrown forward and striking the interior of the car. The result was massive trauma. Therefore the cause of death was, in both cases, compression of the brain resulting from a depressed fracture of the skull."

There was a pause as Dr. Sams wrote his notes. "So the fire was not a factor?" he asked.

Dr. Mackay caught my eye. I saw an expression of sympathy.

"That was a crucial question in my mind," she said. "Obviously, in each case there was much destruction of skin, subcutaneous and muscular tissue. I took blood samples from both Mr. Manning and Ms. Livingstone. Both tested negative for carbon monoxide." She looked toward us. "That suggests the two of them were not breathing after the fire started. I also checked the airways and lungs and found no traces of carbon. Also, although the bodies had suffered the burns I mentioned, they showed no signs of vital reaction. I can give you the technical details if you want but, broadly speaking, the sites of burning showed none of the signs of inflammation you would expect if it had happened while the person was still living." She looked at me once more. "It may be of some comfort to the families to know that the deaths must have been all but instantaneous."

I glanced across at Hugo Livingstone. He didn't look comforted. He didn't even look obviously upset. He was frowning slightly, as if lost in thought.

Dr. Sams asked Dr. Mackay if she had checked Greg's blood-alcohol level. She said she had and that there was nothing untoward. She said it and glanced at me again, as if that was more good news, another thing for me to be relieved about. Dr. Sams asked if anybody had any questions for Dr. Mackay and once again there was an awkward pause.

I didn't really have anything to ask but I had a lot to say. I wanted to say that Greg had always been a careful driver. Blind drunk and engaged in animated conversation, he still wouldn't have missed a turn in the road. He wore his seat belt even when moving the car ten feet. I could have announced this to the court, but then I would have been the person with questions to answer: What did I know about the way he behaved when he was with this other woman? Did I not know about this other relationship, this other life? And if I didn't, what did my knowledge about him count for? I stayed silent.

Dr. Sams released Dr. Mackay and she went back to her seat. He said he was calling no further witnesses and asked if anybody had any statements to make or any questions to put to the court. I looked at my notebook. Without realizing it, I had drawn little stars around "Inquest." Then I had drawn little circles around the stars and little squares around the circles. But I had not written a single note. I had no questions to ask. Nothing to say.

"Good," said Dr. Sams. "There is obviously no confusion about the identity of the victims and the time and place of their death. If there is no objection, I would like to record a verdict of accidental death in the case of Gregory Wilson Manning and of Milena Livingstone. The deaths can now be registered and the bodies released for burial. Written confirmation will follow in a day or two. Thank you very much."

"The court will rise," said the court officer, and we all stood.

I now pronounce you man and wife. You may kiss the bride. It felt so familiar. I looked at Gwen, who managed a brave smile. I felt we should be going out for a lunch to celebrate. We walked out and stood on the pavement in the sunshine.

"Well," said Gwen, "in some ways it wasn't as bad as it might have been."

Chapter Five

"Right," I said, out loud. I had noticed that I was beginning to talk to myself, like a mad woman, trying to fill the silence of the house with a human voice. I didn't care. I had a purpose. I was going to take Greg's life apart and find out what had been going on. He wouldn't escape me that easily. I was going to track him down.

After the inquest I'd persuaded Gwen and Mary to leave and assured them that, yes, I'd be all right and, no, I really didn't mind being left alone—in fact I wanted it. Gwen asked if I was starting work again and I said I was thinking about it. Probably it would have been a good idea. It would have been therapeutic. I restore furniture, from valuable antiques, all oak burr, rosewood or gleaming mahogany, to someone's worthless but beloved piece of junk. I'd taken the kitchen table I sat at now off the top of a skip and mended it; the bed that we—I—slept in. I had done up the bookshelves on the wall. Badly paid though it often was, part-time though it usually was, sometimes overtime, sometimes hysterically so, I loved it. I loved the smell of the wood and the wax, the feel of a chisel in my hand. It was where I'd always gone to escape.

But not now. I started with the tiny mezzanine room. It was next to the bathroom and overlooking the garden, which was small and square, dominated by the rickety shed at the end where I stored the furniture I was working on. This was a study of sorts. There was a filing cabinet full of things like accounts, documents, insurance policies; a bookshelf that mostly held manuals and reference books I used for work, and a table I had found in the junk shop at the end of the road, then sanded and waxed it, on which stood Greg's laptop. I sat down and opened the lid, pressed the starter button and watched icons spring to the screen.

First, the emails. Before I started, I searched "Milena" and "Livingstone" and came up with nothing. I winced at the un-opened messages that had arrived since Greg had died. There were about ninety, mostly junk mail and one sent by Fergus about half an hour before I had rung him and given him the news. He was suggesting they run a half-marathon that week-end before watching the football together. I bit my lip and de-leted it.

I went through his mailboxes methodically, missing none. Even when they had titles like "Customer Service" or "70% off in our Clearance Sale," I read them. There was almost nothing to do with work; he had a separate mailbox for that. Deliv-eries, house stuff, bookings, confirmations of travel arrange-ments. Several were from me and I looked at those as well. They had an easy intimacy about them that seemed far away and unfamiliar now. Death had turned Greg into a stranger; I could no longer take him for granted. Dozens were from Fergus, setting up meetings, swapping bits of gossip, sending references to websites they'd been discussing or continuing a conversation. Joe, of course. Other friends—James, Ronan,

Will, Laura, Sal, Malcolm. Casual greetings and arrangements to meet. Sometimes I was mentioned: Ellie sends her love; Ellie's sprained her ankle; Ellie's a bit down in the dumps (had I been? I couldn't remember); Ellie's away and Ellie's returned. One or two from his brothers, Ian and Simon—usually about some family-related issue, but none from his sister Kate, and none from his parents, who used to communicate with their eldest son by ringing on Friday evening at six o'clock for a fifteen-minute chat. Online articles. Blogs about subjects I hadn't even known he cared about. When there was anything remotely interesting or curious about the emails he had been sent, I pressed the little arrow beside them to see what he'd written in reply. He was normally quite terse—he always used to say that tone was hard to detect in an email; you should be careful about irony or sarcasm. He was careful and factual, even with me.

One of Greg's more regular email correspondents was a woman called Christine, the ex of an old friend, who he sometimes met up with; he wasn't so careful with *her*. I flicked between her messages and his. She lamented approaching her thirty-sixth birthday and he said she was more attractive now than when they'd first met. She thanked him for taking a look at her boiler and he said it was nice to have an excuse to see her again. She said he was a very nice man, did he know that? And he replied that she must bring out the best in him. He was tanned after his holiday; she was radiant after hers. He was looking tired—was he overworking and was everything all right at home? He replied that she, on the other hand, was as fresh as ever and blue suited her.

"But were things all right at home, Greg?" I rubbed my eyes with my fists and glared at Christine's solicitous notes, his flirtatious, evasive responses. "Come on, tell me."

I moved to the sent messages, but the emails still didn't tell me that. They told me he had ordered wood chips for the garden, gray paint for the kitchen, Omega 3 capsules for both of us; also a book on architecture and a new CD by Howling Bells, which I'd never heard of. Maybe he'd given it to someone as a present. Milena? Christine? I called up his music library and scrolled down, and there it innocently was.

I went downstairs. It was still gray outside, and soon enough it would be getting dark again. The lawn was covered with soggy leaves and the pear tree by the back wall dripped steadily. I hadn't eaten since the Danish pastries that morning, so I made myself a piece of toast and Marmite and a cup of camomile tea and took it back to the computer. The phone rang and it was Gwen, with the number of their solicitor for me to call. I couldn't remember the one Greg had used when we'd bought the house. Now there was so much to be sorted out. I wrote it on the notepad I found in the desk drawer and said I'd call her the following day.

Junk mail—but I found nothing apart from advertisements for Viagra, fake Rolex watches, amazing investment opportunities, guaranteed loans, unsecured credit and an invitation to the online casino, where everyone is king.

Trash. Greg was pretty efficient at getting rid of old messages and, anyway, they only went back a few weeks: obviously the ones older than these were deleted at an even deeper level, somewhere in the mysterious circuitry of the computer. I plowed doggedly through them, feeling I was getting nowhere and simply wasting my time. There was a strange little message from Tania, in which she said she didn't really understand his query and he should ask Joe about it.

I got the phone from our bedroom—my bedroom—and called Joe on the office number.

"Yes?" He sounded unusually curt.

"It's me. Is that the way you usually talk to clients?"

"Ellie." His voice softened. "It's one of those days. I was going to call you this evening. Tell me about the inquest. Are you all—"

"Were there any problems with your business?"

"How do you mean?"

I repeated the question, mentioning the email I'd found on Greg's computer.

"What date did you say?"

"A week or so ago."

There was a pause.

"I'm scrolling through my mail and there's nothing I can see from Greg about a worry."

"So, everything was OK?"

"Depends what you mean. If you want me to bend your ear about clients who don't pay up on time, don't give us proper information and then complain, or dealing with the Revenue and the nightmare of bureaucracy . . . But that's just business as usual and you've got problems of your own."

"All the work Greg had to do late at the office, that wasn't because there were problems?"

"Did he often work late?" His tone was cautious, with an underlying note of sympathy.

I felt the blood flame into my cheeks. "That is, he came home late recently. Later than usual anyway."

"Did he seem stressed?"

"No. At least, not really."

"Not really?"

"You know, I keep thinking back and seeing things I didn't notice at the time—or, at least, thinking I can see things. Maybe he was a bit preoccupied. Or maybe I'm making that up."

There was a silence at the other end. I knew what Joe was thinking: that perhaps Greg was preoccupied because he was having an affair. I waited for him to say it, but he didn't. Perhaps he was too respectful of my feelings.

"If he was worried, though," I continued, "I think he would have told me. He wouldn't have protected me. That's not the kind of marriage we had. That I thought we had. We were in things together; we shared things."

"I think you're right," he said. "Greg would have told you."

"You mean about everything?"

Another silence.

"Ellie, I'm finishing up here. Can I come around on my way home? I'll bring a bottle of wine and we can talk this through."

"I won't be here."

I FOUND HER address in his old address book and decided to walk, even though she lived in Clerkenwell and probably wouldn't be in anyway, and even though the drizzle outside was turning into a steady downpour. It didn't feel like something I could express over the phone.

As I arrived, I saw her coming from the other direction, feeling in her bag for her door key. She was wearing a belted mac and a scarf tied around her head, and looked like a fifties film star in one of those classy black-and-white French movies.

"Hello."

I stood in front of her and she looked at me with narrowed, suspicious eyes, then gave an exaggerated little start. "Ellie? My God. I meant to get in touch. I'm so very, very sorry. He was such a lovely—"

"Can I come in?"

"Of course. You're soaked."

I looked down at myself. I was still wearing my inquest clothes and had forgotten to put on a jacket. It was true that I was cold and wet. I must have looked dreadful.

I followed Christine up the stairs and into a spacious kitchen–living room. She took off her mac and hung it over the back of a chair, pulled the scarf off her head and shook out her chestnut hair.

"Do you live alone?" I asked.

"Yes," she said. "Just at the moment." Then she offered me tea.

"No, thanks."

"Or coffee, or a cold drink?"

"Is that the boiler Greg fixed?" I asked. "He never managed to get ours sorted."

"I'm sorry."

Christine sat down opposite me, then stood up and filled the kettle but didn't switch it on. She turned toward me. "Is there a particular reason you came?"

"I wanted to ask you something."

Her face took on the eager, helpful expression I'd become so familiar with since Greg's death.

"You were friendly with Greg."

"That's right," said Christine. "I was devastated when I heard."

"Would you say you were close to him?"

"It depends what you mean by close." Her tone was cautious now.

"I read your emails to each other."

"Yes?"

"He thought blue suited you." Her expression had changed: no longer eager but embarrassed. I pressed on. "How close?"

"You mean . . ." She stopped.

"Yes."

"You poor thing," she said softly.

I stared at her. Shame flushed through me, leaving me clammy. I gripped the table with both hands. "You're telling me there was nothing between you, then?"

"We were friends."

"Even though you told him he was a very nice man and complimented him on his tan and asked him how things were at home, and he said you looked radiant?"

There was a nasty little silence, and then she said, "It didn't mean anything."

"He never tried to make it go further?" I felt abject, and also disgusted by myself.

She gazed at me with a pity that made me want to crawl under a stone.

"I heard he was with another woman," she said.

"Who from?"

"People. I didn't know who she was. Greg and I were just friends."

I thought of Christine and nameless other people talking about Greg and the other woman in the car. A wave of nausea assailed me. "I ought to go. I shouldn't have come."

"Are you sure I can't get you anything?"

"Yes."

"I'm sorry. About everything."

IT WAS DARK outside, with rain still falling and a stiff wind, so I flagged down a cab and sat with my arms wrapped around myself, feeling wretched. When I reached my front door I discovered I didn't have enough money to pay the driver so I ran inside, then came back out to pay the driver with odd bits of money I'd discovered in various drawers and pockets. I'd found a five-pound note in Greg's old leather jacket, which was still hanging in the hall. When was I going to sort out his things? A list of tasks streamed through my mind: contact the lawyer, the bank, the building society, find out about our financial affairs, our mortgage, any life policies, ring up the insurance broker, organize the funeral, answer all the messages I'd received over the past days, learn how to operate the video-recorder, cancel the appointment we'd made together at the fertility clinic, change the message on the answering machine, which still had Greg's voice saying hello and please call back later because Greg and Ellie weren't around just now. Ellie was around, but Greg wasn't and Greg would never be. Greg with his dark eyes and his wide smile and his strong, warm hands. He used to rub my neck at the end of a long day. He used to wash my hair for me, easing out the tangles. He used to bite his lower lip when he read. He used to walk around the house naked, singing loudly and tunelessly. He used to tell me about his days, or so I had thought. He used to watch me as I got undressed, his arms behind his head and a grave look on his face, waiting. He used to lie on his back in bed and snore gently. He used to wake up and turn to me, smiling in welcome as I struggled out of sleep.

Who else's neck had he rubbed, hair had he washed? Who else had undressed for him, taking off garments one by one while he looked at them with the gaze I had thought was for me alone? Who had he lain beside in bed, putting out his hand to touch and comfort? All at once, a jealousy so pure and visceral it felt almost like intense physical desire swept through me, leaving me breathless and shaken. I had to sit on the stairs for a few seconds, trying to breathe normally, before I could make it to the bedroom.

I'd been going to have a bath but I'd forgotten to turn on the hot water. I peeled off my wet clothes and put on a pair of jogging pants and a thick sweatshirt that had belonged to Greg and was vast on me. One of its sleeves was frayed and I put it into my mouth and chewed it. He used to wear it when he went running on winter days and it still held his smell. I went downstairs into the kitchen, feeling a bit dazed. I half expected to see him standing at the hob and this would all have been a feverish nightmare. We had shared the cooking, done it together. Our last meal had been pasta with a chili sauce, nothing special. He only had a few dishes in his repertory: risotto, bean stew, Moroccan lamb, baked potatoes with sour cream and chives, and he cooked them with ferocious concentration, as if they were laboratory experiments that might go badly wrong, with dire consequences.

It occurred to me that since he had died I'd barely cooked beyond making toast. Gwen had made me a vegetable lasagna, Mary had produced salmon fillet with baked tomatoes and watched me as I failed to eat it, and Fergus had brought around a cold roast chicken and garlic bread, which was, I thought, still in the fridge. My neighbor, Annie, had made me too many cakes and soups, as had my mother. Cooking for one is sad when you're used to cooking for two. I decided to poach myself an egg. Eggs are comforting, I thought, as I waited for the water to boil in the pan, then cracked an egg into it, slid a piece of stale bread into the toaster. The meal took about three minutes to make and three to eat. Now what?

Throughout that night I worked very hard, stopping only for a mug of tea at ten, a glass of whisky at midnight (I had somehow acquired three bottles of whisky since Greg had died: it's the drink people think a grieving widow will turn to), a chicken sandwich at two. I sat in the living room and went through his address book again, writing down names I didn't recognize. I went through his diary, though it wasn't his work one, just the old book he kept personal appointments in, and didn't find a single thing that made me suspicious. I went through all of his papers, which had been neatly sorted into categories and then by date. I went through the box of old letters in the junk room that should have been an office. I went through his school reports, his qualifications and diplomas, his photo albums from the years before he met me and before the world had gone digital. He was a sweet, gangly, loose-limbed child; his expectant smile hadn't changed. I emptied the contents of boxes on to the floor and examined them: old vinyl records, compilation tapes he'd made when he was a teenager, books we hadn't got around to putting on the shelves, magazines going back years. I pulled out each drawer in our bedroom and went through his clothes, folding them neatly and putting them back in their proper place because I had discovered I wasn't ready yet to give any away.

I opened the cupboard under the stairs and took out every object there—bike panniers, a squash racket, two pairs of running shoes, an old tent we hadn't used since that trip to Scotland when it had rained nonstop and we had eaten fish and chips and listened to the rain hammering on the canvas. He had told me then that wherever I was that was his home. We had both cried.

At six, because it was too early to go out and I had gone through everything in the house, I started making a list of people I would ask to the funeral. At the end, there were a hundred and twenty names and I gazed at them in despair. How many people would fit into the crematorium chapel, how many into the front room? Should I provide food and drink? Should I ask people to do readings or make little speeches? And what about music? Why wasn't Greg here to advise me?

At eight o'clock I made myself a bowl of porridge—half milk, half water, with golden sugar sprinkled liberally over the top—and a large pot of strong coffee. Then I washed and got dressed in an ancient corduroy skirt that came down to my ankles and a dark blue jersey with a hole in the elbow that Greg had given me when we first met. Because it was cold and gray, I put on a duffel coat, and wrapped a red scarf around my neck. Now I was a bundle of wool and itchy layers.

Kentish Town Road was thick with cars and people on their way to work. I got on to the overcrowded Underground train that took me to Euston, then walked the last few hundred yards to Greg's workplace. It was on the second floor of a recently renovated office block. They had moved in there a few months earlier; when their firm had expanded they had needed more than three desks, three computers and several filing cabinets. Once it had just been Joe and Greg, now there were people I didn't recognize. They needed rooms with doors for clients, lavatories, a coffee-machine and a watercooler. I rang the bell and before long Tania was ushering me in, taking my coat and scarf, pulling out a chair for me, too solicitously offering tea, coffee, biscuits, anything at all, gazing at me with her big brown eyes, shaking her head in horror and sympathy so that her ponytail bounced. She was like a puppy, an eager spaniel trying to please.

"Is Joe here?"

"He's in his office. I'll go and fetch him."

At that moment Joe came striding across the room toward

me, holding his arms out well before he reached me, and Tania seemed to melt away. "You should have told me you were coming," he said. His eyes narrowed. "You look absolutely exhausted."

"I've been up all night. I was looking through Greg's stuff."

"Sorting things out?"

"Trying to find out what he'd been up to."

"Here, come and tell me." He took my arm and led me into his office, which was really no more than a small glass cubicle. On the white wall behind his chaotic desk hung a photograph of his family: his wife, Alison, and his three children, who were teenagers now but in the picture were still small and childish. Alison stood behind them, her arms circling the little group protectively. I saw how the three children were a bit like her and a bit like him, and felt fierce regret and sadness fill me from top to toe.

"There's nothing to tell," I said, as I sat in the chair he pulled out for me. "There wasn't anything strange."

Joe's brow wrinkled. "What were you expecting?"

"I don't know. That was why I was looking. I need to go through his things here as well."

He seemed taken aback. "There's not much personal stuff. I think Tania's already packed up most of it. I really don't think there's anything else except clients' files and government regulations."

"It's his work things I want to go through. His papers, his diary, his appointments."

"I see." He sounded sympathetic but stern, too, and I dropped my eyes under his gaze.

"There must be something to show me he was having an affair with this Milena."

"Ellie . . ."

"Because I'm telling you, Joe, there's nothing at home—I mean *nothing*—that suggests he was having an affair with her or anyone else. You had no idea, or so you say. Neither did Fergus. Or anyone. And nor did I. Even now I look back and can't see it."

Joe nodded a few times, then got up and stared out at the room beyond. Then he turned back to me. On his face was an expression of kind patience that made me squirm. "Maybe he was just good at keeping secrets."

"He can't have been that good. Not Greg. He was incapable of lying about anything. If he was having an affair, someone would have known. There would be evidence somewhere."

"But don't you see, Ellie? Whatever you do, however much you search, you can't prove he *wasn't* having an affair?"

"He couldn't have left no trace."

"Perhaps not. Perhaps you'll turn his whole life upside down and investigate everything and eventually find something."

"Well, then."

"But why do you want to?"

"Why? Because I *have* to. Don't you understand? I loved him. I thought he loved me . . ."

"He loved you."

"I knew him, Joe. I knew our life together. Or I thought I did. And now he's dead and there's this mystery and everyone's pitying me and I look back at our life and I can't see it any longer, can't trust it. It's like the lights have all gone out and everything I trusted I can't anymore. And I can't ask him. I want to ask him what the hell was going on. I can't believe he won't ever be able to tell me, that we won't be able to talk about it together. If he was dead and that was it, no other woman involved, at least I could miss him and remember him with tenderness and feel good about what we had—but even that's muddied by this. I can't even mourn him properly. I feel humiliated, ashamed, tangled up in all these emotions. It's a mess. I'm a mess."

"He loved you," Joe repeated. His voice was gentle, insistent. "Even if he was having an affair, he loved you very much."

"So you think he was, then!"

"I'm saying if."

"I don't want ifs."

"But, in all likelihood, that's all you're going to get."

"I can't accept it."

"Everyone has secrets. Everyone does things they don't want to be discovered."

"Have you, then?"

"What? Had an affair?"

"Yes. Have you?"

"Why would you believe my answer? Do you think I'd tell you if I had? And if I had, would it somehow make it more likely that Greg had as well, and if I hadn't does the same apply?"

"You have, haven't you?" Of course he had, I thought. All those women who crowded around him.

But Joe put his hand on my shoulder. "Stop this, Ellie."

"Sorry. But, Joe, tell me, do *you* think Greg was being unfaithful?"

"Honestly?"

"Yes."

"Well, I . . . Honestly, I just don't know. But perhaps he was, yes. And then, of course, you have the circumstances of his death."

"I see." I bit my lip and sat for a while, composing myself. "Thank you."

"Ellie." His voice was painfully sympathetic.

"I still want to look through his things."

He shrugged helplessly. "If that's what you need. We didn't know you were coming so it's in a bit of a mess, I'm afraid."

It was more than a bit of a mess—it was in disarray. There were files lying open on every surface, piles of paper stacked on the desk and floor, thick accounting books pulled off shelves.

"Sorry," said Joe.

He installed me at Greg's old desk with his computer in front of me, and then his electronic organizer. Tania brought files and folders and I trawled through them as well. I looked at accounts, receipts, letters from clients, recommendations, rules and regulations, lines of figures, application forms, consent forms, VAT forms, tax returns, expenses, queries about trusts and power of attorney. There were pink and yellow Post-it notes stuck on some, scrawled with Greg's slapdash writing. Meaningless. I had no idea what I was searching for and it was quickly apparent to me that I might as well have been reading a hieroglyphic script. I felt my brain throb as I searched for connections I knew I wouldn't find. Joe put cups of coffee beside me and I let them go cold. Tania brought me a cheese and tomato bap and asked me if there was anything that needed explaining.

"One thing," I said. "You sent an email to Greg at home, saying he should ask Joe about whatever it was that was worrying him. Do you remember what it was about?"

Tania wrinkled her button nose and furrowed her smooth brow. "No," she replied eventually, "so it can't have been important, can it? Do you want me to look for the original email he sent?"

"If it's not too much bother."

"I might have deleted it if it was dealt with."

I wished I'd brought Fergus with me—he was some kind of computer whiz and he'd done freelance work for the firm several times. He'd even been here on Greg's last day. He'd have been able to guide me through.

I made a list of all the clients Greg had visited over the last three weeks, with their phone numbers and addresses, and stared at them, the names blurring. I looked at the A–Z and my head buzzed with tiredness and a despairing frustration. Anything was better than not knowing. For how could I say goodbye to Greg when I no longer knew who he was? How could I get him back?

Chapter Six

It was while the undertaker was going through the price options that I descended into a form of mental illness. I experienced the feeling I had once had as a teenager—probably all teenagers have it—that I was the only real person in the world and that everyone else was an actor playing a part. The undertaker's in Kentish Town was much like any other shop in the high street offering a service, an estate agent or a white-goods supplier. But this one had been made over in shades of gray with fake pillars supporting the reception desk and white lilies in vases, so that it looked a bit like a mausoleum. Somber new-agey music, something on Pan pipes, was playing in the background. Of course, Mr. Collingwood, the funeral director, was dressed in a navy suit with a white carnation and, of course, he offered me his condolences in a subdued voice as he pushed the price list across his desk toward me.

In the same subdued voice, he talked about the services they offered, the collection and care of the deceased, the arrangements for visiting the chapel of rest. He murmured that there were decisions to be made: religious or secular, burial, cremation or special facilities, and then there were the extras. As I looked through the section of the brochure devoted to coffins—chipboard lined with plastic, wood veneer, solid wood, cardboard, woven willow—I began to think of Mr. Collingwood as an actor. I wasn't angry about this, or bitter. I didn't want him to dress like an ice cream salesman or to grin as if he was trying to sell me a new car. But I couldn't help thinking that it was almost four thirty. He might have been at a funeral that morning and he must have had lunch, perhaps in one of the new cafés that had opened in the high street in the last two years. He would have seen at least a couple of people before me, and now it wasn't long until the end of the day. Perhaps he was also thinking about the evening, dinner, seeing his children. Maybe one of them was having trouble at school and he would have to sit with them as they did their homework. For all I knew it was his wedding anniversary or his birthday, and he was going out for dinner. He might have been diagnosed with a fatal disease or he might have won the lottery, but now he was playing the role of the undertaker, with the right note of dignity, competence and concern.

He couldn't really care about me. In fact, I didn't want him to. He hadn't known Greg and he didn't know me, and if I suspected he was feeling real emotion about my loss, it would be creepy, as if I had caught him breaking into my house. So he was giving a performance, just well enough, and as I paged numbly through the brochure, it struck me that everyone I had dealt with had been performing as well. The coroner had been respectful and serious but he had finished in time for lunch; he might have gone straight to his club and laughed about the ridiculous case he had just heard or he might have forgotten about it and told dirty jokes, or gone back to his office alone and drunk whisky from a half-bottle in the bottom drawer of his desk. It didn't matter. While sitting in the court he had played the role of coroner in the presence of a grieving widow. The policewomen had acted the way you act when you tell a wife that her husband has died. If they had been returning a lost cat to a little girl, they would have acted in the appropriate style for that. The registrar at the hospital had performed in the way you perform when a relative comes to view a body.

It couldn't just be a matter of behaving according to their emotions because they couldn't feel those emotions anymore, not when they had done it a hundred times. And why should the hundredth grieving family member not get the same treatment as the first? In reality, the hundredth probably gets better treatment than the first. When the emotion is real, you can't handle it: it overflows and comes out in the wrong way. When it's real, you're not dignified and somber: you grin inappropriately and say the wrong thing and make awkward gestures.

I wondered if it was only the doctors, policemen and undertakers who were performing. Wasn't it a bit true of my friends as well? I thought of Gwen and Mary. When something really big happens, like a death, we play parts we're familiar with. They were being the supportive best friends in time of crisis, using the repertoire of concerned expressions, gestures and consoling phrases, taking my hand, touching my forearm. I was the same, of course. I was in the starring role. This was another feeling that almost drove me mad, the sense that I had to act myself, that I had convincingly to impersonate emotions I wasn't really feeling. I hadn't played the part in those terrible seconds when I was told and must have given a bad performance, stammering, forgetting my lines; confused and shocked rather than grief-struck. But when I had entered Mr. Collingwood's office, I had been safely in the role of the widow, just as he had been in the role of the undertaker. This extended to my costume—dignified and restrained, but not black.

"Do you have any thoughts, Ms. Falkner?"

The tone remained subdued, but now he was reminding me that time was limited. Greg hadn't left a will, let alone instructions for a funeral. He hadn't been planning to die. I had tried to think what he would have wanted. "What he would have wanted," that awful patronizing way of talking about the dead, as if they've been reduced to caricatures: Greg would have wanted this, Greg would have been amused by that. If Greg had planned his own funeral, he would probably have come up with something strange and homemade, a Viking pyre, ashes shot out of a cannon, buried at sea. I couldn't compete with him there. I just needed it to be simple.

I made the decisions quickly. Cremation. A non-religious ceremony. Maybe somebody could say something, we could play a piece of music. Then there was the question of the coffin. More irrelevant thoughts kept coming to me. When we had decided to get married, Greg insisted on getting me an engagement ring and we went to Hatton Garden together. It turned out that Greg knew all about types of metal and carats and stones. Things I had never even thought of turned out to be important. I was sure he would have had strong views on the coffin. The mahogany was probably dubiously sourced. The plastic lining on the cheapest would probably contribute to global warming. Maybe all cremations did. He knew things like that.

"Do people really buy cardboard coffins?" I asked.

"Absolutely," said Mr. Collingwood. "Some families like to decorate them, paint them and so forth. They can look"—he seemed to search for the right word—"Remarkable."

I could have done it. I could even have built the coffin. I had made most of the things in our house or, at least, restored them.

"I think I'll spare people that," I said.

I chose a coffin made from woven willow because it didn't look like a coffin. Mr. Collingwood said approvingly that it was chosen by many people who were concerned about environmental issues. For some reason that irritated me and I suddenly wished I'd chosen one made of hazardous waste. Mr. Collingwood excused himself and withdrew into a small office at the back. I heard the grinding sound of a printer and he returned with a piece of paper, which he slid across the desk toward me. "We believe it's important to give a written estimate," he said.

I looked at it and gulped. "Bloody hell," I said. "I'm sorry. I hadn't realized . . ." Then I stopped, suddenly ashamed. It didn't seem a decent subject to haggle over but I had been startled. The estimate was more than we had paid for our car, and that hadn't been particularly cheap. Mr. Collingwood wasn't disconcerted—he must have had worse cases than me. He assured me that the funeral could be as simple as I wanted.

I studied the estimate, item by item. "You will organize the whole funeral?"

Mr. Collingwood nodded.

I took a deep breath. "OK," I said.

I MEANT TO go straight home. There were so many things that needed doing, so many tasks and lists and duties. Instead I went into Kentish Town station, took a southbound train and got off at Kennington. When I came out of the station I felt, as I always did when I came south of the river, that I had emerged in a city in another country, even if the language was deceptively similar, as if I had arrived in New York or Sydney. I knew that the Livingstones had lived at number sixteen Dormer Road, so I went into a newsagent's and bought an *A–Z*. It took only a few minutes to walk there—but in those minutes I went from one world, of high-rise blocks and dilapidated tenements, to another, of discreet wealth and cool grandeur.

The Livingstones' house was large and white, set back from the road. I instantly disliked its pillared porch and raked gravel, and this helped me march up the short sweep of a drive and ring the bell before I had time to think about what I was doing or prepare an explanation. Only when I heard footsteps coming toward the door did I feel a tremble of anxiety go through me.

"Yeah?"

Why had I assumed it would be Hugo Livingstone, Milena's husband, who answered the door? The youth who stood in front of me was tall and skinny, all angles and joints. I thought he must be in his late teens. He had long, dark, unbrushed hair, eyes that were almost black. He was wearing boxer shorts and a faded T-shirt; as on the day of the inquest, he had a stud in his nose. I smiled cautiously at him but he stood blocking the doorway, arms folded over his chest, a flat, assessing stare on his face.

"Is Hugo Livingstone in?" I asked.

"No."

"You're his son, aren't you? I saw you at the inquest."

"Yeah, that's me." He gave a mock bow, knees knobbly below his boxers, quite unembarrassed by his state of undress—indeed, I thought he was reveling in it. "Silvio Livingstone."

"Silvio?" I said.

"Yes," he said, in an assertive tone, as if daring me to comment on it.

"I'm sorry about your mother," I said.

"Stepmother." The way he said it was so blatantly contemptuous that I was startled. He must have seen my expression change for he gave a challenging grin.

"I'm sorry all the same," I managed. "Do you know when he—"

"No. He works from early to late." Everything he said seemed to have a sarcastic ring. "It's only me that *lounges around.*" He was obviously imitating someone when he said the last two words—his stepmother, I guessed.

"Right," I said. "I'm sorry to have bothered you."

"You're his wife, aren't you?"

I didn't pretend not to understand who he was talking about, simply nodded.

"What do you want here, then?"

"I thought we should meet. Given everything."

"You want to come in?"

"It was only if your father was here."

"He isn't." He gave a shrug. "Did you know?"

"Know what?"

"About them, of course."

"No," I said. "Did you?"

"Not about your husband," he said.

For a reason I didn't understand, I found I was more comfortable with this wretchedly sarcastic, angrily self-conscious young man than I had been with anyone else since Greg had died.

"I've changed my mind," I said. "Unless you think your dad would be angry."

"It's my house too."

"Just for a few minutes, then. Maybe you could make me some coffee."

"And you can ask me questions about her instead of asking Dad. At least I'll be honest. I'm not the one she made a fool of."

He led me through the hall and down a corridor lined with photos. They weren't the kind Greg and I have—had—on our walls, improvised patchworks of snapshots showing us at different stages of our lives, but properly framed portraits. I caught glimpses as I passed: there she was, white flesh glowing above a low black dress; there she was again, hair swept up and a tiny smile on her lips. The kitchen was enormous, glinting with appliances; double doors leading out into the garden flooded it with light.

"Black coffee?" He was filling the kettle.

"White," I said. "So, you had no idea about Greg—my husband?"

"Why would we?"

"What do you mean?"

"The point of a secret affair is that it's secret." I was getting very tired of this phrase. "Milena liked secrets." He scooped ground coffee into a cafetière. "It was what she was good at, secrets, gossip, rumor."

"So it wasn't a surprise?"

"Not really. The dying was, of course."

"What about your father?"

"I don't know. Didn't ask. Here, coffee. Help yourself to milk."

I splashed in some milk and took a sip. It was strong enough to make me gasp. "So you're not really sure?"

For the first time a flash of interest, no, intense curiosity, crossed his face. His eyes narrowed slightly. "They died together," he said. "That's pretty intimate."

"Yes."

"So what do you mean?"

"I mean, there's nothing you've found that shows your stepmother knew Greg?"

"I haven't looked. Why should I?"

"And your father?"

"My father?" He raised his eyebrows sardonically. "Dad's been working very hard since she died. He's been busy."

"I see."

"You probably don't," he said.

"I guess not." I sighed and put down my cup, then stood up. "Thanks, Silvio." I wanted to put my hand on his shoulder, tell him he'd be OK, but I didn't think he'd appreciate that.

"You're not what I'd expected," he said, at the front door.

"What you expected?"

"Of my stepmother's lover's wife."

"It sounds like you're making fun of me," I said.

Suddenly he flushed and seemed younger. "I didn't mean that," he said.

A thought struck before I walked away. "What was she like as a stepmother?"

I thought he would shrug or say something sarcastic, but he went red and muttered something.

"I imagine she wasn't normal stepmother material," I said.

"You shouldn't have come here," he said. "It's none of your business."

He pushed the door shut so abruptly I had to step back quickly so my foot didn't get caught.

Chapter Seven

There was one thing I knew I had to do before the funeral. I'd been thinking about it since the inquest, imagining what it looked like, and recently I'd even started dreaming about it—jerking awake from dreams of a deep pit in the middle of London, Greg's red car hurtling to the bottom, bursting into flames there. Porton Way. I'd wake with images of his face pressed against the windscreen, his mouth open in a scream of terror. Or of his body crushed against Milena's as flames licked them.

If I'd asked Gwen or Mary, they'd have been eager to accompany me, but this was something I needed to do alone. And so, the day before the funeral when I was supposed to be making final arrangements, I headed east. It wasn't an area of London I really knew, though it wasn't far from where we lived (where *you* live, I corrected myself fiercely; not "we" anymore) and I mistook the route, getting off at Stratford. It took me about twenty-five minutes to walk to Porton Way, nearly getting myself killed as I dashed across the great arterial routes that lead east out of London. The sky, which had been gray when I left that morning, turned an ominous purple-brown; a storm was coming, and occasional raindrops splashed my cheek. A bitter wind was blowing over the London streets, whipping up litter and the last of the autumn leaves, which swirled along the pavement.

The entire area seemed to have been turned into a building site. Giant cranes punctuated the horizon and swathes of land had been turned into rubble and sticky mud, scarred with wide trenches. There were Portakabins behind high fences, men in hard hats driving diggers, temporary lights redirecting traffic.

Porton Way, lying at the bottom of a steep incline, was dismal, abandoned, full of half-smashed warehouses and the remnants of old houses, which had been brought to the ground in a pile of bricks and cement blocks. One house was still standing among the ruins, though its front wall had been ripped away. Even from below, I could still see the wallpaper and the old bathtub. Once people had lived there, I thought, sat in that kitchen.

I consulted the map, tracing the route Greg had driven with a finger. What a drab, dreary, ugly place to come for a tryst. But private. Even now, in the middle of the morning, there was no one around; it looked as though work had been suspended for the time being. As I trudged toward the fatal corner, it started to rain, the skies opening up and releasing an onslaught, water streaming down my cheeks, seeping into my inadequate jacket. The bottoms of my jeans were soon soaking. Water squelched in my shoes. My hair lashed wetly against my face. I could barely see where I was going.

But there I was, at the steep corner. This was where it had happened. Greg had gone straight across and plunged down that embankment. I closed my eyes, then opened them again.

Where had he landed exactly? Was there anything remaining of the car? I left the road and clambered down the slope, but the mud was like slippery clay and I half fell, putting out my hand to catch myself, ripping my sleeve on a thick bramble. I heard myself give a sob.

It seemed to take a long time to get to the bottom, and by the time I arrived I was muddy and sodden. My forehead stung and when I put a hand up, it came away red with blood, which trickled into my eye, making it even harder to see where I was going. I took off my scarf and held it against the cut.

And what was I doing there, anyway? What could I hope to prove—that Greg wouldn't have come to this place? He wouldn't, but he had. That he wouldn't have taken his eyes off the road on a sharp corner? He wouldn't but he had. That he would have worn a seatbelt? He would but he hadn't. What did I expect to find—to feel? Some kind of—what was that horrible word the coroner had used at the inquest?—closure? Of course not, yet I knew I had to be there anyway, in some ritual that would have no effect and make no difference.

In fact, it was quite clear where the car had landed, although it had obviously been cleared away long ago. There was a charred patch of land, a small crater in the larger one of Porton Way. I made my way across and squatted. So, this was where Greg had died. I stared at the gash in the earth. I blinked away the streaming rain and pushed my hair back. Drops of blood escaped the scarf I still held to my forehead and I could taste them on my lips, their iron tang. The woman at the inquest had said Greg wouldn't have suffered. Did he even know, as he was dying, that this was the end, or had it been too quick even for that? Had he thought of me?

At last I stood up, miserably cold and wet, my jeans sticking to my legs. There was nothing for me here. I turned my back on the site and trudged up the hill. At some point I realized I'd dropped my scarf, and when I turned I could see it, a wisp of color on the muddy ground. The blood trickled down my face like tears, and when I finally reached the Underground station I thought people were looking at me strangely. I didn't care.

When I arrived home, it was midafternoon and my fingers were so numb I could barely turn the key in the lock.

"Ellie?"

I jumped at his voice behind me and turned. "Joe—what are you doing here?"

"What do you think? I've come to see you. But what on earth have you been up to? You look—" He stopped, staring at me with a kind of fascination. "Extraordinary," he said finally.

"Oh, nothing. I just went out and it started pouring with rain," I said feebly. I didn't really want to talk about my day, not even to Joe.

"You've got blood all over your face."

"Oh, that. It's nothing. It probably looks worse than it is because of the rain. Do you want to come in?"

"Just for a minute."

I managed to get the door open and we stepped into the hall. I pulled off my mud-caked boots and struggled out of my jacket, then stood dripping on to the floor.

"Here," said Joe. "It's not important but I thought you'd want this. It was in the kitchen and we missed it."

He'd brought me Greg's favorite mug. It had the photograph of him finishing his marathon last year printed on it, although repeated washing had faded the image. I took it from Joe and looked at it, at Greg's triumphant, exhausted smile. I'd met him afterward and put my arms around his sweaty body and kissed his sweaty face and his salty lips.

"And I wanted to check if there was anything I could do for the funeral."

"You probably just wanted to check, full stop," I said.

He smiled ruefully at me. "Well, I can see you're taking excellent care of yourself. Go and have a bath."

"I'll do that."

"While you're at it, can I do anything for you? Tidy up a bit or make you a warm drink?"

"That's kind of you, but no thanks."

"Ellie?"

"Yes?"

"You're all right?"

"What? Yes. You know."

"You'll tell me if you're not?"

"Yes."

Chapter Eight

Afterward, I remembered the funeral only as a collection of random moments, all of them bad. We had been told we had to arrive five minutes before the eleven thirty start because there were funerals before and afterward. So, we found ourselves standing outside the north London crematorium waiting for our turn. We were a collection of old friends, family members, hovering, not quite sure what to say or do. I noticed people recognizing each other, breaking into a smile, then remembering they were at a funeral and forcing sadness on to their faces.

The hearse arrived, the back door opened and the wicker coffin was exposed. Mr. Collingwood always referred to it as a casket, as if that was more respectful of the dead. It wasn't lifted by pallbearers, but trundled into the chapel on a silly little trolley that looked as if it should be moving packing cases into a supermarket. It rattled clumsily over the cracks between the paving stones. Mr. Collingwood had warned me about it in advance, saying it had been forced on them by their insurers. There had been reports of serious back injury.

A middle-aged woman, who must have been a relative of Greg's, asked if we should follow it in.

"They're going to get it in position," I said. "I'm not sure if the group before us has finished." It was as if we'd booked a tennis court. Greg's relative, if that was who she was, stayed next to me. I felt no need to try any small talk.

"I'm so sorry," she said.

I still hadn't worked out what to say when people said how sorry they were. "Thank you" didn't seem quite right. Sometimes I'd mumbled something meaningless. This time I just nodded.

"It must be so terrible for you," she said.

"Well, of course," I said. "It was such a shock."

Still she didn't go away. "I mean," she said, "the circumstances were so awkward. It must be so . . . well, you know . . . for you."

And then I thought, Oh, right, I understand. Suddenly I felt bloody-minded. "What do you mean?"

But she was tougher than I was. She wouldn't be diverted. "I mean the circumstances," she said. "The person he died with. It must be so upsetting."

I felt as if I had an open wound and this woman had put her finger into it and was probing to see whether I would cry out or scream. I didn't want to give her the satisfaction. I didn't want to give her anything.

"I'm just sad I've lost my husband," I said. "There's nothing else to say." I walked away from her and looked at the gardens. There were shrubs and little hedges of an institutional kind, the sort you might see in the car park of a business center. The building itself had a mid-twentieth-century solidity about it but was noncommittal at the same time, a bit like a church, a bit like a school. But behind, and towering above it, was a chimney. They couldn't hide that. There was smoke coming out of it. It couldn't be Greg. Not yet.

Now I was sure. I had known already, but perhaps I'd forced it out of my mind, especially for the funeral. Everyone, absolutely everyone, knew that Greg had died with another woman and that this meant they had been having an affair. And what did they think about me?

My next memory of the funeral places me inside, right at the front, next to Greg's parents. I could feel the crowd of mourners behind me, staring at the back of my head. They were sorry for me, but what else did they feel? A little bit of embarrassment, contempt? Poor old Ellie. She hasn't only been made a widow: she's been humiliated, abandoned, her marriage exposed as a sham. Would they be speculating about us? Was it Greg's roving eye? Was it Ellie's failings as a wife?

Greg's brother Ian and his sister Kate had both rung me with suggestions for the service. I had resented this at first. I felt possessive, territorial. Then, suddenly, I'd thought of the funeral as a nightmare version of *Desert Island Discs*, choosing music and poetry to show what a sensitive and interesting person Greg had been and how well I'd understood him. The idea of choosing poems with an eye on what it would make people think of my good taste repelled me so I rang Ian and Kate back and said I'd leave it to them.

Ian came to the front and read some Victorian poem that was meant to be consoling but I stopped paying attention halfway through. Then Greg's other brother, Simon, read something from the Bible that sounded familiar from school assemblies. I couldn't follow that either. The individual words made sense, but I forgot the meaning of the sentences as they unfolded. Then Kate said she was going to play a song that had meant a lot to Greg. There was a pause that went on too long and then a rattling in some speakers on the wall as someone pressed play and then what was clearly the wrong song came on, perhaps a song from the funeral afterward or the one before. It was a power ballad I remembered having heard in a movie, one with Kevin Costner. It was completely alien to Greg, who had liked scratchy songs played on steel guitars by wizened Americans who had served time in prison, or looked as if they had. I glanced across and saw panic on Kate's face. She was visibly wondering whether she could run out and switch off this awful song, find the right CD and put it on, then deciding she couldn't.

It was the only bit of the funeral that really meant anything to me. For just one moment, I had a vivid sense of what it would have been like if Greg had been there, and how he would have looked at me, and how we would have struggled not to laugh, and how we would have cackled about it afterward, and how it would have become a standing joke. It was the closest I got to crying all day, but even then I didn't cry.

When we were spilling out afterward, we collided with another group about to come in and I realized that in another hour they would be colliding with yet another. We were on a conveyor belt of grief.

Everybody was invited back to my place where we had the worst party of all time. It wasn't that the food was bad, far from it. At first I had planned to hit a supermarket and buy everything ready-made but then I'd decided to do it myself. I'd spent the evening and night before making tartlets with goat cheese and red onion and cherry tomatoes and mozzarella and salami. There were toppings on little pieces of dried toast. I'd stuffed red peppers and baked cheese straws. I'd bought a kilo of olives with anchovies and chilies. I'd bought a case of red wine and another of white. I'd baked two cakes. There was coffee, tea, a selection of infusions, and yet it was still the worst party of all time.

It combined the ingredients of different kinds of bad party. For a start, quite a lot of people didn't turn up. Some friends weren't even at the funeral. Others didn't come to the house. They might have felt embarrassed by the circumstances, by the humiliation. It gave the party a forlorn, rejected atmosphere.

Once people started arriving, I was reminded of those awful teenage parties where the boys cluster in a corner, giggling among themselves, staring at the girls but not daring to approach them. Something tribal had happened. Maybe my perspective had been poisoned, but I felt that it was as if Greg had left me for Milena and there were those who were taking his side against me.

Gwen and Mary were there and, of course, they were entirely in my camp. They fetched drinks and food and hovered around me, murmuring words of support. I half expected us to put our handbags on the floor and dance around them.

My parents were there, old and crumpled, and my sister Maria, looking furious—as if Greg had done her a personal wrong by dying in the way he had. Then there was Fergus, whose eyes were swollen with grief; I envied him that. He had wanted to read something at the funeral but at the last moment pulled out. He said he didn't think he'd manage it. I got the impression from Jemma, his hugely pregnant wife, that he had been sobbing on and off since it had happened.

There were people like Joe and Tania, who drifted between the camps, making heroic and doomed efforts to bring them together. There were groups of Greg's and my friends, but everything seemed forced and awkward.

In a strange way, the people I took most comfort from were not friends, certainly not family, but those I had never met before. There was an old primary-school friend whose name I recognized as the James with whom Greg had run three-legged races; there was a large man with a face like a bloodhound's who had taught Greg piano when he was a teenager. There were several clients, who came up to tell me how much they had depended on Greg, trusted him, liked him, and would miss him now that he was gone. It was such a relief to be with people who didn't know the backstory to his death, and were there simply to say goodbye.

"He was a very dear young man," said Mrs. Sutton, in a piercing voice. She wore a black silk dress and seamed stockings, and had a creased face and silver hair in an immaculate bun. She looked very old and very rich, with an aquiline nose and straight-backed bearing that seemed to belong to a different era.

"Yes, he was," I agreed.

"I always looked forward to his visits. I'm going to miss him."

"I'm sorry," I said absurdly.

"As a matter of fact, he was going to visit me the day after he died. That was how I heard—when he failed to arrive I rang his office to ask where he was. It was such a shock." She gave me a piercing glance. "I'll be eighty-eight in two months' time. It doesn't seem right, does it? People dying out of their turn."

I couldn't speak and she lifted a hand like a claw and placed it lightly over mine. "You have my sympathy, my dear," she said.

For the main part, however, it was a funeral party where nobody seemed able to do the sort of things that funeral parties are for. They couldn't offer their condolences without seeming embarrassed or creepy; they couldn't engage in uncomplicated, emotional reminiscences about the deceased. They couldn't do anything else either. Some picked at the food, others gulped the wine (the woman who had approached me outside the crematorium had much more than was good for her, whether in remorse or some perverse kind of revenge). And gradually they just peeled away.

In the end, Gwen, Mary and I were left with a handful of Greg's relatives I didn't know; they had ordered a taxi that kept not arriving. They sat on the sofa with empty glasses, refusing top-ups and more food because it would spoil their dinner. They phoned the cab company repeatedly while we cleared and wiped and finally vacuumed around them. In the end they left, muttering something about finding a taxi in the street or catching a tube.

Gwen and Mary stayed on and I opened some more wine and told them about the woman outside the crematorium and what she had said, and Mary said, "You don't have to fight it, you know." I asked her what she meant by that and she said I had nothing to feel bad about. Men were bastards. My friends loved me and would support me. I would get through this. I can't remember making much of a reply. Instead I just poured myself glass after glass of wine and drank it as if I was insatiably thirsty. They asked if I wanted them to stay and I said I wanted them not to stay, so they left and I think I drank one more glass of wine, a big one, though, filled almost to the lip, so that I had to hold it with both hands.

When I was ten my grandfather had died. I didn't want to go to the funeral but my mother said funerals were where we went to say goodbye to people who had died. We thought about them and we cried for them and we said goodbye to them and then we went back to our lives.

I lay on my bed fully clothed and couldn't decide whether the room was rotating around me or whether my bed was rotating inside the room or whether in deep, philosophical terms it made a difference. But as I lay there, drunker than at any time since my first year at university, I knew that on that day I hadn't cried for Greg, and, above all, I hadn't said goodbye to him.

Chapter Nine

In the middle of the night I suddenly sat up in bed, straining my eyes in the darkness. I didn't know what time it was. I had turned off the digital alarm clock because, over the past weeks, I had come to dread waking in the small hours and gazing at the time clicking past. I only knew that it was dark and that something had roused me. A thought, which must have wormed its way into my dreams. A memory.

Like most couples, I'm sure, Greg and I used to have conversations about which of our friends were unfaithful. After all, if one in three partners cheats on the other, or something like that, we figured we must be surrounded by people who were betraying each other. Now I remembered a conversation so vividly it was like being there again, and there we were in bed together, warm under the duvet and facing each other in the grainy half-light, his hand on my hip and my foot resting against his calf.

"My parents?" he was saying, and I giggled: "No way!"

"*Your* parents?"

"Please!"

"Who, then?"

"Fergus and Jemma?" I suggested.

"Impossible. They've only been together for a couple of years and he's not that kind of guy."

"What kind of guy is that? And, anyway, it doesn't need to be him, it could be her."

"She's too moral. And too pregnant. What about Mary and Eric?"

"She would have told me," I said firmly.

"Sure? What about if it was him?"

"She would *definitely* have told me that too. Even if she didn't, I'd know."

"How?"

"I just would. She's a very bad liar. Her neck goes blotchy."

"What about me—would you be able to tell with me?"

"Yes—so watch it."

"How would you know?"

"I just would."

"Trusting fool."

We smiled at each other, sure of our happiness.

I got out of bed, pushed my feet into slippers, went downstairs and into the kitchen, turning on the overhead light and blinking in the sudden dazzle. I saw from the wall clock that it was nearly three o'clock. It was windy outside and when I pressed my face to the window, trying to make out the shape of the roofs and chimneys, I imagined all those people out there, lying safely in bed with each other, warm and submerged in their dreams. I could still hear Greg's voice and see his smile, and the contrast between the intense comfort of that memory and this cold, empty darkness was like a blow to the stomach, making my eyes water. No one tells you how physical unhappiness can be, how it hurts in your sinuses and throat, glands, muscles and bones.

I made myself a mug of hot chocolate and drank it slowly. Greg's face faded. I knew he wasn't here, wasn't anywhere. His ashes were in a small square box with a rubber band around it. But I heard his teasing voice. Trusting fool, he called me.

"Fergus."

"Ellie?" His eyes widened with surprise. He was still in his dressing gown, unshaven and puffy with sleep. "Are you OK?"

"Did I wake you?"

"What's happened?"

"Can I come in?"

He stood back, pulling his dressing gown more tightly around him, and I walked past him into the kitchen, where the four of us had sat so many times, eating takeaways, playing cards, drinking almost until it got light. The supper things were still on the table: two stacked plates, an empty serving bowl, a half-drunk bottle of red wine. Fergus started to collect them up, dropping the forks on the tiled floor with a clatter.

"I know it's a bit early."

"It doesn't matter. Coffee? Tea? Breakfast? Devilled kidneys? That last one was a joke. Jemma will be in bed for ages. She's on maternity leave now." As he said this, I saw anxiety cross his face: Jemma was on maternity leave and I was childless, barren, shamed and alone.

"Coffee, please. Maybe some toast."

"Marmalade, honey, jam?"

"Whatever. Honey."

"If we've got any. No. No honey. Or jam, actually."

"Marmalade's fine."

"The funeral seemed to go off all right," he said cautiously, as he filled the kettle and slid a slice of bread into the toaster.

"The funeral was crap."

He smiled ruefully at me.

"No one knew what to say to me."

"It's over, at least."

"Not really."

He looked at me, eyebrows raised. "What d'you mean?"

"I've decided to believe him."

The kettle started to boil, sending puffs of steam into the air. Very methodically, he measured spoonfuls of coffee into the pot, then poured in the water. Only when he had handed me the hot mug did he look me in the eye. "Come again?" he said.

"Greg didn't have an affair."

"Oh," said Fergus, putting his mug carefully on to the table with a click, then wiping his mouth with the back of his hand. "Right."

"On the one hand there's how it appears, him dying with this other woman."

"Yes."

"And on the other is my trust."

"Yes."

"I'm keeping faith. I'm not abandoning him."

I waited for Fergus to say that he was dead, but he didn't.

He said, "I see," and picked up his mug again, staring at me over the rim. "Well, that's good, I suppose."

"Yes, it is."

"Good, I mean, if it lets you come to terms with what's happened."

"No."

"No?"

"Because what has happened?"

Fergus frowned and ran his fingers through his hair, so it stood on end, giving him the look of a sad clown. He dipped his finger into his coffee and licked it. "Why don't you tell me what you're thinking, Ellie?" he said eventually.

"When you were doing work for him, in the office, did you see any sign that he was . . . you know—involved?"

"No."

"Nothing?"

"Nothing. That doesn't mean—"

I interrupted what I knew he was going to say. "Look, Fergus, Greg died with another woman. But he wasn't having an affair with her. He wasn't. OK? So, what were they doing together? That's the question, isn't it? For a start there are other possibilities." Fergus looked at me and didn't speak. "Just off the top of my head she might have been a hitchhiker."

Fergus thought for a moment. "Not wanting to be a devil's advocate, but this woman—"

"Milena Livingstone."

"She was some sort of businesswoman, no?"

"Sort of."

"Do they tend to hitchhike? In London?"

"Or just some business contact."

"Absolutely."

"That he was giving a lift to."

"All right."

"So you believe him?"

"Ellie, he's not here to believe. Your husband—my best friend, the man we both loved and miss like hell—is dead. That's what this is really about, isn't it? It's as if by somehow persuading yourself that he wasn't fucking another woman, he won't be dead after all. You'll go mad if you keep on like this."

"You only think that because you believe I'm wrong, deluding myself, and that Greg was unfaithful to me."

"You're never going to find out what happened," he said wearily.

I should have kept a tally of how many times that had been said to me. "I trust him," I said. "That's enough for me. The toast is burning, by the way."

AT SUNDAY LUNCH with Joe, Alison and one of their three children, Becky, who had her father's blue stare, her mother's pallor and reticence, I repeated what I'd said to Fergus. It was harder in front of three people. I sounded forced and overinsistent. I saw Joe's shoulders sag, and I saw him throw a helpless glance at Alison before he turned to me, a lettuce leaf dangling from his fork. "Sweetheart," he said.

"I know what that means," I said. "*Sweetheart*. It means you're going to tell me very patiently why you think I'm behaving in a wrong-headed and self-destructive way. You're going to tell me I'll never find out the truth and must learn to live with that uncertainty and move on. And probably you'll tell me this is a form of grieving."

"That's pretty much it, yes. And that we love you and want to help in any way we can."

"Do you want to put the kettle on, Becky?" Alison said, in a mild tone. "I'll get the cheese."

"You don't need to be tactful, Alison." I smiled at her. "We've known each other too long and too well for that. It's fine. I'm fine. Really. I just thought you should know that Greg wasn't being unfaithful."

"Good."

"It would be better if someone believed me."

THE MAN STOOD on my doorstep, barely visible behind the battered wooden rocking chair he was holding.

"Terry Long," he said. "I've got the chair for you." He looked at me expectantly.

"I don't—" I began.

"For my wife. It's her Christmas present. You said you'd repair it for us. It's a bit of a mess, as you see. It was her grandfather's, though, so it has sentimental value."

"There's been a mistake."

"I called you at the beginning of September. You said it would be fine."

"Things have changed," I said. "I'm not taking on new work."

"But you *said* . . ." His face had hardened. He put the chair on the ground, and it rocked gently between us, making a clicking sound. One of its runners was badly damaged. "You can't just let people down like that."

"I'm sorry."

"That's it? You're sorry?"

"I'm very sorry. I just can't. I really can't. I'm sorry." I kept repeating the word: sorry, sorry, sorry. In the end he went, leaving the broken chair behind. Even his back looked angry.

I picked up the rocking chair, shut the door, and went through the house and into the garden where I unlocked my shed; the door was reinforced and there had been three padlocks on it since the time a year ago when a gang of youths had broken into it and stolen some of my tools. Inside, there were several ladder-backed chairs, a corner cupboard in dark oak, a lovely little ash cabinet without a back, a carved chest with an ugly gash along its lid and scars where some of its raised designs had been, and a Georgian desk. They were waiting for my attention. I went in, without turning on the light, and ran my finger across the wooden surfaces. Even though I hadn't been in there for days and days, there was still the wonderful smell of sawdust and wax. Curls of planed wood lay on the floor. I squatted, picked up a pale rind and fingered it for a while, wondering if I'd ever come back to work here again.

Greg and I had argued about stupid things. Whose turn it was to empty the rubbish bin. Why he didn't rinse the basin after he'd shaved. Why I didn't know how irritating it was when I cleaned up around him, huffing just loudly enough so that he'd hear me. When he interrupted me in the middle of a sentence. When I'd used up all the hot water. We argued about clothes that shrank in the wash, botched arrangements, overcooked pasta and burnt toast, careless words, trivial matters of mess and mismanagement. We never fell out over the big things, like God or war, deceit or jealousy. We hadn't had long enough together for that.

"So you don't believe me?"

Mary and I were walking on the Heath. It was cool and gray, the wind carrying a hint of rain. Our feet shuffled through drifts of damp leaves. Robin, her one-year-old, was in a carrier on her back; he was asleep and his bald, smooth head bobbed and lolled on her neck as we walked. His pouchy body swung with each step Mary took.

"I didn't say that. Not exactly. I said . . ."

"You said, 'Men are such bastards.'"

"Yes."

"Meaning?"

"Meaning that men are such bastards. Look, Ellie, Greg was lovely."

"*But?*"

"But he wasn't a saint. Most men stray if they get the chance."

"Stray?" I said. I was beginning to feel angry and rattled. "Like a sheep that's got out of its field?"

"It's all about opportunity and temptation. This Milena probably made the first move."

"This Milena didn't have anything to do with him. Or him with her."

Suddenly Mary stopped. Her cheeks were blotchy in the

cold. Over her shoulder Robin's eyes opened blearily, then closed again. A thread of saliva worked its way down his chin.

"You don't believe what you're saying, do you?" she said. "Not really."

"Yes, I do. Though you clearly don't."

"Because I don't agree with you, it doesn't mean I'm not on your side. Are you trying to push us all away? It's rotten, what's happened. Really horrible. I have no idea how I'd be dealing with it in your situation. Listen, though." She put a hand on my arm. "I do have a bit of an understanding of what you're going through. You know Eric? Well, obviously you know Eric. You know what happened just after Robin was born—and when I say 'just after,' that's what I mean. Three and a half weeks, to be precise."

A feeling of dejection settled on me.

"He slept with this woman at work. I was woozy and weepy and tired, my breasts were sore, I'd only just had my stitches out so I could hardly sit down, sex was out of the question—I was a moony, overweight cow. And yet I was happy. I was so happy I thought I'd melt. And it wasn't just once, a drunken mistake or something, it went on for weeks. He'd come home late, take lots of showers, be overattentive, overirritable. It's such a bloody cliché, isn't it? Looking back, I can't believe I didn't realize what was going on. It's not as if the signs weren't there. But I was blind, in my own little bubble of contentment. I had to practically see them together before I knew."

"Why didn't you tell me before?" I remembered again the conversation with Greg, in which I had insisted I would have known if Eric had been unfaithful to Mary.

"Because I felt humiliated. And stupid." She glared at me. "So fat and ugly and useless and ashamed. You must understand that feeling now, after what's happened to you. That's why I'm telling you."

"Mary," I said, "I'm sorry. I wish we'd talked about it before. But it's not the same."

"What makes you and Greg so different?"

"He wouldn't have behaved like that."

"That's what I used to say about Eric."

"I have an instinct."

"You can't face the truth. I'm your friend. Remember? We can tell the truth to each other, even if it hurts."

"It doesn't hurt because it's not true."

"Has it occurred to you that maybe he was sick of having sex to get pregnant?"

I couldn't stop myself: I flinched in pain, as if Mary had slapped me across the face.

"Oh, Ellie." Her face softened; I saw there were tears in her eyes, whether from the cold or emotion I couldn't tell.

WPC DARBY SHOWED me into a small room. There were red and pink plastic flowers in a jug on the desk, and more flowers—yellow this time, a copy of Van Gogh's *Sunflowers*—in a framed picture on the wall. I sat down and she sat opposite me, folding her hands on the desk. They were broad and strong, with bitten nails. No rings on her fingers. I looked at her face, weathered, shrewd and pleasantly plain under her severely cut hair, and was satisfied that she was the right person to tell. There was some meaningless chat and then I stopped.

"It's not the way it seemed," I said.

She leaned toward me slightly, her gray eyes on my face.

"I don't believe he was having an affair with Milena Livingstone."

Her expression didn't waver. She just went on looking at me and waiting for me to speak.

"Actually I don't think they even knew each other."

She gave a nervous smile and when she spoke it was clearly and slowly, as if I was a small child. "They were in the same car."

"That's why I'm here," I said. "It's a mystery. I think you ought to look at it again."

In the silence, I could hear the voices in the corridor outside. WPC Darby steepled her fingers and took a deep breath. I knew what she was going to say before she said it.

"Ms. Falkner, your husband died in a car crash."

"He wasn't wearing his seat belt—but Greg *always* wore it. You have to investigate further."

"The coroner was perfectly satisfied that it was a tragic accident and that no other vehicle was involved. I understand that the fact he was with another woman is unsettling and upsetting for you. As a matter of evidence, how they knew each other doesn't matter."

"There's no evidence at all, of any kind," I said. "Nothing to show that he knew her."

Again, I anticipated what she was going to say. "If he was having an affair and keeping it secret, then perhaps that's not surprising."

"I'm telling you, he didn't know her."

"No. You're telling me you don't *believe* he knew her."

"It amounts to the same thing."

"With all due respect, it does not. What you believe and what is true are not necessarily the same thing."

"So you're just going to let things lie?"

"Yes. And I would advise you to do the same. You might consider seeing someone about—"

"You think I need bereavement counseling? Professional help?"

"I think you've had a terrible shock and are having difficulty in coming to terms with it."

"If anyone says 'coming to terms' to me again, I think I'll scream."

Chapter Ten

I read through Greg's emails so often that I almost knew them by heart. I thought they might give me a sense of his mood in the days and weeks leading up to his death. Was there a hint of anxiety? Anger? Apprehension? I couldn't find anything and gradually they became familiar, like songs you've played so often you don't hear them anymore. Then I noticed something blindingly obvious, something that everybody in the developed world apart from me must already have known. Every email showed the exact time he had pressed the send button. Each email, whether from his home or his office computer, was a fairly accurate guide as to where Greg had been at a particular moment.

Within half an hour I was back from the stationer's with two bulky carrier-bags. I tipped their contents on to the carpet. There was a large roll of poster-sized card stock, rulers, different-colored pens and Magic Markers, highlighters, and sheets and sheets of little stickers—circles, squares and stars. It looked like the raw materials for a nursery-school art project.

I spread four of the cards in a row on the floor, using heavy books to hold the corners down. Then, using a ruler and a fine architect's pen, I started to rule grids across them, each representing a week in the last month of Greg's life. I traced seven columns, then drew horizontal lines cutting them into halves, then quarters, then eighths and so on, until I had chopped each column into a hundred and twenty rectangles, each representing ten minutes in a day starting at eight and finishing at midnight. I didn't bother about the nights because we hadn't spent a night apart in the last month.

Just from memory, I was able to cross out entire evenings I knew we had spent together. On the weekends there were whole days I eliminated with a bold stroke of black: the Saturday we had taken the train to Brighton, walked on the beach, eaten some awful fish and chips, bought a secondhand book of poetry and I'd fallen asleep on his shoulder on the journey back; the day we walked along the Regent's Canal from Kentish Town all the way to the river. Those were two days when he hadn't been having sex with Milena Livingstone.

Then I started on the emails. At work, Greg had written twenty or thirty a day, sometimes more. Based on each one, I wrote "O" for office in the appropriate slot on the card. Some were in clusters. He had a habit of sending a flurry of messages as soon as he arrived at work, another just before one o'clock and another at around five, but others were dotted through the day. It didn't take me much more than an hour to work my way through the emails, and when I was done, I stood back and surveyed the result. The chart was already satisfyingly shaded in, and there was still so much to do.

The next day I invited Gwen around. I said it was urgent but she was at work and didn't reach me until almost six. When she arrived I hustled her through to the kitchen, boiled the kettle and made a pot of coffee.

"Would you like a biscuit?" I said. "Or a slice of ginger cake? I made both this afternoon. I've been busy."

Gwen looked amused and a bit alarmed. "Some cake," she said. "A tiny slice."

I poured the coffee and gave her the cake on a plate. I wasn't hungry. I'd felt I needed to cook but not to eat.

"So what's up?" said Gwen. "Did you summon me here to try the cake? It's great, by the way."

"Good, have some more. No, it's nothing to do with that. Drink your coffee and I'll take you through."

"Take me through? What is this, a surprise party?"

"Nothing like that," I said. "I've got something to show you. I think it'll interest you."

Gwen took a few quick gulps of her coffee and said she was ready. I steered her along the hall and into the living room.

"There," I said. "What do you think of that?"

Gwen stared down at the four large pieces of card, now covered with marks and stickers, all different shapes and colors. "It looks lovely," she said. "What's it meant to be?"

"That's Greg's life in the month before he died," I said.

"What do you mean?"

I explained to Gwen how the charts represented days and sections of days. I told her about the timed emails and my own memories and how I'd even found receipts from the sandwich bars where Greg had bought his lunch. All the receipts, whether for food or petrol or stationery, gave not just a date but an exact time, to the minute, when the purchase was made. "So all these stickers, the yellow circles and the green squares, they show moments when I know exactly where Greg was. It's pretty amazing, isn't it?"

"Yes, but—"

"A couple of times a week Greg drove to visit a client. But I pretended to be Greg's assistant, rang up and said that for tax reasons I needed an exact time for when the meeting had taken place. People were very helpful. I've marked all those in blue. Even then I was left with the gap between him leaving the office and arriving at the client. But I found a website. If I type in the postcode of the office and the postcode of his client, it gives an exact driving distance and even an estimated journey time. I've marked those in red. Obviously, driving in London traffic during the day, it's not an exact science, but even so it fits pretty well. It took me a day and a half—and look."

"What?"

"What do you see?"

"Lots of colors," said Gwen. "Lots of stickers."

"No," I said. "It's what you *don't* see. There's barely a gap over four weeks when I don't know where he was and what he was doing."

"Which means?"

"Look at the chart, Gwen," I said. "It shows Greg working very hard, traveling, eating, buying stuff, going to the movies with me. But where's the bit when he's having an affair? Where's the space for him even to meet the woman he died with?"

There was a long pause.

"Ellie," she began, "for God's sake—"

"No," I said. "Stop. Listen for a moment. I talked to Mary about this—not about this," I gestured at the charts, "I mean my feelings about Greg. She wasn't sympathetic. She was even angry with me, as if it was some insult to her that I wasn't immediately accepting that my husband had been having an affair and had had a crash with the woman he really loved."

"No one's saying that," said Gwen. She looked at my charts almost with an expression of pity. "I don't really know what to make of this." She took my hand. "I'm not an expert but I've heard that there are stages of grief and at the beginning it's anger and denial. It's completely understandable that you feel anger. I think the point of mourning is to get through that and reach some kind of acceptance."

I pulled my hand away. "I know all of that," I said. "I read a piece about it once in *Cosmo*. And you know what I was thinking when I was doing all this crazy stuff with colored stickers and ringing people up under false pretenses? What would make it easy would be to find just one deleted email, just one scrap of paper in a pocket, that would show Greg had been having an affair. Or even just one occasion when he wasn't where he was meant to be, or a missing afternoon when nobody knew where he was. Forget denial. Then I could just get angry and be sad, and my life would continue. There's no trick to proving somebody's having an affair. You catch them at it, just once. But how do you prove somebody's innocent? What do you suggest?"

Gwen shook her head. "I don't know," she said.

"You have to do something like this," I said. "Something obsessive and excessive. You have to fill in all the gaps, then the gaps between the gaps so there's just no space for this relationship. You know I went to see the police?"

"Ellie, you didn't!"

"I told this woman officer I was convinced my husband wasn't having an affair. She didn't seem to believe me. I don't think she thought it even mattered whether he was or not. The case was closed. This wasn't something she wanted to hear about. But if I showed those charts to the police, do you think it would make a difference?"

Gwen frowned at the charts for a long time. "Honestly?" she said.

"Yes."

"This is amazing," she said. "Scary but amazing. I don't think the police would pay much attention to it, but if they did, they might say, 'Perhaps he was seeing the woman while he was doing other things. Perhaps she met him while he was buying his sandwich, perhaps she went with him in the car to his meetings. Or you might be right. Maybe they didn't meet in that month. She could have been away and they were meeting up again on the day they crashed.'"

I took a deep breath. My first impulse was to be angry with Gwen, to shout at her and show her the door, but I stopped myself. She might have humored me. Instead she had said what she really thought.

"And if they said anything," Gwen continued, "it would be that you're ignoring the only piece of evidence that really matters, which is that Greg and the woman died together. What in the end can you really say to that?"

I thought for a moment. "That it's difficult to be innocent," I said. "And to prove you're innocent is impossible."

Chapter Eleven

I knew before I rang the bell and knocked with the heavy brass ring that no one was there: there were no lights on in any of the windows, no car parked in the driveway; the house had an unoccupied look. But I stood, stamping my feet in the cold, waiting to make sure. I opened the letterbox and saw only the polished floor. I peered through the downstairs window and saw the tidy, empty living room, the swept hearth, the gleaming top of a grand piano with photographs on top in silver frames. It was too arranged and perfect, like a stage set rather than a home. I wondered what Hugo Livingstone was feeling now. Was he lonely, angry, sad? Did he think about Greg as I thought about Milena, with hatred, jealousy and puzzlement? Did he think about me? Did he know something I didn't?

That morning, when I had sat over my unsatisfactory breakfast of slightly stale bread and the last scrapings of marmalade, I had decided I needed to look at the picture from the other side. I had examined Greg's life and found nothing, but what about Milena's? Although to say that I had "decided" is inaccurate, because what had actually happened was that I had drifted around the house, at a loss as to what to do with myself, picking things up and putting them down, opening the fridge and closing it, shuffling out through the garden,

which was neglected and piled with soggy leaves, unlocking
the shed door and gazing at the furniture waiting for my attention. Then I'd put on my coat, wrapped a scarf around my
neck and walked to the Underground station, without even
saying to myself that I was going back to the Livingstones'
house and certainly without knowing what I hoped to find
there. Silvio, smiling sarcastically, a signed and dated love letter from Greg to Milena, with a photo of the besotted couple
together? His father, assuring me that his wife had never had
an affair with Greg and he could prove it with—with what?
Nothing could prove that.

There I was, on a damp, gray November morning, staring
at the blank windows of the large house and wondering miserably what to do next. Because I couldn't return to my own
small, cold house and deal with the things that were piling
up: bills, letters, phone messages, laundry, dead leaves, broken
chairs, dust, dirt and drabness. I found myself consulting my
map and walking the half mile or so from the Livingstone
house to the address of Party Animals, the business Milena
and her partner had run together.

I'd looked at the company website, read about parties at
the Tower of London and the zoo, fancy-dress balls, color-
coordinated golden weddings, Burns Night celebrations, with
haggis created especially for people who didn't like haggis,
and dinners for your most valued clients with six elegant
courses. I thought about the parties Greg and I had had—you
invite people around at the last moment to squash into the
front room, ask them to bring wine, then cook chile con carne
and garlic bread, put on some music and see what happens.

Tulser Road was a quiet residential street just down from Vauxhall Bridge. It didn't look like the kind of place for offices and, indeed, number eleven was clearly just a house, like the other houses on either side: large and semi-detached, with a side alley leading to its garden, a basement floor and bay windows. There was only one bell, and no sign saying that this was where exciting and original happenings, tailor-made to suit every individual customer, were organized. But there were lights on in the downstairs window; someone was there, at least. I raised my hand to ring the bell and saw my wedding ring. I looked at it for a moment, almost dispassionately, as if it had suddenly appeared. In fact I hadn't taken it off since—with a great deal of effort—Greg had pushed it over my knuckle in the register office. I had thought it would be difficult to get off but I'd lost weight and it made no resistance. It was an object now, not part of me. I put it into my purse and rang the bell.

The woman who answered the door was slightly older than I had expected; she was tall and slender, with long legs and unexpectedly full breasts. Her highlighted blond hair was cut short in a chic style with soft wisps framing her triangular face. Her pale skin was just beginning to line, and she wore thick, rectangular specs. She had on beautifully tailored black trousers and a pale blue linen shirt, tiny studs in her ears and a thin silver chain around her neck. If she was wearing makeup, it was the invisible kind. There was a classy look to her, a restrained and intelligent attractiveness that I liked immediately.

"Yes?" she said. "Can I help you?" Her voice was low and husky; her manner was polite, but a little impatient. From somewhere in the house there was a loud bang, the sound of something dropped. I saw her wince and bite her lip.

"Is this where Party Animals is run from?"

"That's right. Are you planning an event?"

"No," I said. "I've come about Milena Livingstone."

I saw her eyes widen and then she made a visible effort to control herself. She reminded me of me. I recognized the weary sense that the story would have to be told yet again.

"Are you a friend of hers?" Without giving me time to answer, she said, "Didn't you know?"

There was a fraction of a moment when I could have said, yes, I knew, because the man she died with was my husband. But something stopped me. "Know what?" I said.

"Come in for a second. Sorry, my name's Frances Shaw."

She held out a hand and I shook it. Her grip was warm, strong; I saw that her nails were painted the palest pink. I stepped over the threshold and she shut the door behind us, then led me along a corridor.

"Better come downstairs into the office, if you can call it that. I'm in total chaos, I'm afraid." She led me into the basement, a large room with a long table in the center; on its surface were several roughly stacked heaps of paper and files. There was a sofa covered with brochures and a desk pushed up against the wall, also piled high with folders.

A phone was ringing and a young woman, with dramatically dark eye shadow and very high-heeled boots, came out of the adjoining room. "Shall I get that?" she asked.

"No, let the machine answer it," said Frances. "I tell you

what, though, Beth, perhaps you could make us a cup of coffee. If you want coffee, that is," she added, turning to me.

"Coffee would be lovely." I was a bit dazed.

"Have a seat." Frances scooped up the brochures from the sofa, looked at them helplessly, then laid them on the floor. "When did you last see Milena?"

"I don't want to give you the wrong impression . . ." I said.

The phone rang again and then her mobile, which was lying on the table. "Damn. Sorry. I'll be with you in a second." She flipped it open and turned away from me. I heard her murmuring something. Upstairs, cupboard doors banged and Beth's heels clicked across the floor. I sat on the sofa, taking off my jacket. The warm, cluttered room was like a nest.

Frances snapped shut her mobile and sat beside me. "I'm surprised you haven't heard. I'm so sorry to have to tell you that Milena died."

That was my last chance to say who I was, but I didn't. I wasn't even sure why. Perhaps it was a relief to be the onlooker for a while, rather than the victim.

"Oh!" I said, and rubbed my face because I wasn't sure what my expression should be.

"This must be a shock."

"I wasn't exactly close to her," I said, which was true.

"She died recently in a car crash."

"How terrible," I muttered. I felt like an actor, saying lines that made little sense to me.

"It was awful. She was with a man." There was a pause. "Someone nobody knew even existed."

"So young," I said. The possibility of putting Frances straight receded, and then—as she told me Milena's husband and her stepchildren were coping as well as could be expected and I expressed sympathy—it vanished altogether.

"Hence the chaos," said Frances, gesturing at the room.

"It must be hard for you," I said. "Were you close?"

"When you work together the way we did, you have to be close." She grimaced. "For better or worse. She wasn't exactly . . ."

Frances stopped herself. I wondered what she'd been going to say. What wasn't Milena? I wanted to ask what she had been like, but I was supposed to know that. So instead I nodded and said, "Yes," in an I-know-just-what-you-mean kind of way.

The door was flung open and Beth tottered in, carrying a tray on which there were a cafetière, two mugs, a milk jug, a bowl of sugar lumps and a plate of biscuits. As she approached she stepped on a file and stumbled. She tried to keep control but disaster was inevitable, as in the seconds after a building has been dynamited from beneath. There was a moment of quiet and then it got noisy and messy. The cafetière banged on to the wooden boards and exploded, sending arcs of coffee everywhere; the jug shattered and a river of milk ran across the floor toward Frances; the mugs broke on impact and shards skidded across the room; sugar lumps bounced up at surprising angles.

"Fuck," said Beth, from the floor. "Oh, fuck and fuck."

"Are you hurt?" said Frances. She didn't seem particularly surprised, just very, very tired.

"Sorry," said Beth, scrambling to her feet with an expression of almost comical surprise. "It's a bit of a mess, isn't it?"

"Let me help," I said.

"Don't be ridiculous," said Frances.

I took Beth's arm.

"Come on," I said. "Show me where your cleaning stuff is."

"Would you? That's really kind. There's a mop in the tall cupboard in the kitchen, paper towels in a dispenser, and a dustpan and brush under the sink."

We went upstairs into the long kitchen that smelt of coffee and fresh-baked bread. When we returned, Frances was on the phone, protesting about something. When she'd hung up, she took off her glasses to rub her eyes.

"Trouble at work?" I laid wads of kitchen towel over the puddles of milk and coffee and started to pick up pieces of glass and china and drop them into a bag. Beth hovered around me, avoiding broken china.

"What I need," said Frances, "is the world to stop for about a week while I get the backlog sorted out and my life in some kind of order. Milena—may she rest in peace—wasn't the most organized of women. I keep discovering things she's done or promised that there's no record of. At least," she glanced around the room, "no record that I can lay my hands on." She watched me as I picked up the sugar lumps one by one, swept up the biscuit crumbs, picked up the mass of sodden kitchen roll and dumped it in a bin-bag. "You shouldn't be doing this."

"I quite like clearing up mess," I said. "With your work,

though, you should chunk it up. You can't clear it all at once. Maybe you should get extra help in, for the time being at least."

"I can't do anymore," said Beth, grumpily.

"I wouldn't expect you to," said Frances.

I gathered some loose sheets of paper from the floor. "What do you want me to do with these?"

"Nothing. You've done more than enough as it is. I'll sort them out later."

"I can put them into piles for you, if you want. I'm quite good at organizing stuff."

"I couldn't possibly ask you to do that."

"You're not asking. I'm offering. I'm not doing anything right now. I'm . . ." I hesitated . . . "between jobs."

"You'd do that?" For a moment she looked as though she was about to burst into tears or hug me.

"Just to sort this lot out. After all, it wouldn't have happened if you hadn't offered me coffee."

Beth pottered around to not very much effect while Frances and I sorted the papers: venues, catering companies that Party Animals used, parties being planned, quotations. There was nothing that gave me any hint of the personal life of Milena Livingstone, although there were papers with her dashingly scrawled signature, and Frances referred to the dozens of sympathy letters she'd received and hadn't yet replied to.

Beth made coffee in a jug and brought it in mug by mug, with an air of triumph. I felt strangely, absurdly relaxed, even though I was there under false pretenses. It was a relief to be helping someone instead of being the one in need. Maybe it also felt good to have a holiday from being me, the grieving widow and "betrayed wife," pitied friend with a great big bee in her bonnet. When the time came for me to go, Frances, seeming slightly embarrassed but also a bit desperate, asked if there was any chance I could pop back. I replied, trying to sound casual, that I'd be glad to help out and suggested the next day.

"Yes, great," said Frances. "Oh, Lord, that's amazing. You're my savior. I was on the point of—Hang on, I don't even know your name."

And I answered, without a beat, "Gwen. Gwen Abbott."

Chapter Twelve

As soon as I arrived home, I looked up Gwen's name in the phone book. It wasn't there, probably because she teaches math in a secondary school. If her name was in the book her phone would never stop ringing: What's the homework for tomorrow? I can't do question three. Why did my child fail his exam? And, now, baffling messages from the party-organizing company she didn't know she worked for.

Then I looked up Hugo Livingstone and, before I could stop myself, punched in his number. On the second ring it was answered by a woman with a strong Eastern European accent.

"Hello?"

"Hello," I said. "Could I speak to Hugo Livingstone?"

"He's not here."

"When would be a good time to call back?"

"He will be away for many days. He is in America."

"Oh. Sorry to have troubled you."

I put a baking potato into the oven, poured myself a glass of wine and then another as I thought about what I had done. Had I committed a crime? I didn't think so. As long as I wasn't doing it to perpetrate a fraud or theft, I couldn't actually be arrested. Was that right?

Was I being dishonest? Well, obviously.

Was it morally wrong to give a false name, and not just a false name, a name that belonged to somebody else, in fact, to one of my best friends? But, then, borrowing a name wasn't like borrowing a sweater without asking. I wasn't depriving Gwen of it. I wasn't going to damage it or get it dirty. I had misled Frances and Beth. But if I had been open about who I was, they might have thought I was insane. Which brought me to the question . . .

Was I insane? Or had I just done an insane thing? Or both? Or neither? And if I was insane, could I myself tell—from the inside, as it were?

After an hour or so, I took the baked potato out of the oven and mashed it with lots of butter, then sprinkled it with salt and pepper. I ate the soft inside first, then the crunchy skin. It was delicious. The phone rang.

"Where the hell are you?" Mary said.

"What do you mean?"

"You're coming here for dinner," she said.

"Am I?"

"I asked you several days ago. You said yes."

"Are you sure?"

"We're all about to sit down."

"All?"

"There are seven of us. Or, rather, there will be when you get here."

"Ten minutes," I said. "Fifteen at the most."

I was absolutely sure Mary hadn't asked me. On the other hand, such was the chaos of my life, the fact that I was absolutely sure didn't necessarily mean she hadn't asked me. Every impulse in my mind and body was screaming at me not to go. What I really wanted was a bath, bed and hours of heavy, dreamless sleep. What was more I had already eaten a solid meal and drunk several glasses of wine. I cursed obscenely and loudly as I had a thirty-second shower, pulled on a dress and ruffled my hair in the hope that it would look artfully arranged. I put a coat on, ran out of the house and got a taxi at the end of the road.

Mary greeted me rather frostily as she opened the door, but she couldn't shout at a widow in front of Eric and her four other guests. I knew two of them: Don and Laura were old friends of Mary and she always seemed to invite us together so that we could become friends with each other, but for reasons I didn't understand it had never quite happened. Then there was Maddie, who worked in Mary's office, and Geoff, who explained to me that he had met Mary and Eric on a cycling holiday in Sicily a couple of years back and that they'd stayed in contact. I wondered, with a touch of resentment, if Mary was already trying to set me up, then quickly became cross with myself. What was she meant to do? If she had invited two couples, I might have been cross at being excluded.

As Mary introduced me, I saw the now-familiar concern passing across everybody's face. It was clear that Mary had briefed them in advance about my situation. But I soon had other things to worry about. Mary said we must eat and muttered something under her breath about everything being spoiled.

I was grateful, in theory at least, to Mary for inviting me. It can't have been the most enticing prospect. She must have known I wouldn't be the life and soul of the party. The others seemed constrained as well, perhaps with the effort of avoiding any subject that might seem inappropriate: death, funerals, marriages. And I now knew rather too much about the state of Mary's marriage; I kept glancing at Eric, then looking away when he caught my eye. Geoff told me in unnecessary detail about the cycling holiday he had gone on in the year after he had met Mary and Eric, and in even more unnecessary detail about the cycling holiday he was planning for the summer. "Do you cycle?" he asked finally.

"No," I said, which was a bit of a conversation stopper—at least, that was what it was intended to be. I turned to Laura who leaned toward me, put her hand on mine and said, "Ellie, how *are* you?"

"I'm fine," I said. "I mean, as fine as can be expected."

"I just wanted to say," said Laura, "that if there's anything I can do, then just ask."

I made myself respond appropriately to her: I thanked her and said it wasn't really about help, just about getting through it and about friends being there for me, and by the time I'd got to the end of the sentence I couldn't remember how it had begun. In the meantime, I wasn't doing full justice to Mary's cooking. The first course consisted of a selection of Greek mezes: hummus, rice wrapped in vine leaves, taramasalata, little slices of fried haloumi, olives attached to lumps of feta with cocktail sticks. It would have been mouthwatering if I hadn't just eaten a huge buttery baked potato. Eric filled my plate for me, as if double helpings were a cure for grief. I nibbled at things, cut them up and rearranged them on my plate, in the hope that this would give the impression of lots of eating.

The Greek theme continued with the main course. Mary had cooked a hearty moussaka, and Eric spooned a huge slab on to my plate. I made him spoon half of it back and devoted much ingenuity, effort and clutter to cutting up the food and occasionally moving it toward my mouth. I put the same effort into not drinking the wine, because I was already about three drinks ahead of everybody else.

I toyed with the cheese and biscuits, too, and Mary finally asked if I was feeling unwell. I said I was fine and she let it go at that, probably attributing my lack of appetite to grief. I didn't hold back on the coffee, though. I drank three strong mugs, after which my hands were trembling and I felt fiercely, inhumanly awake, yet tired at the same time.

At the end of the evening, I turned down Geoff's offer of a lift home. I wanted to walk to clear my head, work the coffee out of my system. Anyway, I liked walking at night in the city and I needed to think, to sort things out in my head.

I'd half decided I wasn't going back to Frances's office, because it was wrong in every way, but looking back on the evening at Mary's, I also felt I couldn't continue like that. From the outside, I probably seemed all right, like a robot that had been fairly well programmed to behave like a human being: I hadn't made a scene, I hadn't cried, I hadn't embarrassed anybody. From my point of view, from the inside, it was a different story.

Perhaps it was a sign of success to make it through the day and then to the end of the evening without cracking up, or screaming, or having a flaming row. But that wasn't what I wanted from my life, that horrible feeling of dissociation, of acting a part that didn't belong to me, of being a person I no longer knew. That and not knowing the truth about Greg. They seemed to be separate things, but in my mind they were linked. If I could just discover that Greg and that woman had been having an affair or that they hadn't, I could start my new life as a real person. If I could find the letter or the email or the postcard that showed he had slept with her, because I had been too much for him or too little, I could be angry with him and maybe, just maybe, forgive him.

So THE NEXT day I put on clothes that were business clothes, but not too much like business clothes because, anyway, I didn't own any—you don't dress up for restoring furniture in the shed in your garden. I selected black canvas trousers with a thin, pale-gray jersey, and tied back my hair in a messy bun, put on earrings, a silver chain around my neck, even eye-liner and mascara. Now I wasn't Ellie but Gwen: helpful, calm, practical, discreet, ever so mathematical. I took my purse out of my bag; if, for no reason I could envisage, I needed it, I could pretend to have forgotten it. I just took a fistful of cash. I went through my shoulder bag carefully, removing anything that identified me by name. I looked at my left hand. No wedding ring.

At five past ten, when I arrived at her house, Frances opened the door with a smile of such welcome and relief that it made me smile back. "I thought you wouldn't come," she said. "I thought maybe I'd hallucinated you yesterday, out of desperation. It's such a disaster zone. I have to work here but you don't."

"I'll help out for a day or two," I said. "I've got work of my own to get back to, but you're having a bad time, so if there's anything I can do . . ."

"I am having a bad time," said Frances, "a terrible time, and part of what's terrible about it is that I don't know what you can do to help, what anyone can do, apart from putting a match to it all."

"I can't organize a party," I said, "or dress up as a waitress, or cook a five-course meal for forty people, but if someone could give me a cup of coffee, I'll go through every piece of paper in this office and reply to it or do something about it or put it in a file or throw it away. And then I'll get back to my own life."

Frances's smile changed to something of a frown. "What have I done to deserve you?" she asked.

I felt the tiniest shiver of apprehension. Was I being too obvious? "I'm trying to do as I would be done by," I said. "Does that sound too yucky?"

Frances smiled again. "I'm a drowning person being dragged to the shore," she said. "Who cares?"

Chapter Thirteen

Beth arrived just after eleven. She apologized, saying she had been out late, but she looked entirely fresh and rested. And she was immaculately dressed, entirely different from the day before: a dark gray pencil skirt with a little slit up the back, shoes with very low heels, and a waistcoat over a crisp white shirt. Her skin glowed, her hair tumbled over her shoulders. She made me feel shabby, old and boring. She seemed surprised and not completely pleased to see me. "Where's she going to work?" she asked Frances.

"She's going to hover," I said, before Frances could reply. "Just sort out a few things and not get in anyone's way."

"I was just asking," said Beth, and was interrupted by a merry tune from her mobile phone. She opened it and turned her back on me; I noticed there were seams on her black tights.

It was immediately obvious that it would take more than a day or two to restore order to the chaos of the office. It surprised me that Frances had let everything get into such a mess: she seemed the kind of person who would be calmly and instinctively organized: knickers folded in her underwear drawer, herbs and spices arranged alphabetically on the kitchen shelf, car insurance and MOT documents neatly filed.

"Did Milena do the organizing and filing?" I asked, as we drank our first coffee of the day, poured from a new cafetière.

"That's a laugh," said Frances. "No. Milena was the gorgeous public face of Party Animals. It was her job to schmooze the clients, flirt with the suppliers and come up with the brilliant ideas."

"What did you do?" I asked.

"We picked up the pieces," said Beth, from across the room.

"She sounds quite a character," I said.

"You must have seen that," said Frances.

"I meant that you don't know what people are like at work," I gabbled, cursing myself silently. "You must miss her."

"She's certainly left a gap," said Frances, as she picked up her phone and punched numbers into it.

I found some space by a work surface at the back of the office that gave out on to the steps that led up to the garden. I began to add to the piles of paper I had created the previous day. I tried to avoid speaking for a while, worried I might give myself away again. I felt startled and shifty every time Frances called me Gwen. Couldn't she tell that I was not a between-jobs Gwen but an out-of-control Ellie, that my black trousers, gray jersey and eyeliner were a feeble disguise? I kept expecting a stern hand to fall on my shoulder.

"How did you know Milena?" Frances asked me.

"Oh." My mind raced. "I met her at a fund-raising event. For breast cancer," I added. "It was boring and she was fun so we kept in touch. Vaguely. I can't remember when I last saw her, though." I glanced at Frances: she didn't seem to find my words incredible.

"What do you do normally, Gwen?" she asked.

"I'm a math teacher at a comprehensive school." So far so Gwen Abbott.

"No wonder you're good at this kind of thing. But why did you leave?"

"I don't know if I have left, not permanently. I'm taking a break. I like teaching but it's so stressful." Frances nodded sympathetically and I warmed to my theme, remembering things Gwen had said, TV documentaries I'd watched, and my own schooldays, when I'd hated math. "I teach in an inner-city school in . . ." Areas flashed through my mind and I seized on one that was far to the north but still in London. "Leytonstone. Half the kids don't want to be there. Some hardly speak English and need much more support than they're actually getting. Instead of teaching them, I try to keep order. I thought I'd take a few months out and think things over. If I'm going to make a change, it should be now. Maybe I'll travel."

"Lovely," said Frances, staring at a brochure and frowning. "Where?"

"Peru," I said. "Or I've always wanted to go to India." Without warning, tears stung my eyes. Greg and I had talked about going to India together. I blinked furiously and pushed two receipts into the appropriate folder.

"Are you married?"

"No. I was with someone for a long time but it didn't work out." I gave a rueful shrug. "Between jobs and between relationships. So, you see, I have this rare moment of freedom."

"No children yet?"

"No," I said shortly. And then I added, without realizing that I was going to, the words taking me by surprise, "I always wanted children," and for one fearful moment my defenses were down and I was being me, Ellie, with a pain in her heart because she hadn't been able to have children and now . . . I sat up straighter, snapped a folder shut. "Maybe one day," I said—Gwen said—with brisk cheerfulness.

"I never wanted children," said Frances. "It seemed so time-consuming, so wearing, trading your freedom for someone else's well-being. I watched friends turn from fun-loving, care-free creatures to people who talked about nappy rash and started yawning at eight o'clock and thought, That's not for me. And David agreed. I used to thank God I was born into a time when it was permissible to admit to possessing no mater-nal feelings. But then, just a few years ago, I suddenly thought how nice it would be to have someone to care for like that. Would have been, I should say. Too late now. Tick-tock," she said, with a sad little laugh.

I didn't get much information about Milena from the pa-pers I went through on that first morning, just slapdash sig-natures on copies of letters about the cost of finger food and the hire of champagne flutes, although I wrote down every relevant date and place in my little notebook. I decided to go for a more direct approach.

"Tell me," I said, as we sat drinking another of the mugs of coffee that punctuated the day, "this man Milena died with: who was he?" I ran my finger around the rim of the cup, try-ing to appear casual. Was my voice wobbling?

Frances shrugged. "I don't know anything about him. I think he was married. Silvio said something about meeting his wife once. He seemed rather taken with her—but, then, Silvio's an odd fish."

My face felt hot. How would a normal person react? Should I ask who Silvio was? No. I was meant to know Milena. "You never met him?"

"I never even knew he existed."

"Strange," I said.

"Not in Milena's world."

"How d'you mean?" I put my mug down and shuffled papers, as if I wasn't particularly interested in the answer.

"Milena's private life was always a bit complicated. And mysterious."

"You mean she was unfaithful."

Frances's face was flushed with either embarrassment or distress. "Basically, yes."

"Oh," I said. "I didn't know. Didn't her husband mind?"

Frances gave me an odd look. "I don't know if he even knew. People see what they want to see, don't they?"

"So she didn't confide in you?"

"When she wanted to. I guessed she'd met someone new. She had the familiar radiance about her." She gave a small, sour smile. "You probably think I'm being heartless, speaking ill of the dead."

"You're being honest. Milena was a complicated woman." I worried that I'd gone too far. I didn't want Frances to think I was prodding her into being rude about her friend. "And messy," I said, standing up and crossing the room to fetch another pile of unsorted papers. "I'd better crack on with this lot."

"Gwen?"

"Yes."

"It's really nice to have you here."

I tried to smile. "It's nice to be here."

AT LUNCHTIME, BETH went upstairs to the kitchen and made us the kind of meal I've always imagined women eat after they've had their hair done: a light salad of green beans, butter beans and beansprouts, scattered with health-giving seeds and dressed with a lemon vinaigrette, and when we'd finished, I was hungrier than I had been before.

Answering Frances's questions, I found out more about my life as Gwen: it turned out that she had grown up in Dorset, the youngest of five children, gone to Leeds University and studied math and physics, that she liked gardening and even had an allotment (stop! I commanded myself—you know nothing about allotments), that her father was dead. I felt a growing anxiety as I made up a life on the spot. It would have been much simpler to stick to the facts of my own life—or that of the real Gwen at the very least. Now I had to remember what I had said. Beth didn't speak but just looked at me. Had I made a mistake? All it would take was for Beth or Frances to be a bit too familiar with Dorset or Leeds or Leytonstone, and who knows what would happen? At the same time, I felt a thrill of pleasure as I concocted a life for myself. I'd always wanted to be the youngest in a large, close family, rather than the eldest in a small, distant one, and now, for a few days, I was. And maybe I'd get an allotment. Why not? Anything is possible when you decide to be someone else.

At about four o'clock, when the day outside was thickening toward twilight, Beth answered the phone, then muttered something to Frances.

"Bloody hell," said Frances. "All right, we'd better go." She sat lost in thought for a moment, then looked at me as if she had forgotten my existence. "Gwen," she said, "something's come up. We've got to pop out. Would you mind holding the fort?"

I wouldn't mind holding the fort. I positively wanted to hold the fort. I waited until the front door closed and I saw them—or, at least, their lower halves—walking past the basement window. Then I jumped up and started to prowl. I didn't know what I was looking for, but I knew it probably wouldn't be in any of the folders and files I was ploughing through. Maybe in the desk drawers. I yanked the first open and started rummaging among the stationery, finding nothing except envelopes, paper clips, ink cartridges and Post-its. But in the second I came across two vodka bottles, one empty, the other half full. I sat for a minute or so, considering them, then replaced them and pushed the drawer shut. I turned my attention to the computer. I pinged it on and waited for it to load.

The doorbell rang, making me jolt in my chair, my heart pumping wildly in my chest and my throat suddenly dry. I turned off the computer, watched it count down and go blank. The bell rang again. I licked my lips, smoothed my hair, put on a Gwen-expression of calm inquiry and went to answer it.

The man standing on the step seemed surprised to see me. He was quite small and slim, almost gaunt, and dressed in a gray suit with a white shirt. He had hollow cheeks, quick gray eyes and brown hair that was starting to thin.

"Can I help you?" I asked.

"Who are you?"

"Why do you want to know?"

"Are we going to go on just asking each other questions? Is Frances there? That's another."

"No. I'm helping her out for a bit. I'm Gwen."

"Johnny." He reached out a hand and I shook it. He didn't meet my eyes but looked over my shoulder as if he didn't believe I was on my own. "Did Frances forget I was coming?"

"She's a bit distracted by everything. She'll be back soon."

"I'll wait."

He walked past me, obviously at home in Frances's office.

"Do you work with Frances?" I asked.

"I sort out most of the food for her."

"You don't look like a chef," I said. It came out sounding rather rude.

He looked down at his suit. "You think I'm pretending? I've been kicked upstairs into management, in line with which I've brought her a menu for next week. Do you want to see it?"

"I'm not really the person to—"

"You're here, aren't you?"

We sat together on the sofa and he showed me the menu. He told me how to make soufflés in advance; he said he sourced his ingredients locally; he put his hand on my arm; he told me his restaurant was called Zest, his signature dish was stuffed pig's trotter and I had to pay him a visit there soon; he listened attentively when I spoke; he laughed and looked me in the eye; he called me Gwen with each sentence—" . . . don't you think, Gwen?" and "I'll tell you what, Gwen . . ." And Gwen flushed with self-consciousness and awkward, complicated pleasure.

When Frances came back, damp with the rain that had started to fall, she looked at the two of us on the sofa with affectionate amusement. "I see you haven't missed me." She took off her beautiful coat and threw it on the back of the chair, then kissed him on both cheeks.

"I always miss you," he said, "but I've been well looked after." He put his hands on her shoulders and held her away from him, gazing at her seriously. "You seem worn-out, Frances. Are you taking proper care of yourself?"

"No, but Gwen is," she replied, and they smiled at me, warming me with their approval.

JOHNNY DROPPED ME at the Underground station. He took my hand in both of his and said it had been a real pleasure to meet me and we would certainly see each other again soon. I muttered something in reply, and avoided his bright gaze. Why should I feel guilty because a nice man was flirting with me—or, at least, with me pretending not to be me? After all, I was a free woman, and it had been a long time since anyone had looked at me without pity and embarrassment. But I didn't feel free: I felt that I was still in a relationship with Greg, and that to respond would be, in some perverse sense, a betrayal.

It was dark and drizzly as I walked home from the tube.

Puddles glistened under the streetlamps. In a few weeks, it would be the longest night of the year; the days were closing in and Christmas was coming. There were decorations in the shop windows and lights strung between the lampposts. I wondered drearily what I would do for Christmas. For a moment, the thought of waking up in my wide bed on Christmas Day, alone, made me gasp with pain. I stopped and put a hand against my heart. I turned into my road and saw my little house ahead of me, with its unlit windows and its soggy, uncared-for front garden.

As I went in I heard my mobile ringing. I saw it was Gwen calling and, for a moment, was confused.

"I've been trying to get hold of you all day."

"Sorry, I've been busy."

"That's good. Have you forgotten it's your birthday in a few days' time?"

"No," I said. "I just haven't really thought about it."

"It would be nice to have a little drinks party for you."

"I'm not sure about that."

"At your house. You don't have to do anything but be there. I'll do everything else. I'll even clear up for you."

"You're making it sound as though you've already organized it."

"Not exactly. But I've made sure that people like Mary can come."

"What do you mean, 'people like Mary'? Who else?"

"Just a few. Me, Mary and Eric, Fergus and Jemma, of course, Joe and Alison, Josh and Di. That's about it. And anyone you want to ask."

"I don't know, Gwen."

"I'll do little eats and Joe said he'd provide the wine."

"When's this supposed to be happening?"

"Day after tomorrow."

I gave up protesting. "I'll check my diary," I said ironically, "but I'm pretty sure I'm not busy then."

"Good. That's settled. I'll come around at five, straight from school, and we'll get everything ready."

Chapter Fourteen

When I arrived at the office, Frances was on the phone. She waved me in frantically. It sounded as if she was on the receiving end of a lecture. "Oh, yes," she said. "Yes, I can see that . . . Is that really true? . . . Didn't we? . . . Is it serious? . . . So what do we do?"

I tiptoed across the room, made two mugs of coffee and handed one to Frances. She pulled faces at me like a silent-movie actress, signaling thanks for the coffee and, at the same time, frustration and exasperation. "Yes," she said. "But things have been a bit difficult, you know, with what's happened . . . Yes, but couldn't you explain it to them? Would that make things better? . . . Oh, I see . . . Yes, all right."

Finally she put the phone down. I thought she was going to cry.

"I never wanted to be a businesswoman," she said, her voice almost a wail. "Did I tell you I went to art school?"

"No, you didn't."

"I was going to be a painter. That was the plan. I was good at it, but in the end there's only room for about four painters in England at any one time and it was clear I wasn't going to be one of them."

"Who was it on the phone?" I said.

"That was our horrible accountant," she said. "He's meant to be working for us—we certainly pay him enough—but all he does is shout at me. He's like a disappointed parent. Apparently we're late with our VAT and apparently that's bad. I thought the point of accountants was that *they* were meant to deal with that sort of thing. Oh, God, Gwen, I hate this—I'm out of my depth."

I remembered an early conversation with Greg, when we were getting to know each other and obsessed with every detail about each other's life. I'd teased him about being an accountant. Wasn't it just about adding up columns of numbers and filling in forms? He'd laughed. It wasn't like that at all, not with the clients he had. It was a mixture of being a psychiatrist and a magician, a hostage negotiator and a bomb-disposal expert, with a bit of form filling at the end.

"Beth's not handling this very well," said Frances. "The thing about Beth, who, incidentally, has not arrived yet, is that she's very young, very decorative and very confident. You can take her anywhere and she seems very busy all the time but at the end of a day it's never particularly easy to work out exactly what she's done. She's good at events. The clients are very keen on her. The male ones, I mean. It's to do with her being twenty-two. And her breasts."

"They're very nice."

"Well, breasts don't get the VAT done. And Christmas is coming at us like a train. Gwen, are you sure I can't give you a job? Or a three-month contract to get us through this?"

I shook my head and tried to think of what Greg used to say about situations like this. "What you really need," I said, "is to know exactly where you are just now. What you owe, what you're owed, what you've got, and what your plans are. We can sort that out in a couple of days and then you'll be fine again."

"I wanted to be an artist," said Frances, "and when I met Milena, it was all going to be fun. We liked going to parties, we liked having parties, so why not do it as a living? And I could be an artist on the side. It didn't turn out like that. You know how you never properly enjoy your own party? You always worry that the drink's going to run out or that someone's not happy? It's like that all the time."

"Was it like that for Milena?" I asked.

"No," said Frances, with a sad smile. "Milena didn't let the details get her down."

"The details are my job now," I said. "At least for the next few days."

Somehow, when it isn't your own life, it isn't so hard. For two hours, I behaved like Frances's view of an accountant. There was nothing magical involved, no smoke and mirrors, no cleverness. I just piled up pieces of paper that looked alike. I made lists of dates, which I also, surreptitiously, transferred to my own notebook, I checked receipts against bank statements. At eleven o'clock Beth arrived. I gave her a list of phone calls to make to check delivery dates. She was as shocked as if I had asked her to clean the drains. She pulled a face and glanced resentfully at Frances, but she did what I said.

Twenty minutes later, Johnny arrived; he nodded at me, then sat next to Frances and talked menus. I barely looked up. I was holding a lot of information in my head temporarily. If

I spoke or thought about something else, even for a moment, most of it would dissipate and I would have to start again.

My sense of time was imprecise, but a short while later I felt a presence beside me. It was Johnny.

"I'm a bit worried walking around here," he said, gesturing at the piles of paper circling my chair.

"Then don't," I said, frowning at the distraction.

"This isn't—"

"Stop," I said, holding up my hand. I wrote down a date followed by an amount of money and then the VAT. Then I looked at him. "Yes?" I said.

"I was going to say that you're doing all the boring bits of the job and none of the fun bits."

I waved at the office. "That's what seems to be needed," I said.

"Whereas," said Johnny, "my own strategy is to do the fun bits and leave the boring bits to sort themselves out."

"That sounds like a recipe for going bankrupt."

"All restaurants go bankrupt in the end."

"That doesn't sound much fun."

"It's great," said Johnny, and added thoughtfully, "until the end. And then you start again. It's got a sort of rhythm to it. But what I really wanted to say, really wanted to ask, in fact— you remember I mentioned my restaurant—was whether you might want to come over and I could show you the sort of food I do. Some time. Today or tomorrow or whenever."

He was handsome in a louche sort of way, well dressed, a man who went bankrupt and didn't let it get him down. He was perfect, in a certain fashion. Perfect if I wasn't me—

although, of course, the person he was talking to wasn't actually me. "I can't," I said. "Not at the moment. I'm not in the right place for that. In my life."

"Oh, no," he said, unruffled. "I wasn't suggesting a date. I'm not harassing you. I just thought, as one professional to another, it would be interesting and useful for you to see the kind of food we do."

"I'll think about it," I said. "My life's a bit confusing right now, but I will think about it."

In my own job, I had got used to scraping away at a chair, varnishing a chest, with no company but the radio, which drifted in and out of my consciousness. The Party Animals office was almost a public space, with people coming and going, packages being delivered, clients or potential clients dropping in. Sometimes the potential of the client seemed very vague indeed. I came to feel that Frances had exaggerated the degree to which she was burdened by the bureaucracy of the business. Much of the morning and the early afternoon disappeared in a series of long, loud conversations, on the phone or in person.

Some clients seemed to know Beth as well, and I saw a different side of her, a glow about her, confidence, as she flirted with the men or gossiped with the women. As I listened to her—and it was impossible not to—I came to realize I had entered a different world, a richer one than mine, with its own rules and standards and culture.

Of the visitors, several were smartly dressed women who seemed to have a lot of time on their hands. I might have felt a jab of resentment at this if I hadn't forced myself into this situation. Anyway, the less Frances and Beth did, the more chance I had to learn something. I sat on the far side of the room, with my back to them, my head in my hands, covering my ears so that I could concentrate.

Shortly after three I heard a visitor come in. I was faintly surprised to hear a man's voice and looked around, and was jolted.

It was Hugo Livingstone. A man I had seen just once, at the inquest. For a moment I was pointlessly and ridiculously angry: what on earth was he doing there? Then I cursed my stupidity. He was Milena's husband. Wasn't it natural for him to visit his dead wife's office? Hadn't I done the same thing myself? I tried to think of a way, any way, of getting out of the room without him seeing my face. I could crawl; I could climb out of the window. But I knew it wasn't possible. All it would take was a glance. The idea of being seen, recognized and forced to attempt an explanation was so terrible that I felt feverish anticipating the nuclear explosion of exposure and embarrassment.

I tried to continue working or, rather, to make it look as if I was working. I bent over some papers as if I was scrutinizing them with particular attention. Other people had come and gone without paying me any heed. If I could just sit tight, maybe he'd go away. I tried to make out what he was after, but he was speaking in a mumble from which I could only hear the occasional word. There was no such problem with Frances. I heard murmurs of sympathy and talk about the chaos she was in, and then I knew what was coming.

"Oh, that's Gwen," she said. "She's been an absolute treasure. She came from nowhere and she's sorting things out. Gwen?"

Frozen in panic, I grasped for something, anything, that could prevent me having to turn around. There was no trap-door, no rope to climb, but my mobile phone was on the desk. Switched off, so nobody could ring me. I picked it up.

"That's right," I said into it. "Could you check it? Yes, it is urgent. Yes."

I turned my head about half a degree and raised my free hand in a gesture much like the one I'd seen from Frances earlier. I hoped it meant, "Sorry, I'd love to be introduced, but I'm caught up in this absolutely crucial phone call and can't possibly be disturbed." I decided I was talking to a builder who was doing some emergency work on my bedroom. I tried to picture him at the other end of the line so that I would seem more convincing. I continued to say yes and no, to murmur half-sentences. Even though I was becoming more and more used to living in a fantasy world, and now a fantasy world within a fantasy world, it still sounded pathetic and unconvincing to me.

In the gaps between my fatuous outpourings, I tried to listen to what Frances was saying. My fear was that she would tell him I had been a friend of Milena's and then he really might stay, however long I remained on the disconnected phone, to find out how I knew her. But then Frances started talking about people I had never heard of, and after a few minutes more I heard footsteps, then the front door opening and closing. I made myself continue the conversation for a bit longer. "So we'll talk about the colors when we meet?" I said brightly, loudly. "That's great. Maybe I'll see you when I get back . . . Oh, you'll be gone, then? All right, tomorrow. "Bye."

"Everything okay?" Frances said sympathetically.

"It's my so-called builder," I said. "You know how it is."

I hoped desperately that Frances did know how it was, because I couldn't bear to lie any more. There would be too much falsehood to fit into my brain. She just nodded. I don't think she wanted to find out too much about my life.

I really was organizing the company's papers. I wasn't lying about that. But at the same time I was also jotting down every reference to where Milena had been on a particular day. If I compared it to the chart I had constructed for Greg, perhaps I could find somewhere they had been together, or nearly been, or a route that had crossed. It didn't have to be a night in a hotel, it could be a train, a petrol station. Indeed, as I worked I decided I would stop off at the stationer's on the way home for more card and colored pens and that I would make a separate chart for Milena.

I worked with such concentration that when I heard Frances say my name it was as if I had fallen asleep and woken up to find the world dark.

She wasn't alone. A man was standing with her, tall, distinguished, rich. He made me feel disheveled and a little ill-at-ease. He must have been in his mid-fifties, with short dark-gray hair, silvering at the edges. He was wearing an overcoat with a navy blue scarf.

"This is Gwen, my good fairy," said Frances, and once again I had to stop myself looking around to see where Gwen was. "This is my husband, David." He gave me a slightly wry smile and held out his hand. It was beautifully manicured but, then, everything about him looked beautifully manicured, his hair, his black leather slip-ons. His handshake was dry and limp.

"David, you've got to persuade Gwen to stay."

He regarded her coldly, then gave a small shrug. "Don't you see how much you're valued?" he said, in a voice that managed to combine sarcasm with indifference.

"It's just a holiday for me," I said.

"Funny sort of holiday," he said.

"She's a math teacher," said Frances.

"Oh," said David, as if that explained everything.

"Time to go," said Frances. "But wait a second." She went to her desk and scribbled on something. Then she came back and handed me a check.

"I can't take this," I said.

"Don't be ridiculous," she said.

"No," I said. "I *really* can't take it."

"Oh, I see," she said. "You mean the tax? David, could you give me your wallet, darling?"

He sighed and handed it over. She riffled through it, pulled out some notes and offered them to me. I wanted to say no but I thought that a person who comes and works for you, sorting out your office, then refuses any payment, stops looking like a saint and starts looking a bit creepy, maybe even suspicious. I took the money. "Thank you," I said.

"Tomorrow?" she said.

"Tomorrow, at least," I said.

We left the house together.

"You know how we all love you," said Frances.

"Don't be silly," I said.

"I mean, Johnny completely adores her," she said to her husband, who smiled distantly and moved away from the hand she laid on his arm. I saw her wince as she registered the slight. She was too eager with him, I thought, and too anxious, while he treated her with something close to contempt. I felt a spasm of pity for Frances—a beautiful woman in her privileged life, yet she was clearly unhappy.

THE OLD LADY behind the counter at the Oxfam shop in Kentish Town Road seemed disconcerted when I gave her the banknotes and said I didn't want to buy anything. She tried to make me take a dress or even a book, but I wouldn't be persuaded and she reluctantly gave up. I left feeling as if I'd been shoplifting, but in reverse.

Chapter Fifteen

D o you think," I asked, "that it would be a good idea for me to go through Milena's emails and check there aren't any more nasty surprises waiting to jump out at you?"

Frances had just discovered that she and Milena had been expected at a client's large house in Kingston upon Thames to discuss plans for her daughter's wedding. Even from the other side of the room, I could hear the woman's voice coming down the phone, high and irate.

"Milena never mentioned it," said Frances, dejectedly, after she had ended the conversation and promised she would be there the following day. "She was supposed to write everything in the office diary."

"Can I see the diary?" I asked. "Just to double-check things."

"Would you?"

I took the large, hard-backed book, which had a page for each day and was covered with scrawls, crossings-out, reminders, and tried to memorize appointments so I could cross-reference them with Greg's chart, but I soon gave up. I'd have to write them down later.

Frances had no objection to me sifting through Milena's messages, but the computer did. I found that to access her email I had to enter a password. "What was it?" I asked Frances.

"I haven't a clue."

"Oh." I stared at the screen in frustration. I had this idea that the answers I needed were locked in that slim little box, if only I could find the key. Idly, I tried the names of her two stepchildren, with no success. "No ideas?" I asked Frances.

She shrugged helplessly. "You could try her maiden name. Furness."

"No," I said, after a few seconds.

"Her date of birth: the twentieth of April 1964."

So she was forty-four, a decade older than me. I typed it in. Nothing.

"She used to talk about a dog she had when she was a girl."

"What was its name?"

"She never said. But, look, aren't there ways around things like this?"

I couldn't help smiling at that. "Probably, but if there were, do you really think I'd know about them?"

"Oh, well, I guess we'll just have to hope there aren't other appointments waiting to be missed. In the meantime I need to get quotations on marquees before tomorrow morning."

THAT DAY I had told Frances I needed to leave early. Even so, when I hurried up the road Gwen was waiting at my door, several carrier-bags at her feet. "Happy birthday!" she said, kissing me on both cheeks. "But where've you been? I was worried you'd forgotten or got cold feet."

"Just trying to catch up with a few things," I said vaguely.

She looked at me curiously. "You're being rather mysterious."

I felt flustered. "I don't mean to be. It's just I've been having to sort out things, like—like money." Untrue, although, of course, that was what I should have been sorting out, and if I thought of my financial situation, I felt dizzy with anxiety.

"Horrible for you," Gwen said sympathetically.

"It's got to be done." I fished my key out of my pocket. "Let's get inside out of the cold. I'll carry some of these. What's in here? I thought you said just a few people." We went into the kitchen.

"That's right. Fifteen, twenty at most." She started unpacking the bag on to the kitchen table. "Hummus with pita bread, and guacamole. I've bought the avocados for that. Tortilla chips with salsa, pistachio nuts. Nothing much to do except put them in bowls."

"What time is everyone coming?" I was filled with panic. I was used to being Ellie-and-Greg facing the world together. I'd lost the ability to cope on my own—unless, that is, I was pretending to be someone else, in which case I seemed to be managing much better.

"About six, six thirty."

"What shall I wear?"

"Calm down. It's just your friends. We'll have a poke through your wardrobe in a moment, but it's casual. People will be coming straight from work. You can wear what you've got on now, if you want."

"No," I said, with a sharpness that surprised even me. Because I was wearing my Gwen-clothes: my black trousers again, the stripy gray shirt, a sleeveless jersey over the top, and slouchy black suede boots. "I can't wear these. I'd feel all wrong."

"I've got something for you," Gwen said. "A birthday present." She held out a small packet. "Go on, open it."

I tore off the wrapping paper and found a little box. Inside there was a plain silver bangle. "It's beautiful." I slid it over my wrist and held up my arm so Gwen could admire it.

Her face changed, but not in the way I'd expected. "Ellie, you've taken off your wedding ring."

I felt a terrible flush spreading over my face and down my neck as we stared at my bare finger. "Yes," I said finally.

"Is that because—"

"I don't know why," I said. "It's in my purse. I might put it back on. Shall I?"

"God, Ellie, I don't know. We'll talk about it when everyone's gone home. Now we're going to choose your clothes."

In the end I dithered and fretted in front of the mirror until Gwen chose for me: jeans and a thin white shirt that was quite new and I'd never worn because it was too nice, too crisp and clean, and I was always saving it for a special occasion. I brushed my hair and piled it on top of my head. "There, will that do?"

"You look gorgeous."

"Hardly."

"No, you do. I invited Dan. Is that all right?"

"Who's Dan?"

Gwen blushed deep crimson. "Someone I met."

"That's great," I said. "As long as Dan knows how lucky he is to be invited by you." Gwen didn't have much luck with men. I always told her she was too good for them and, in a way, it was the truth. Men, I thought grimly, go for women like Milena, who treat them badly, who don't care. It's caring too much that's our downfall.

The doorbell rang.

"Who's that? Is it time already? I wish it was nine o'clock and everyone had gone home and it was just you and me again, discussing how it went. And Dan, of course."

"It'll be Joe. He said he'd arrive early with the drink."

Sure enough, it was Joe, his car parked by the pavement with the boot open. He gave me a bear hug; his stubble scratched my cheek and his overcoat itched against my skin. "How's the birthday girl?"

"Doing fine."

"Right, I'll put it in the kitchen, shall I? Twelve bottles of champagne—well, sparkling wine, to be honest. Twelve bottles of red."

"That's twenty-four bottles, Joe!"

"You can keep the rest for later. Let's open a bottle now, shall we?"

He peeled off the foil and wire and eased the cork out of a champagne bottle, letting the foam rise out of its mouth and subside. Then he poured three glasses, which we lifted and chinked together. "To our dear Ellie," he said.

"To Ellie," said Gwen, grinning at me fondly.

Why did I feel so much like crying? Why did my eyes sting and my sinuses ache and a block of sorrow lodge in my throat?

PEOPLE ARRIVED IN dribs and drabs, and then a small flood, leaving umbrellas in the hall, tossing overcoats over the banister and on the back of the sofa. Soon my little house was full of people. They were in the living room, in the kitchen, sitting on the stairs. They'd all brought presents: whisky, biscuits, plants, earrings, a little ceramic bowl. Josh and Di arrived with a rocket that they set up in readiness in the garden, even though the instructions said it had to be fifty meters away from any building.

These are my friends, I thought, and this is my life now. Fergus was a bit subdued but very sweet and affectionate, Joe was in an expansive mood, throwing his arms around people, pouring too much wine into their glasses. Gwen was talking to Alison, but glancing surreptitiously at her watch every few minutes because Dan had not yet turned up. Mary had cornered Jemma and was telling her what to expect from childbirth in every agonizing gory detail. Laurie and Graham were playing chess in the corner. I went from group to group with a bottle in my hand. That way I didn't have to stay with anyone for long: just enough time to say hello and kiss them before I moved away. I didn't drink and I didn't talk to anyone properly—and no one mentioned Greg. He was the ghost in the house.

At seven thirty—just after Gwen had answered the door and returned, shy and pink, with a man I assumed to be Dan—Joe clinked his fork against a glass and stood on a rather flimsy chair, which creaked ominously beneath his weight. "Gather around," he roared.

"Oh, no."

"Don't worry, Ellie, this isn't a speech, just a toast."

"Good."

"You don't know what Joe means by 'toast,'" warned Alison, standing beside me.

"No, really—all I wanted to say was you've had a terrible time and I know I can speak for everyone when I say that we're always here for you, through thick and thin. Happy birthday, Ellie."

"Happy birthday," came the ragged chorus.

"Speech!" someone shouted.

"Just . . . thank you," I said. "All of you."

"More wine," commanded Joe.

"Here." At the other end of the room, Fergus pulled a cork out of a bottle and a spume of froth flowed over its neck and on to the small table by the window. "Oh, shit, I've spilt it— what is this, anyway?"

"Oh," I said, cursing myself for not having put it away. "That's—Well, it's my chart."

Fergus bent over it, dabbing at the wine with his sleeve. "It's very colorful. Is it work?"

"No." I hesitated. "Actually, it shows where Greg was during the last few weeks of his life."

"Seriously?"

"Yes."

"Fuck, Ellie." He seemed dazed. "It's amazing. It must have taken forever. But why?"

"Because . . ." I was glad I hadn't put out Milena's chart: it was still a work in progress.

"What is it?" Jemma had joined us and so, a few minutes later, had most of the others in the room.

"There's almost no time unaccounted for!" Josh sounded either impressed or scared, I couldn't tell which.

I took a deep breath. These were my friends, after all, and

suddenly it seemed important to make a public declaration. "I did it because I wanted to work out when Greg would have been with that woman. And you see"—I waved at the chart—"He wasn't. There are barely any gaps. He simply didn't have the time."

I stared at them. Nobody was smiling or nodding; everyone was looking at me gravely, or with embarrassment. "So, something else was going on," I said ominously, hearing my words fall into the silence. "Something bad."

"Bad?"

"I think he was murdered."

You could have heard a pin drop.

"Let me pour you some wine," said Joe at last, taking the bottle from Fergus.

"No, thanks. You all think I'm mad, I can tell."

"No!" said Fergus. "We think you're . . ." I could see him searching for the right word. "Tremendously loyal," he concluded. Jemma, beside him, nodded urgently.

"I made a cake," Mary said, into the awkwardness. "Is now the right time to cut it?"

Everyone made overenthusiastic noises; I blew out the symbolic candle on top of the coffee and walnut sponge, then slid in the knife.

"It's bad luck if we hear it touch the plate," warned Di, just as the knife audibly clinked against the china.

"Fuck that," said Joe, scowling at her as if she was a criminal. He wrapped an arm around my shoulders. "It's only good luck from now on," he said, kissing the top of my head.

"Do you think I'm mad?"

"Not mad. Sad."

"And a bit of a party-pooper."

"Meet Dan," said Gwen, appearing beside me. "Dan, this is Ellie."

He was big and shy, with a quiet, rumbling voice. I liked him at once for the way he looked at Gwen.

"Josh is about to light the rocket," said Gwen, tucking her arm through mine. "Come out and see it, and then I'll send everyone home. Right?"

"Right," I agreed, for suddenly I felt desperately tired and dejected. And lonely, too—lonelier now, in this crowd of too-eager friends, than I ever did when I was alone.

"But I'll stay and clear up. We can get a takeaway or something if you want. So steer clear of that cake for the moment."

THAT WAS THE best bit of the party: after everyone had left and the glasses were washed, the empty bottles put out for collection, sitting at the kitchen table with Gwen and her nice new man, eating curry out of foil cartons and not having to make an effort anymore. There aren't many people you can just be silent with.

At several points, I nearly told Gwen I had stolen her name and was passing myself off as an unsettled-math-teacher-turned-office-assistant to the business partner of the woman who had died alongside Greg. But I stopped myself. It made me sound crazy.

Chapter Sixteen

After Gwen and Dan had left, I did the last of the washing-up and took out a bin-bag full of slimy, smelly party relics. I made a mug of tea and put the TV on, and by the time I got to bed it was after two. It didn't matter because the next day was Saturday. My plan, if it could be called a plan, was to sleep until I woke and then to go back to sleep. If I left my bed it would be to eat and then I would return to my state of hibernation. Instead, I was woken from strange dreams—gray, hard-edged, dark, slow—by the doorbell. I pulled on a dressing gown and went down the stairs, muttering to myself like a bag lady. I was expecting to have to sign for something but instead I found Fergus on the doorstep.

"Did I wake you?" he said.

I was still fuddled with sleep. "Did you forget something?"

"No, nothing like that," he said.

"What time is it?"

"Breakfast time," he said, smiling. "Can I come in?"

I was genuinely tempted to say no and slam the door. But I stood aside for him, then went upstairs, had a shower and tugged a pair of jeans up over my tired, pale legs. I put on an old sweatshirt of Greg's and found some slippers in the back of a cupboard. I could already smell coffee.

When I came down to the kitchen Fergus had cleared the kitchen table and laid out mugs and plates. "I found a muffin in the freezer," he said. "I'm defrosting it. Unless you want bacon and eggs."

"I don't even want a muffin," I said.

"Of course you do," he said. He took the muffin from the microwave and spread it with butter, then raspberry jam, and put it on a little side plate and gave it to me. He poured a mug of coffee for me and one for himself. He sat down opposite me.

"Am I that bad?" I said.

He smiled and sipped his coffee. I felt cross and tired and blurry, and his insistent cheeriness was irritating, like music playing too loudly. "We've been having a conference," he said.

"We?"

"The usual suspects. I was the one delegated to come and see you. Well, I delegated myself, really."

"It's the chart, isn't it?" I said. "I should have put it in a cupboard."

"We've not been looking after you properly," he said.

"Everyone's been looking after me," I said. "You came to my birthday party. I've been invited to dinner. People have put up with my deranged behavior."

"You've not been deranged," said Fergus.

"I'm just going through the stages of mourning: anger, bargaining, denial. Lots of denial." I paused. "Are they really the stages of mourning or are they the stages of dying? It doesn't matter. I think I've had enough help. Maybe it's time now to help myself."

"I'm not allowed to take no for an answer," said Fergus.

"Says who?"

"Says me and Gwen and Joe and Mary and no doubt other people as well."

"This is since the party?" I said.

"Some of it was at the party. But the lines have been buzzing as well."

"I wish people would just talk to *me*."

"I *am* talking to you."

"So what's the plan? Is someone going to take me to the seaside? Are you clubbing together to pay for a massage?"

"You shouldn't be sarcastic," said Fergus. "It's the lowest form of wit. The immediate plan is for you to eat your muffin, then show me around your house."

"You know what it looks like."

"Please, eat up."

I nibbled at the muffin, feeling like a child who had been told off. It was dry in my mouth, hard to swallow. "I don't need all this help," I said. "I shouldn't need it. He was your friend. You knew him much longer than I did. Losing him must have been as bad for you as it was for me, maybe worse."

Fergus looked reflective. "I don't think I'll ever have a friend like him again. I couldn't. It was something about who'd seen me drunk and being embarrassing, at my low points." He smiled. "And there were good things as well. Trips, girl-friends . . . Well, I probably shouldn't go there. Anyway, this isn't a competition."

"I should be looking out for *you*," I said.

"First things first," said Fergus. "That'll do. That's enough muffin. Let's go upstairs."

As I walked upstairs with him, I suddenly remembered being about seventeen and my mum coming into my bedroom. "You're meant to have tidied your room," she would say.

"I *have* tidied it," I'd say.

"Well, it doesn't look like it."

And so it would go on. It seemed to me that I had spent days and days dealing with my affairs, sorting out Greg's stuff, generally getting things ordered, but as I saw my bedroom, the junk room and the spare bedroom through Fergus's eyes, I had to admit that it didn't look like it. If there are stages of mourning, there are also stages of tidying. The first stage is your basic untidiness. The second stage is deciding to do something about it. The third stage involves getting everything out of the drawers, cupboards and shelves so you can see what you have to deal with it. The third stage necessarily looks much worse than the first. I wasn't sure about the fourth because I hadn't yet got to it.

There were piles of Greg's clothes in the bedroom. The spare room functioned as a sort of office. It had a nice view over the garden toward the plane tree that stood next door. We had never made it a proper office because we'd been going to make the junk room into an office and turn the spare room into a nursery, put up silly wallpaper with clowns on it or something like that. The spare bedroom and the landing were piled high with files, papers, folders and books, some of which were connected with Greg's work. "It looks bad, I know," I said. "I'm in the process of getting it sorted."

There was so much I couldn't say, starting with the supposed excuse that one of the reasons I hadn't cleared up the house was that I had been down in Camberwell, sorting out Milena Livingstone's office.

"Don't worry," he said. "I've already heard about this from one of my spies."

"Who was it? I bet it was Mary. If I live to be a hundred and spend the entire time doing housework, I'll never live up to her standards of cleanliness."

"I'm not saying," said Fergus. "I'm not able to reveal my sources. What I can do is tell you the plan."

"The plan?"

"Are you at home today?"

"I hadn't thought of going anywhere."

"Good. You might have some visitors."

"Who are they? What are they going to do?"

"I think you'll recognize them. What they'll do, basically, is help you deal with this. Some of it they'll do on site, as it were, but mainly we don't want to be in your hair. We can take things away, sort them out. If you trust us, that is."

I stepped forward and put my arms around him and my face into his shoulder, the way babies do when they're held. I couldn't see his expression. It might have been horror, for all I knew, but I felt his arms go around me. I stepped back.

"This is lovely of you," I said, "lovely of you all. But it's something I should be able to do myself. And it's not just that. I want to sort this out, Fergus, obviously I do. But what I don't want is to have Greg surgically removed from my life. I want his stuff around me. Not necessarily in piles on the floor. But for me to move on, I don't need to have all this stuff taken out of the house and dumped in a skip."

"That's not what it's about. We just want to help you deal with it. If it's a matter of privacy, if you don't want us nosing through your things, then just say so and we'll back off."

"That's not what I mean. There's nothing I want to hide from you guys. It's too late for that. It's just that I should be able to deal with it myself. It feels wrong."

"It shouldn't," said Fergus. "Let us do it for you. When Jemma finally gives up on me, you can do the same for me."

A horrible thought occurred to me. "Is there anything you're not telling me?" I asked. "Do you all think I need help? I mean psychiatric help."

Fergus laughed and shook his head. "Just us. Honest."

IT STILL FELT uncomfortable to have been talked about, as if a conspiracy had been hatched against me. An hour later Joe, Gwen and Mary arrived, looking a bit sheepish. I told them I felt terrible. This was their weekend. Didn't they have obligations, people to be with? They hugged me and made apologetic sounds. I wasn't sure whether it was more difficult to receive help or to give it. I made more coffee and we went upstairs to survey the chaos. There was some discreet muttering.

Joe gave me a friendly nudge. "It's not so bad," he said. "Just think of it as some decorating that needs doing and we've come around to hang wallpaper and paint."

"Do you want me to show you what everything is?" I asked.

"What we want," said Gwen, "is for you to go out and do some shopping or have a swim, anything, and we'll go through everything, and some of it we'll put in boxes and take away. In a couple of days we'll bring it back and then, at least, we'll have been able to sort out one bit of your life. We hope."

I thought for a moment.

"I feel I should say no to all this, or feel resentful, but really it's such a relief."

"Then go away," said Mary, and I did, though not before I'd rolled up Milena's chart-in-progress and put it into my bag. There are some things even friends shouldn't know about.

I swam in the public pool, washed my hair in the showers afterward and put on some clean clothes. I found a café, ordered a pot of tea and read the newspaper. I walked up Kentish Town Road and bought vegetables and salad. When I got home, they had left. I went upstairs and it was miraculous. Almost everything was gone and everything that wasn't had been arranged neatly on a shelf or a desktop. Someone must have found the vacuum cleaner as well, made my bed and done the washing-up. There was nothing for me to do but make myself a salad, then clear up thoroughly after myself, in case someone came back to check.

The next morning Joe rang. He'd gone through Greg's work stuff and most of it could be dealt with at the office. Anything personal he would drop back later in the week. There was nothing urgent. In the afternoon Gwen came around with a pile of files under her arm, all household papers. She had gone through them, reordered them and, on a piece of paper, she had written a "to do" list: people to be phoned, bills to be paid, letters to be written. She had drawn a star next to the ones that needed to be dealt with immediately. She was being Gwen to me in the way that I was being Gwen to Frances, but I couldn't tell her that.

I didn't check my mobile phone the entire weekend. On Sunday evening I phoned Frances and told her I wouldn't be in on Monday. I wasn't sure I would ever be in again, but I didn't say so. On Monday morning I went into the workshop, put on the CD player with something baroque, and began to attend to that man's rocking chair. I sanded it down with far too much care, not because I wanted the job to be perfect but because I found it reassuring to be doing something so physical and precise that I couldn't think about anything else. Almost automatically, in a dream, I continued with the job, and when I woke from the dream, the chair was there, finished and perfect, almost too beautiful to part with.

When I got into the house, I rang the owner of the rocking chair and said that, after all, I had found time to mend it for him, and he could collect it whenever he wanted. Then I had a long bath and afterward I remembered I hadn't checked my answering machine, as if I'd wanted to keep the world away, just for the moment. There was a message from Fergus. I rang him.

"Are you home?" he said.

"Yes."

"For the next ten minutes?"

"Yes."

He hung up. I'd barely got dressed when the doorbell rang. It was Fergus, but he was different from when I'd seen him in the same spot on Saturday morning, distracted, not meeting my eye. He walked straight past me and into the living room. He sat on the sofa and I sat beside him. Without speaking, he took something from his pocket and placed it on the low table in front of us. It resembled a large narrow playing card.

"I think you should look at that," he said.

Chapter Seventeen

It's funny, the things you notice. Your brain can't stop working. When I picked the card up and turned it over, my hands were shaking but, even so, I saw it was a menu with the date—September 12—scrawled across it. There was a choice between goat's cheese and walnut salad or watercress soup for starter, followed by either sea bass with roast Jerusalem artichokes or Welsh lamb with mashed sweet potato and steamed baby vegetables. Then, for dessert, chocolate fondant or fruits of the forest. I saw all of this, even as I was reading the bold handwritten message across the top. "Darling G, you were wonderful this evening. Next time stay the night and I can show you more new tricks!" I didn't have to read the signature to know who had written it: I had spent days looking at the handwriting on bills, receipts, business letters.

I laid the menu back on the table, face down.

"Ellie," Fergus began.

"Wait," I said. I stood up and went to the chest where I'd put the chart. I took it out, unfolded it and examined the grid for September 12. An hour and twelve minutes was unaccounted for. At first I thought this was an amazing coincidence but quickly I realized it wasn't a coincidence at all, because that's the way reality fits together. I folded the chart and put it back in the drawer, then came to sit beside Fergus again.

"Where was it?" I asked him. My voice sounded quite calm. My hands were no longer trembling.

"Inside one of his running books. I was going through them this afternoon. Jemma said I shouldn't clutter up the house. I feel dreadful, Ellie. Was I right to show you?"

I gazed at him, although it was as if I was trying to see him through a fog. "You were quite right."

"I'm so sorry, Ellie."

"Thank you," I said politely, and folded my hands in my lap. I looked at the fingers laced together and thought I would be keeping my wedding ring off my finger after all.

"You were wonderful, the way you trusted him."

"I did, didn't I?"

"At least you know now."

"That's true."

"Can I get you a cup of coffee?"

"No, thank you." He looked so wretched that I forced myself to make an effort. "This must be really horrible for you, Fergus. But I'm glad you told me. It would have been terrible not to. I'm grateful."

"He was a fool. An idiot. But he loved you, Ellie, I know he did. You mustn't forget that."

"It's nice of you to say so. If you don't mind, I'd quite like to be alone now, Fergus."

He stood up, and I remained where I was, so that he had to bend down awkwardly to kiss me on both cheeks.

"I'll phone later," he said.

After he had gone, I continued sitting on the sofa with my hands clasped together. I don't know how long I stayed like that, or what I thought about. Perhaps those words: "I'll show you more new tricks." What kind of love note was that, with its tacky and teasing suggestiveness, as if Greg was a circus pony and she the ringmaster with the whip and black boots? I squeezed my eyes shut, trying to stop the images that were flooding through me. Perhaps I thought how extraordinarily, stunningly and flawlessly good he had been at keeping it secret from me, like a professional spy. Perhaps I thought it didn't make sense, or that it made perfect sense, at last.

Finally I stood up and pulled out the chart again, staring at the gap in the schedule that I could now fill in: Greg was with Milena. I unrolled her much less filled-in chart as well. Nothing for September 12 there either. So. She had wanted him to stay the night next time. Had he? I couldn't see when he would have done, but neither could I see why it should matter anymore. I had the evidence I'd been searching for and dreading. As clearly as if she was in the room, I heard Mary's voice: "Now you can get on with the rest of your life."

Right. I stood up abruptly and went upstairs into our bedroom; into *my* bedroom. I opened the wardrobe and pulled out Greg's handful of smart shirts, most of which I'd given him over the years, and his jackets. They would do for a start. I had been going to share them out among friends but now that didn't feel right. On my way downstairs, I grabbed his old toweling robe from the back of the door. I wouldn't be snuggling up in it on a cold evening anymore.

In the garden, I bundled them into a pile and put a match to them. You'd have thought clothes would burn easily, but not those. It was nearly dark, and it was drizzling, which didn't help matters—and the neighbor on the right, who had once complained to us about our loud music, was looking at me inquisitively while he put vegetable peelings on to his compost. I went into the shed, took paraffin from the top shelf and splashed a bit over the damp pile. I didn't even need to add another match; an ember must still have been glowing in the folds of a jacket, because there was a bang, a "Whoa!" from over the fence, and a violent orange flame roared several feet into the air. I could smell burning and realized my hair was singed. Who cared? Who cared what the neighbor thought, or his wife, who had now been summoned to watch the scene that was taking place? Who cared that acrid clouds of smoke were now rising from my fire, and petals of ash were floating in the air? Not me. I threw on his lovely leather brogues. They made a terrible smell. As I watched them blacken, I had a sudden picture of Greg buffing them with a soft cloth, that look of concentration on his lovely face, and wanted to rush forward and rescue them, but it was too late for that.

The elation had drained away and I felt empty, bleak, grim, defeated. Tired of the whole sorry business, of being angry, being ashamed, being sad, being lonely. Being me.

PERHAPS THAT WAS why I returned to Frances's the following morning. Because there, for a time, I wouldn't have to be me. I could be Gwen: practical, calm and in control, helping other people sort out the mess of their lives. The previous night I had gone to bed early, without eating anything and hugging a hot-water bottle because although it was not a particularly cold evening I felt chilly and shivery. I lay there, wide-eyed, in the darkness. I wanted to cry, in the same way that sometimes, when I feel horribly nauseous, I want to be sick, but the tears didn't come, wouldn't. Several times, I had heard the phone ring and voices leave messages: Fergus, Gwen, Joe, Gwen again. They must have heard on the grapevine. Soon everyone would know.

It took me a long time to choose what to wear. I tried on skirts, tops, different shoes. I stood in front of the mirror, examined myself critically and didn't like what I saw. I was pale; there were tired smudges under my eyes; my hair hadn't been cut for months and was long and wild. In the end I put on a dress that looked a bit like a pleated chocolate-colored sack, ribbed tights and my only pair of boots, although one of the heels was a bit loose. I put an amber pendant around my neck, because Greg hadn't given it to me, and tied my hair back into a messy bun. I put on muted eye-shadow, eyeliner, mascara, lip gloss. Finally, when it was after eleven o'clock and a pale sun had come out from behind the clouds, I looked enough like somebody else to venture out of the house.

FOR A MOMENT I thought Frances was going to hug me, but she contented herself with a hand on my shoulder and a warm, relieved smile.

"Hello," I said. "Sorry about yesterday."

"I'm just pleased you're here now. Come downstairs. Johnny's made us a pot of coffee."

"Johnny?"

"Yes. Listen, I need you to do me a favor. Anyway, it'll be more interesting for you than just trawling through the papers."

"What is it?" I asked. Trawling through the papers was exactly what I wanted to do: I hadn't finished with Milena Livingstone yet. Her chart was incomplete. My need to know about her had not been extinguished by that single coarse message scrawled so carelessly on the back of one of her menus. Now I wanted to know why—why had Greg fallen for her? What did she have that I didn't?

"I've got to dash out." She waved her hand vaguely in the air. "Crisis. But I'd promised Johnny I'd go to sample some of his suggested dishes, make the final choices. You can go instead of me."

"Wouldn't it be better if Beth did it?"

Frances frowned. "Beth isn't here yet. Besides, she doesn't deserve it."

"I don't know anything about food."

"You eat, don't you?"

"Kind of."

"Then it'll be a treat for you. Are you hungry?"

I tried to remember when I'd last eaten a proper meal.

"Good. That's settled, then," said Frances, as if she had read my mind.

Johnny arrived with the coffee. He kissed me on one cheek, then the other, and said I was looking lovely. I stammered something and caught Frances's amusement and something else. Tenderness?

JOHNNY'S RESTAURANT WAS in Soho, down a little side alley. I knew it must be exclusive because it was almost impossible to spot from the street. The dining room was small, maybe ten tables, only one of which was unoccupied as we came in. With its low ceilings and deep-red wallpaper, it had the air of being someone's private house rather than a public place. There was the hum of conversation, the chink of cutlery on china; waiters padded through, hovering deferentially over diners, pouring the last of the wine from bottles into glasses.

"Nice," I commented.

"They're all here on expense accounts," Johnny said dismissively. "They don't even taste what they're eating. Why do we bother?"

"Shall I sit here?" I gestured to the single empty table.

He shook his head and whisked me through the door at the back and suddenly I was in an entirely different world, a brightly lit space of gleaming stainless-steel surfaces and scrubbed hobs. It was like a laboratory where men and women in white aprons bent over their work, occasionally calling instructions or pulling open vast drawers to reveal ingredients. I stared around me in fascination. Johnny pulled out a stool and sat me down at the end of a counter. "I'll give you some things to try."

"Am I meant to choose the menu for Frances?"

"No, I've already decided it."

"Then what am I doing here?"

"I thought you were sad. I'm going to look after you. Wait." He disappeared through a small swing door and returned holding a large glass with a tiny amount of gold liquid in the bottom. "Drink this first."

I took an obedient sip. It was sweet, pungent, like apricots.

"Now, some soup. Radek, soup for the lady here!"

It didn't come in a bowl, but a tiny teacup, and was frothy like cappuccino. I drank it slowly, finishing it with a teaspoon. "What is it?"

"Do you like it?"

"It's delicious."

"Artichoke."

Lunch came in miniature portions: a sliver of sea bass with wild mushrooms, a single raviolo sitting in a puddle of green sauce in the middle of a huge bowl, a square inch of lamb on a spoonful of crisped potato, a thimbleful of rice pudding with cardamom. I ate very slowly, in a dream, while around me the bustle gradually died down as the restaurant emptied and the kitchen filled with racks of washed plates and glasses. Johnny fussed over me, wanting my approval. The mess of my life receded; in this warm space I felt I need never venture to be Ellie again.

"I've never eaten like this in my entire life," I said, over strong black coffee and a bitter chocolate truffle.

"Is that in a good way?"

"I feel looked after," I said.

"That's what I wanted." He put a hand on my shoulder. "What is it, Gwen?"

Our eyes met. For a moment, I so badly wanted to tell him

the truth that I could feel the words in my mouth, waiting to be spoken. Then I shook my head, smiling at him. "Everyone has their sad days," I said. "You've cheered mine up."

"That was what I wanted." His hand was still on my shoulder. "Tell me something, please."

"What?"

"Is there anyone?"

"There was," I said. "For a long time there was. But not anymore. That's all over now."

I felt so sad as I said the words. Cocooned in sadness, tiredness, food, warmth and the admiration of this nice stranger.

I let him take me home. Not to my home, of course, but his: a flat near the restaurant, up two flights of stairs and looking out onto a street market that was just packing up. It wasn't out of desire but need, and the sheer, raw, monumental loneliness that had engulfed me: to be held as the day faded, to be told I was lovely. I shut my eyes and tried not to think of Greg's face, tried not to remember and compare.

Afterward, when he tried to hold me, stroke my hair, my body wouldn't let me stay still. I got out of bed and dressed with my back to him, so I couldn't watch him watching me. An hour later, as I opened my front door, I felt a sudden unease, as if the house itself would be angry with me for what I'd done.

Chapter Eighteen

W hat was it like with Johnny?" asked Frances.
I looked up from some files and wondered if she could
see my cheeks going red. Had he blabbed? "What do you
mean?"

"The food," she said. "What did you think?"

"It was fine," I said.

"Just fine? Is that all?"

"It was good," I said. "It was really nice."

"Details, details," said Frances. "I need to know everything."

Frances poured a cup of coffee for me and one for her, and I
went through every dish Johnny had served me, describing its
appearance, its texture. Under Frances's intense questioning I
was forced to recall the ingredients, the garnishes, the presen-
tation. And as I talked, she leaned forward, her lips parted, as
if she was tasting the food in her imagination. I suddenly saw
her as a hungry woman—not just for the meals I was describing, but for intimacy, affection.

"Mmm," she said, when I'd finished. "Lucky you. Do you
think it's stuff we can use?"

"It might be a bit ornate," I said.

"Ornate is good," she said.

"Johnny never showed me a menu, but I guess it's expensive."

"That's the whole point," said Frances, briskly. "You've been looking through the bills, haven't you? In the bonus season, the problem for most of our clients is finding things that are expensive enough. And that look expensive as well, without being vulgar. But you know that. What I really wanted to talk to you about was Johnny. Did you see him at work in the kitchen?"

"That was where I ate."

"On a first date?" said Frances.

"It wasn't exactly a date."

"Whatever," said Frances. "But wasn't it wonderful, watching him cook? I remember the first time he made supper for David and me—it was a revelation. It was like knowing someone and thinking they're fairly normal, then discovering they can juggle or do magic tricks. He was so at home. Just the way he chopped vegetables or handled a piece of meat. I couldn't see how he did it all so quickly and casually. Except it wasn't casual. When I saw him cook, I thought he loved food more than he loved people."

"I know what you mean."

"Preparing a meal, tasting it . . . I think he misses that, being management rather than spending all his time in the kitchen, hands on, getting his fingers sticky."

"I get your point," I said. I was trying to think of a way to change the subject.

"David is one of the restaurant's main backers," she continued. "I'm afraid it's all very incestuous."

"Is that what David does for a living?"

"Sometimes. It's hard to explain—I don't think I really understand it myself. David is a rather mysterious man." She gave a little frown, as if an unpleasant thought had occurred to her. I saw the way she plaited her hands together tightly, so her thick gold band cut into her wedding finger. "He buys things, changes them a bit and sells them again, usually for much more than he bought them. And he makes problems go away for people who've got into a financial mess."

"What's that called?"

Frances laughed. "I don't really know. He earns a horrible amount of money from it, though. When you met him he was on his best behavior. I'm not sure I'd like to be in one of those companies while he's doing the sort of things he does to them, cutting away the deadwood or the fat, whatever he calls it. Anyway, that's what gives me the freedom to do things like this."

"You make it sound like a hobby," I said.

"From David's point of view it is," she said, a bit wistfully, I thought. "Not mine. But he keeps an eye on me, for what it's worth. Matter of fact, I think he's having lunch with Johnny today."

"Why?"

"I don't know," said Frances. "Just to talk things over. I don't think he'll get to eat in the kitchen, though."

IT MUST HAVE been a very long lunch because it was late in the afternoon when the two of them wandered into the office, looking very relaxed. I didn't trust myself to meet Johnny's eye. I wondered if he would come over and kiss me or put his arm around me, do something to suggest what had happened, but he didn't acknowledge me at all, so far as I could tell with my head down and pretending to concentrate. Instead I heard him talking to Frances in a low voice about a party that was coming up. At the same time I detected another presence close by me. I smelled a wave of aftershave and alcohol.

"How do you take your coffee?" David asked.

I looked around. He was wearing a fawn-colored suit made of a peculiar material that was probably rare, expensive and enormously desirable. "No milk, no sugar," I said.

"That's easy, then," he said, and handed me the mug he was holding.

I expected him to join the others but he pulled up a chair and sat next to me. I sipped the coffee while he leaned over my desk. He picked up a piece of paper. It was just a summary of invoices with details of what had been received and not, paid and not, but he scrutinized it with a frown. He replaced it with a grunt I couldn't interpret.

"Is something wrong?" I asked.

"Far from it," he said. "Looking at this, I can't imagine what Frances and Milena were up to. But you're in danger of turning this company into a going concern."

"I'm just tidying up."

He gave a languid smile. "That's about ninety-nine percent of what it takes to run a business." He looked across at his wife who was huddled in conversation with Johnny. "You're wasted here," he continued. "I could use someone who can do work like this."

"It isn't what I do for a living," I said.

"You mean you want to get back to teaching a class of young hoodlums? Let me tell you, they're not worth it."

I felt I ought to leap to the defense of those kids, even if they didn't exist; even if the person who was defending them didn't really exist. "I don't agree," I said.

"You like teaching logarithms and trigonometry year after year?"

"Um—yes!" I replied wildly, praying he wouldn't ask me anything technical. I knew about addition, subtraction, simple multiplication and even simpler division, and that, more or less, was it.

He ran his fingers through his thick, graying hair as if it was an architectural feature he was quietly proud of.

"Johnny was talking about you at lunch. No, don't worry," he said quickly. Perhaps he noticed an expression of alarm on my face. "He's very impressed with you. He says you've got a flair for the job and that Frances was lucky to find you."

I didn't reply. Like so many conversations I was having in that office, I didn't want it to go any further, any deeper. I did worry and, more than that, I didn't like the idea of being discussed over lunch by those two men, as if I was a specimen. And I didn't like the way that Johnny had brought David back to the office, as if they were going to look me over together, or so that Johnny could show off his latest conquest.

"You're an enigma. That's what Johnny says. We lose Milena suddenly and tragically, and you appear like a white knight. It's Fate."

I snatched at the opportunity to push the conversation in a

different direction. "It's strange for me," I said. "Milena feels so present here, and absent as well. What did you make of her?"

"You knew her, didn't you?" His tone was curt.

"Not well," I said. "Were you close to her?"

I expected David to smile and make a joke but his face took on a stony expression.

"No," he said. "I wouldn't say I was close to her."

"But she was a remarkable character, wasn't she?"

He allowed himself a very small, very forced smile. "In some ways, yes."

"You don't sound as if you liked her very much."

"'Liked' is rather a tepid word when talking about someone like Milena. People either found her whole act appealing and attractive, or . . . well, they didn't." He looked at me more closely. "It's funny to think of you as connected to Milena because you're as opposite from her as it's possible to be."

And yet, I thought, she'd been involved with my husband. Perhaps that was what he had been looking for: someone as different from me as it was possible to find.

"You see?" he said. "You've got me changing the subject. You've got me talking about Milena, when what I want to talk about is you. Milena would have liked that. She wanted to be the center of attention. She would have liked the idea of us talking about her even after she was dead and buried. Or dead and scattered, in her case. To get back to you, what Johnny said is that he thought very highly of you—as I've said—but he couldn't make you out. Reserved, mysterious, those were the words he used about you."

I tried to force a laugh. I felt I was being backed into a corner. "There's nothing mysterious about me," I said. "I wish there was. I'm really just a glorified cleaner here. I wanted to help Frances, that's all."

"Why?" said David. "Why did you want to help her? From a general love of humanity? A religious calling? Do we have a Good Samaritan here?"

"It's nothing complicated," I said. "When I was little I used to like clearing up my room, putting things in piles and arranging them. When I saw the mess this office was in, I wanted to sort it out. When the job's done I'll return to my old life."

David glanced at me more sharply. "We'll see," he said. "I reckon you'll find it harder to walk out on this than you think."

He had used a silky, detached tone that made it difficult for me to decide whether he was paying me a compliment or threatening me. He moved away and I tried to continue working but he poured himself a cup of coffee and returned to my side. He looked at the receipts, letters and invoices with me, made comments and suggestions. He was helping but it felt as if he was assessing me at the same time for a test I didn't know how to pass because I didn't know what the questions meant.

After a few minutes I felt a hand on my shoulder and Johnny pulled up a chair. I muttered a greeting without meeting his eye. I needn't have worried about looking awkward because the two men chatted casually as if I wasn't there. They were talking about another restaurant they were planning to revamp. Then they wandered around the room, making phone calls, drinking coffee, chatting until it was five o'clock. As I stood up to go, David said, "Do you fancy coming for a drink with us?"

"I can't," I said, deliberately not making an excuse, something that could be argued with.

Johnny stepped forward. "I'm about to drive in your direction," he said. "I could drop you."

I shrugged, and he led me outside. We sat in his car.

"I thought you needed rescuing from their clutches," he said.

"I can look after myself," I said.

"That's probably true." There was a pause. "I meant it about driving you, though. Where shall we go? My place or yours? I'd like to see where you live. I'd like to learn something about you."

The idea of Johnny prowling around my house trying to learn about me, about the real Gwen who wasn't Gwen, was unbearable.

"Let's go to your place," I said.

He watched me as I undressed, as if seeing me naked was a way of seeing me as I really was. But even with my clothes off, even when we were entangled in his bed, I tried to make myself believe I wasn't really there.

Afterward, I lay with my back to him and felt his fingers running through my hair, down my spine.

"This doesn't mean anything to you, does it?" he said.

I turned to face him. Suddenly I felt hard and cruel. I had spent too long trapped in my own misery, behaving as if I was the only one who was real and everybody else just a supporting actor in my drama. "I'm sorry," I said. "But—well, I am in the wrong place. Wrong place, wrong time. Working for

Frances was meant to be an interlude. I need to stop it and get back to my own life."

Johnny raised his hand and ran a finger down my nose, my cheek, the side of my jaw. "I dont know what you're talking about," he said. "What's this if it's not your life?"

That wasn't a question I could answer. "I feel I'm filling in for a dead woman and it's not right."

"That's crap."

"Milena was the one the company was built around, she's the one everybody talks about. She needs to be replaced, and that's not something I could do, even if I wanted to."

Johnny laughed. "You mean you're not a drama queen. You're not chronically disorganized. You're not totally self-centerd. You're not manipulative. You know she thought she looked like Julie Delpy, the movie actress?"

"I think I've seen her in something."

"She didn't at all, of course. It was about wanting to be French and Bohemian. You're not unreliable. You're not dishonest."

"Reliable. Organized. Unselfish. Lovely. It sounds like I should get a Girl Guide badge."

"I didn't mean it like that."

I leaned forward and kissed him, but only on the forehead. "I've got to go." I climbed out of the bed and began to pull on my clothes, with my back to him so I couldn't see him watching me.

"There was one thing, though," Johnny said. "She didn't leave in the middle of the night."

I looked around sharply. Knowledge coursed through me,

bitter and toxic. "You didn't?" I said, though of course I knew he had—and how had I not understood before? Milena had got into everyone's lives, and was still there now, as powerful dead as she had been alive. "Tell me you didn't."

"Is that a problem?"

"Milena?"

"Milena."

"Why didn't you tell me?"

"You mean, tell you about an affair with someone who's not alive anymore and that happened before you and I knew each other?"

I pulled my sweater over my head. "You should have told me," I said.

"Why would it have made any difference? It was before we met," he repeated, pulling on a pair of jeans and a sweatshirt, then following me downstairs and out on to the street. We stood in silence until the taxi arrived and he handed me in. Being angry, even unfairly angry, made it easier to leave.

The next morning, as soon as I arrived, I opened Milena's computer and clicked on the email. When the window appeared asking for a password, I typed "juliedelpy." I was in.

Chapter Nineteen

Was it a dream? A mistake? Shall we do it again? J xx."
I pressed the semicircular arrow beside Johnny's message to see what Milena had written in reply: "Tonight, 11:30 p.m. your place. Light the fire."

The following day: "You left your stockings. Next time, can't you stay?"

And Milena replied: "Maybe you've forgotten that I'm a married woman."

Two days later: "I can't leave the restaurant at 10, I'm afraid. Later any good? Thinking of you every minute of the day, J xxxx."

And the reply, a terse "No," to which Johnny responded, "OK, OK, I choose you over the crème brûlée. 10 then."

Three emails she didn't answer. The first was anxious: "Why didn't you come? Has he found out? Please tell me." The second beseeching: "Milena, at least tell me what's going on. I'm frantic." The third angry: "Fuck you, then."

There were dozens and I read them all. Their affair had lasted weeks. They usually met late at night, but sometimes they grabbed an hour or two in the day. They used Johnny's flat, Milena's house, when Hugo wasn't there, a hotel a few times, and once, according to Johnny's rhapsodic account, which I read with wincing shame, the back of Milena's BMW. I noticed that whereas Johnny's emails were often emotional—besotted, elated, grateful, angry or hurt—Milena's were almost always the same: short, practical, and often in the form of orders or careless ultimatums. She rarely mentioned her husband, and when she did it was as an irritating obstacle; she gave Johnny dates, times, places, that was it. I felt sorry and embarrassed for him: Milena was very sure of her power over him, and in his messages to her, he was not the sardonic and assured man I knew but someone insecure, needy, painfully submissive. By the end his messages deteriorated into abusive accusations about other lovers, deceit and calculating cold-heartedness. To these, Milena did not bother to respond.

In her work, Milena had been untidy and disorganized, not writing down appointments, expenses or even formal agreements, operating on a private whim that, often, she had not even shared with Frances. But her personal emails were scarily well ordered, almost playfully businesslike in their arrangement of betrayal, jealousy and loss. The first thing I discovered, when I entered Milena's virtual world, was that she had a special mailbox for her love affairs, labelled "Miscellaneous." Johnny was in there, and so was a lover from the previous year, who had begun as a client. It struck me that she rarely called them by their name: it was never "Dear Johnny" or "Dear Craig."

Gradually I came to feel a certain grudging, appalled admiration for the woman who'd taken my husband: she might have been predatory and cold, but she wasn't a hypocrite. She didn't say "make love" but "fuck"; she didn't pretend to feelings she didn't possess; she never used the word "love." I was struck by the apparent absence of pleasure, the energetic joylessness of her affairs. And she'd had so many. How had she managed it? All that planning, all that deception, all the lies she must have told, different lies to different men and having to remember which version of herself she was meant to be with which man. It made me weary just to think of it.

I searched for Greg by name, but wasn't discouraged when nothing turned up: if I'd learned anything over the past grim weeks, it was that their secret was buried deep. I wouldn't stumble across it but would have to uncover it with patience and guile. I glanced at the mailboxes, one by one. Johnny, the client Craig, someone called Richard, with whom Johnny had overlapped and who had unceremoniously faded out. There was a mailbox labeled "Accounts," which set my heart pounding so ferociously that I pressed my hand against my chest to calm it, feeling dizzy with the terror that I was finally about to enter the hidden world of my dead husband, but it turned out to be just what it said: increasingly exasperated messages from Milena and Hugo's financial adviser about her accounts, which were clearly in a mess. There were also several people who didn't sign off with their own names and whose addresses didn't give any immediate clue as to their owners' identity—perhaps, I thought, one might turn out to be Greg, masquerading under an assumed name. And then, of course, there were other people who hadn't been given their own special compartment, but were scattered randomly through the in-box, or who had been moved to the catch-all

"Personal" mailbox, which also held messages from friends, acquaintances and family.

"What are you doing?"

I started. I had been so engrossed that I hadn't noticed Beth arrive. I felt as if I'd been caught with my hands in the till. Perhaps, in some way, I had. "Checking some stuff out," I said.

"You want some coffee?"

"Great."

While Beth was gone I wondered if what I was doing was wrong. Well, of course it was. The question was how wrong, and whether it mattered. Frances was my employer and she probably thought of me as a friend. Here I was, under false pretenses, snooping through her office, rifling through her dead friend's personal life, behaving like a spy. When Beth returned, she gave me the coffee but she didn't head off, as she normally did, to potter around and talk on the phone. Instead she pulled up a chair and sat close to me, cradling her mug in her hands. I quickly closed Milena's email window.

"What are you doing here?" she said.

I made myself laugh. "What do you mean?"

"I'm working here because Frances is an old friend of my mum's. It doesn't pay much but the job's good for making contacts. And it's Frances's life. But I don't understand what's in it for you."

I couldn't tell whether Beth was teasing, curious or suspicious. Had she picked up on some mistake? I tried to change the subject. "What about Milena? What was she in it for?"

"Why are you so curious about her? It's like an obsession with you—Milena this, Milena that."

"It's strange her not being here," I said. "It's like going to a play that's missing the star."

"It's funny," said Beth. "I'd never really known anyone before who died. There was a girl at university who was killed in a car crash but she wasn't really a friend. I worked with Milena for a year and I'd never met anyone like her and I still wake up in the morning and suddenly remember she's dead and it comes as a shock each time."

"Yes, I know," I said, although I wasn't thinking of Milena anymore.

When we'd finished our coffee, and Beth had taken my mug away, I told myself I mustn't look at Milena's emails, that it was too risky while Beth was there, but I couldn't help myself. I arranged the screen so that she couldn't see it and opened a notebook, so that I appeared to be doing accounts, and returned to it with dread and overpowering curiosity.

First—or first in this computer's memory, going back two years and nine months—there was Donald Blanchard, barrister and colleague of Hugo's, who called Milena "Panther" and suffered from bursts of anxiety about betraying his friend, not to mention his own wife, which hadn't stopped him taking Milena to Venice for a weekend.

I was able to follow one of the affairs, with a man who signed himself J, as if it was a piece of music. It began, as several did, with memories of "last night" and anticipation of the next time. It wasn't like reading love letters, more like a series of diary entries, times and places. Then it gradually petered out, although there was a sudden flurry at the end, as the affair finished. The last message consisted of the single ominous sentence: "Well, I can just phone her up, then." Milena clearly didn't like being left.

This overlapped a more drawn-out affair with Harvey, who was visiting from the States. He went home and Richard arrived on the scene. During her time with Richard, Milena had a couple of flings: one was with a man much younger than herself, whom she referred to as her "toy boy" and sent packing when he became too insistent. After Richard there had been Johnny. And after Johnny, in the crucial month before Greg and Milena had died together, there was only one other significant player: he never used a name, simply put a couple of crosses at the end of a message. I wrote his address in my notebook.

I stared at the screen until my eyes hurt. Was the anonymous lover Greg? He signed off with kisses and his Hotmail address was "gonefishing"—there were dozens of messages from him, spaced out over three months. They were love letters: they commented on her hair, her eyes, her hands, the way she looked when she smiled at him, the way he felt when he saw her before she lifted her head and saw him too. For a moment I had to stop reading. There was a lump in my throat and my vision blurred. If this was Greg, he had never written to me in that way. And if this was Greg, he was writing to a Milena no one else had known: someone more tender and lovable than the bright, glittering, heartless woman everyone else seemed to remember. And that made horrible sense to me: I couldn't imagine Greg having a coldhearted affair, but I could imagine him falling in love with a woman, and by his love transforming her into someone different, better. I used to think he had done that to me—discovered a version of myself that only existed when I was with him and that had disappeared when he had died.

Gradually the pain in my chest eased and I could look at the screen again. I put away the messages from the anonymous lovers for the moment and browsed through the in-box to see if anything relevant cropped up. There were various messages from "S," cranky and intemperate. I looked at a couple of messages from her to him and recognized the flirtatious tone she reserved for certain men, very different from the brisker style she adopted with Frances, Beth or female clients. It seemed a very particular sort of betrayal to be reading Beth's mail while she was sitting in the same room but, then, I was becoming something of a connoisseur of betrayal.

I was about to open a message from Milena's husband when I heard the front door open and Frances hurried down the stairs, looking flushed. "Hi!" she said, tossing her coat on to the sofa and coming over to kiss my cheek, which felt hot with shame and anxiety. "Sorry I was away so long."

"That's OK."

"What have you been up to?"

"Just clearing things up a bit," I mumbled. Couldn't she tell that everything was exactly as it had been when she had left, not a single piece of paper moved or dealt with?

"Good," she said. "You mustn't work too hard, though."

"No, no, I didn't."

She looked at Beth. "Could you make us some tea, darling?"

Beth pulled a face, got up and left the room with obvious reluctance.

Frances came over and stood close by me. "It's been good having you here," she said, in a subdued tone. "I haven't said this to you—well, I haven't said it to anyone—but when Milena died I thought I might give up the business."

"Really?"

"To be honest, even before that things hadn't been going well. Milena had . . ." Frances paused. "Let's just say that a lot of what brought me into the business seemed to have gone away."

"So things were bad before she died?"

There was another long pause, in which Frances's face took on a troubled expression I hadn't seen before. "It's all in the past now," she said finally, "and it's not what I wanted to talk about. Maybe another time. We could go out for lunch—or dinner, even."

"I'd like that," I said.

"You're easy to talk to and, to be honest, I need advice. There are things I need to say out loud."

I didn't know how to respond; I felt my deceit must be written across my face. I made an indeterminate sound and stared at my hands, my ringless finger.

"What I was going to say," Frances continued, "is that I know David was talking to you but I wanted to ask you formally if you'd think of staying on."

"Here?" I asked stupidly.

"That was the general idea."

"I've given you the wrong impression," I said. "I'm just a teacher taking a bit of time out."

"I like having you around. Most people irritate me. You don't."

"Thank you." I couldn't meet her eyes. "But I don't think it's possible."

"Don't say no at once. Think it over at least. Are you in tomorrow?"

"There are things I need to do."

"I'd be grateful if you could manage an hour or so in the morning. I've got to go out."

"All right," I said. "Now I ought to leave. Things to do."

"But before you go, I think I should pay you for the last few days."

"Later."

"Gwen! Anyone would think you were doing this for nothing."

"Don't worry, I'm not a saint."

"Johnny seems to think you're pretty perfect." My face burned. I heard myself mutter something unintelligible. "Don't worry. He hasn't said anything to me. He's pretty discreet. I've just seen the way he looks at you."

"I'll see you tomorrow," I managed to say, and dashed out.

I TOLD MYSELF I mustn't go back, but it had become an addiction. I had to go back, just to look through the rest of Milena's emails. I arrived home in a restless and agitated state. My answering machine was flashing but I didn't bother to listen to the messages. I made myself a cup of tea and drank it while I paced around the house. I opened the fridge and had one of the liquid yogurts Mary had brought. She said it would be good for my digestion; it tasted of coconut and vanilla and coated my tongue. I went into my neglected little garden. Darkness was drawing in, giving everything a mysterious air. I noticed the drifts of sodden leaves on the lawn, the nettles growing up against the back wall. There were a few yellow roses left on the bush by the back door. The bedraggled little blackbird was singing its heart out in the gloom. I reminded myself that I still had time to plant bulbs for spring. The previous autumn we'd planned snowdrops, winter aconites, daffodils and red tulips. Greg had loved tulips—he said they were the only flowers that were as beautiful dying as they were unfurling. I realized that I no longer had any difficulty in thinking of him in the past tense. When had that happened? On what day had he slipped between the cracks of memory to lie with other departed people in the deeper places of my mind?

Back in the house, I laid my two charts on the kitchen table and looked at them, my brain tingling uselessly. I took my notebook out of my bag and stared at the two addresses. What should I do now? The phone rang and I didn't answer it. I waited to hear the message but there wasn't one. Then it rang again, but still I didn't answer. It rang yet again. It was like a game of chicken. Finally I gave up and answered.

"I knew you were there." It was Fergus.

"Sorry, I was tired."

"I wanted to ask you for supper. Jemma's put a chicken in the oven, I've lit a fire."

"As I said, I'm a bit tired."

"If you don't come, we'll put the dinner in the car and drive over to you. And if you don't let us in we'll eat on your door-step and embarrass you in front of your neighbors."

"All right, all right, I'll come."

"I'll come, *thank you*."

I laughed. "Sorry for being so rude. Yes, thank you for ask-ing me."

JEMMA WAS VERY, very pregnant. Every so often she winced as the baby kicked her. At her invitation, I put my hand on her belly and felt it writhing and jabbing. She told me it kept get-ting hiccups.

"There are so many things people won't say to me," I said, after two glasses of wine.

"What do you mean?" Fergus leaned forward to top up my glass but I put my hand over it.

"Well, for example, you two don't talk to me about the baby unless I press you. You think it might upset me—because of Greg, because we never managed it and now it's too late. And of course it upsets me, but it's not as if I forget about it until you remind me. It's much better to say things, otherwise I feel shut out from life. Mary used to go on about Robin at every hour of the day—his snuffles, his nappies, the way his fist closed around her finger—and now she barely mentions him. Gwen used to tell me about her love life. Joe would regularly complain to me about having a cold or some bloody rich client. Not anymore."

"In that case," said Fergus, glancing sideways at Jemma for her approval, "we wanted to ask you something."

"Yes?"

"Will you be its godmother?"

"Godmother?"

"Yes."

"But you don't believe in God."

"Well, that's not really the point."

"Neither do I."

"Is that a no?"

"Of course I'll be its godmother! I'd love to." I was crying, tears sliding down my cheek and into my mouth. I wiped the back of my hand across my face and held out my glass for more wine. "Here's to whoever-it-is."

"Whoever-it-is," they echoed.

Fergus got up and hugged me. "I'm so sorry about everything," he whispered.

I shrugged.

Chapter Twenty

When I got home, I had decided what to do. It would have been easy to send emails from Milena's account, simply replying to the messages she had received from old lovers, but that felt too risky. Even if I stayed anonymous, it would have to be sent by someone who knew Milena's password. It might even establish a connection with Milena's computer or her office. The safest idea seemed to be to set up a Hotmail account for myself. I had no idea how easy it was to trace emails, but I probably wasn't dealing with computer experts here. Creating the new email address, I simply jabbed randomly at the keyboard and ended up with j4F93nr4wQ5@hotmail.co.uk. I entered my first name as J and my second name as Smith. As a password I wrote out sequence of numbers and upper-and lower-case letters. When I was done, I sent myself an email, just to check. There was just "J Smith," the subject line, the date and time and the address. That seemed safe enough.

I entered the first of the email addresses I had retrieved from Milena's computer, wrote "re" beside "subject," and then, after a few moments' thought, typed: "Dearest Robin, I am LONGING to see you and . . ." I tried to think of a plausible name. "Petra." No—wasn't that a dog's name? And a tourist destination. "Katya." Sounded a bit exotic. I realized I was thinking of names that sounded too like "Milena." I looked at the books on the shelf. "Richmal." Hopeless. "Elizabeth." Was anyone called that anymore? "Eliza." "Lizzie." "Beth." "Bessie." They all sounded ridiculous. Anyway, what did it matter. "Lizzie" would do. And then I remembered. No, it wouldn't do. The name needed to start with a J. Jackie then. "Jackie again after all this time. Ring as soon as you arrive, love Jackie xxxxx PS I hope this is your email address and if it isn't will whoever is reading it let me know!!!!!"

I read it over and then again. I pressed send and it was gone. I wrote the same message to the second address as well and sent it. I thought of when I was a child and sometimes I had been afraid to post a letter because when I pushed it through the slot and heard it fall, I would realize it was still there, a few inches away, but lost to me, beyond change or recall.

THE NEXT MORNING, when I arrived at the office, Frances was talking on the phone. She was preparing a party for a firm of City lawyers that was being held in an old warehouse by the river. As I switched on Milena's computer, she slammed down the phone and strode over to me. "They want a Shakespearean theme," she said. "I don't even know what that means."

"Can't you just hire some young actors?" I said. "They can walk around with the canapés and say lines from Shakespeare. About cakes and ale and, well, there must be some other references to food."

"And they want Elizabethan food. I mean, honestly! I had this ridiculous woman on the line just now and I said, "What do you mean by Elizabethan food? Carp? Pike? Capon?" She

said, "Oh, no. They just want normal food with an Elizabethan twist."

There were shelves of books and magazines in the office
for just such a crisis and Frances started to rummage through
them, speaking half to herself and half to me. I went to my
new account. My new email address and password were impossible to remember. I had to copy them painstakingly from
the piece of paper on which I'd written them.

"What exactly *are* sweetbreads?" said Frances. "Some kind
of gland, aren't they?"

"I'm not sure if they're right for finger food," I said. I had to
make an effort to keep my voice level because I had noticed
there were two messages for me. The first was welcoming me
as a new account holder. The second was from "gonefishing."

Frances walked across the room toward me, reading aloud
as she did so.

"Jugged hare," she said. "Lobster. This is hopeless. We
might as well be cooking larks' tongues."

"You just want little things that have an old-fashioned
look to them," I said. "Quail's eggs. Bits of bacon. Dump-
lings. Scallops."

I clicked on the message.

"Who are you?" it read.

I clicked "reply" and quickly typed. "I'm Jackie, as you can
see. Have I got the wrong address? Who are you?"

I highlighted and underlined the last word: "Who are <u>you</u>?"
I pressed send.

"That sounds right," said Frances. "We can just put Ye Olde
English garnishes on the plates. Bits of parchment. Branches

of rosemary. Little ruffs. We can hang some tapestries and garlands on the wall. Pickled walnuts," she added, warming to the subject. "Medlars. Quinces. The problem is, people won't know what they are."

"It'll give the staff something to talk about," I said. "In fake Elizabethan language, of course. 'Odds bodkins.' You know."

There was a ping from Milena's computer. A message from "gonefishing."

"Who are you?" it said, same as before. I pressed reply again.

"Don't understand," I typed. "Did you get my last message? Have I got the wrong address? Could you give me your name?" I pressed send.

I waited one minute, two, but there was no response.

Meanwhile Frances was flicking through another book. "Did they have oysters in Elizabethan times?" she asked.

"I think so."

"I'm a bit wary of shellfish. You don't want to poison a roomful of lawyers."

My attention drifted away and I suddenly heard Frances's voice raised, as if she was trying to rouse me from sleep.

"I'm sorry," I said. "I didn't hear what you were saying. I was trying to sort something out in my head."

She looked at me with concern. "Are you all right? You're rather pale."

"I'm fine," I said. "Maybe a bit tired."

Frances fussed over me as if she was my granny. She felt my brow with her thin, cool hand. She made me coffee and even asked if I'd like a touch of brandy in it. "Now, that might be the thing for the end of the party," she said. "Did they have coffee in Elizabethan times? They must have had brandy."

Reluctantly I left my desk and we thumbed through the cookbooks for ideas. We discussed goujons of sole, deviled whitebait, creamed mushrooms and smoked eel, baby tomatoes stuffed with crab, and new potatoes stuffed with caviar. Frances was doubtful about the last. "I'll need to run this past the wretched Daisy at G and C's," she said. "This might be a bit steep even for them. I saw some caviar at Fortnum's the other day. It was about a million pounds a thimbleful."

As she was talking, I heard a ping from Milena's computer and suddenly it was as if I was in a dream and Frances's words were meaningless background noise. I had to force myself to talk normally as she put the cookbooks down and wandered across to the shelves for an exhibition catalogue.

"Can you give me a moment?" I said, and walked across to Milena's computer. I clicked on the new message. "Nobody has this address," it said. "How did you get it?"

I collected my thoughts and made myself take on the character of Jackie, a nonexistent person conjured up by another nonexistent person. "Maybe I got it wrong," I wrote. "I just wanted your name to see if I've mixed it up with someone else. But if it's a problem, don't worry about it."

I sent it and returned to Frances, who had found an old catalogue for an exhibition of Elizabethan miniatures. She smiled and pointed at an exquisitely delicate oval image of a woman wearing a tall hat with a white ostrich feather, a lace ruff, sleeves bunched and embroidered with gold thread and a rigid, richly decorated bodice. "She looks like you," she said. "I'd like to see you in that."

"I haven't the waistline for it," I said.

Frances looked at me appraisingly, as if I was a pig she was considering buying. "Oh, yes, you have," she said. "How do you do it? Exercise and good living?"

Not eating, not sleeping, constant anxiety, I thought, but just smiled with what I hoped was rueful modesty. We leafed through the gorgeous catalogue, pausing over men in doublets and ruffs, stockings and breeches; women in cloaks and petticoats, corsets and farthingales.

"If we can dress some of our young actors in these," said Frances, "and get them to learn a few lines, it should be magnificent. If we want to be really authentic, we should probably have the women played by men as well."

"I don't think the lawyers would like that," I said. "When they asked for Elizabethan they were probably thinking of wenches dispensing flagons of ale and behaving bawdily. It might be a grueling evening for some of them."

Frances grunted. "The drama-school girls we employ are pretty unshockable," she said. "You know, if they were laid end to end in the garden, et cetera et cetera."

I heard another ping from the computer and got distracted again. "Et cetera what?" I said.

"I wouldn't be the least surprised."

"What?"

"It's an old joke. I've ruined it now. If the girls were laid end to end in the garden. You know. I wouldn't be in the least surprised."

"Oh, yes," I said. "I think I've heard it."

"Dorothy Parker, I think."

"Yes," I said. "Excuse me a moment. Someone's sent me a message." I couldn't pretend to continue a conversation. I walked over to the computer and clicked on the new message.

"Sorry for being paranoid," the message read. "It's a security issue. Just give me your phone number and I'll give you a ring and tell you my name."

As I read the message, I felt as if I had immediately, and without warning, become immensely more stupid. I was like a person in a foreign country who just about understood what basic words meant but couldn't make out what lay behind them, what was implied, what were the customs everybody took for granted. I found it impossibly difficult to assess what the message meant, its implications. Was there any possible way I could give some phone number or other to this person? Was it conceivable that they would ring and tell me who they were and I would know who this lover of Milena's was?

Suddenly everything was made up of puzzles I wasn't equipped to solve.

Was it possible that whoever it was believed my message had been a mistake? Could that be a security issue? Was it likely they would go to the trouble of phoning to clear the matter up? My thoughts were slow, trapped in sludge, but in the end, with Frances hemming and hawing and waiting for me on the other side of the room, I decided, no, it was not possible. I had gone too far. I had laid myself open.

My password seemed safe. Certainly it was safe from me, as

there was no chance I would ever remember it. But just to be absolutely safe I deleted all of the messages, both those I had received and those I had saved, and then deleted the deletions. If I could have, I would have deleted those as well, but as far as I could tell, they were as pulverized as anything can be in cyberspace.

I rejoined Frances and we made more Elizabethan plans, then went out to lunch where we ate a meal that seemed as far from Elizabethan cuisine as it could have been, all tiny slices of tuna carpaccio and miniature heaps of spicy noodles. But, then, I know nothing about Elizabethan cuisine apart from what I've seen in historical dramas on TV. For all I know, Elizabethans might have had delicate side orders of bean sprouts with their haunches of venison. We also had a small jug of warm sake which Frances drank quickly and greedily, barely looking at her food before ordering a second. I remembered the vodka bottles in her desk drawer. She talked about whether we could hire a jester from the Comedy Store and wondered whether health and safety regulations would allow flaming torches on the walls, whether we could hire Elizabethan musicians—and what was Elizabethan music like? What about morris dancers? Were they Elizabethan?

"It's all about money," Frances said thoughtfully, as we lingered over the coffee. "If you're in London and you've got money, you can have anything." And then she pushed her food, barely touched, away from her and said, "Except happiness, of course. That's a whole different story."

I didn't know what to say. In normal circumstances I would have reached across the table and touched her arm, asked what she meant, tried to draw her out. But these weren't normal circumstances. If she turned to me for support, she would be turning to someone who didn't exist and, what was more, someone who would leave her before long. So I wrinkled my brow and murmured something meaningless.

"Would you say you were happy, Gwen?" she asked, raising her pale, delicate face to me.

"Oh, well." I stabbed my fork into the final sliver of tuna. "That's hard to say. I mean, what's happiness?"

"I used to be," she continued. "It seemed easy once. Or maybe I wasn't really happy. Maybe I was just having fun. That's different, isn't it? I think I used to be very selfish. I didn't understand that actions had consequences. When Milena and I first met, before we were married, we were a bit like Beth, I suppose—out every night, lots of men, lots of parties, lots of drink. But then it all changed. You reap what you sow, that's what they say. But I wish I'd understood then what I was sowing. Shall we have a dessert wine?"

"I'm fine," I said. "If I drink during the day I fall asleep. But go ahead if you feel like one."

"No, you're probably right, and we should get back to work, I suppose. Sorry to ramble on. Sometimes I feel so . . ." But she stopped, shook her head as if to clear it, put her spectacles back on, gave me a wry smile. "Right. Let's go and talk doublets and hose."

When we returned to the office, I felt Milena's computer drawing me as if I was attached to it with invisible cords. But I didn't work on the computer that afternoon. I sketched our thoughts for the party into a coherent proposal. It was so trivial and so interesting that I felt regret that this would surely be my farewell to working with Frances. I finished the proposal and had almost cleared my desk when David arrived to collect her. He was in a bad mood and scarcely glanced in my direction. Frances made an apologetic grimace. I muttered an excuse and left.

When I got home, I ran up to the computer without even taking off my jacket. I went through the tiresome business of typing in my new email address and password, copying each character one by one. There was a new message and I clicked on it.

The previous messages had been written above the one before but now the old ones had been deleted. The subject line said, "Who are you?" and the message repeated, "Who are you?"

Chapter Twenty-One

Against my better judgment, I had promised to be at the latest Party Animals happening because Beth was away for the long weekend she'd been planning. A very long weekend that was actually one day short of a week. "Just to give you a better feel for what we do," Frances had said, the afternoon before. "You don't need to do anything, really. Just be in the background and keep an eye on things." She had examined me dubiously. "It's that women-in-commerce thing you costed," she said. "You know, dozens of high-powered women networking and complaining about men. So if you could . . ." She faltered.

"Wear a suit?"

"Yes. Something like that. Thanks, Gwen."

I didn't own a suit, or even anything that could be put together to look like a version of one. I hauled myself out of bed and showered under tepid water because the boiler operated in a mysterious and sporadic way and I didn't have the money to get it adjusted—I didn't have the money, as it happened, even for food, but I couldn't think about my bank balance now. It would have to wait, just as everything else would have to wait: friends, a job, real life.

Sure enough, there was nothing in the cupboard that Frances might possibly approve of. The only suit there was Greg's green-gray one that he had worn when we married and that, even in my rage-filled binge, I hadn't been able to bring myself to burn. I took it out and examined it. It was lovely, simple and lightweight. I'd helped him choose it and it was the most expensive item of clothing either of us had ever bought. I held it against myself: it was a bit long but I could roll up the legs and put a belt around the waist. When I tried it on, I was startled by how different I looked, how jauntily androgynous. I put on a white shirt and tied an old bootlace around my neck in imitation of a tie. A trilby would have completed the effect, but I didn't own one, so I put on a corduroy newspaper-boy's cap that we'd found in Brick Lane one spring morning, tucking my hair underneath it, and putting studs in my ears. Now I didn't look like Ellie or Gwen, but someone entirely new.

I had time before I needed to leave for the City, so I made myself instant coffee and had the last fragments of the now-soft cornflakes that Greg used to eat sometimes. The light was flashing on my answering machine but I decided not to listen to the messages. I already knew that half of them would be from Gwen and Mary and they would say, "Where are you?" and "Ring me back as soon as you can," and "What's going on?" Then, like a crack addict, I went back to the computer and looked at the email I'd received last night. I didn't need to, of course. There were still only those three words: "Who are you?" I had no idea what to do next, and although common sense insisted that I leave well alone—leave Frances and Party Animals, leave my snooping and prying, leave my hapless pretense at being someone else, return to the life I'd left behind and try to build a sustainable future—I knew very well that I wasn't going to. Not yet, anyway. But I couldn't think of a way to find out the identity of "gonefishing." Obviously, I couldn't give him my number, home or mobile. I didn't want to speak to him, to have him hear my voice. But I had to give him some number to ring me on.

Perhaps I could ask Gwen to talk to him, while pretending not to be Gwen, of course, because I was Gwen. But I dismissed the idea, because I didn't want to be told—as I most definitely would be—that what I was doing was misguided and wrong, and I should stop at once. I already knew that.

I stared at the screen until the words blurred. I stared at my new Hotmail address: j4F93nr4wQ5@hotmail.co.uk. And it came to me: what I should do was simply repeat what I'd already done with my email and get myself a new mobile, whose number I wouldn't give to anyone except "gonefishing." When he rang, I wouldn't answer, but I would have his number on my phone. That was a step forward, at least.

I had time to buy the pay-as-you-go phone and still be early at the women-in-commerce lunch, which took place in a vaulted basement in the heart of the City, a dimly lit, handsome space of ancient brick, cold stone and muted echoes. A fire blazed in the hearth at one end of the room, and vases holding velvety red roses stood at intervals on the long table. Slender wine glasses—which nobody used because they drank sparkling water—and silver cutlery glinted. It all felt very old-fashioned and masculine, which, as Frances had explained to me, was the point: this was to be like a stereotypical gentlemen's club taken over by the ladies. It was typical of

Frances to make something so establishment simultaneously ironic.

Sure enough, the women, when they arrived, had on the club uniform. They all wore beautiful skirts and jackets and dresses, in black and gray and dark brown, with white shirts, elegant shoes, sheer tights, discreet flashes of gold at their ears and on their fingers. They flowed down the stairs, handing cashmere coats, leather gloves, slender briefcases and furled umbrellas to the staff, and stood in their massed, discreetly ostentatious wealth. I felt shabby, angry, out of place—like a court jester. I wanted to go home, put on my oldest jeans and plane curls off pale, seasoned wood.

But when Frances saw me she raised her eyebrows. "You look very fetching," she said, smiling. "You certainly have your own style, Gwen." I didn't know if that was a compliment or a veiled insult.

It hardly felt like work: I drifted from kitchen to cloakroom and back to the dining room, keeping an eye on things, making sure the lunch ran smoothly and courses were delivered at the right time. Yet by the end I felt weary and stale, in need of fresh air, natural light. When I stepped out on to the street, I gasped and shrank back into the doorway. Joe was walking along the pavement toward me, his coat billowing around his solid figure. He was carrying his bag and seemed deep in thought; there was an angry frown on his face. I felt as though someone had struck me. My mouth was dry and my heart pressed against my ribs. He mustn't see me, not when I was dressed in Greg's wedding suit and being Gwen, not when, in a few moments, Frances would come up the stairs behind me and witness him greeting me as Ellie. I bent double, pretending to tie up the laces of my shoes, which didn't possess laces, and when I glanced up, he had passed by on the other side of the road, although I could still see his familiar figure striding away, toward some banking client perhaps. I stood upright and tried to collect myself, although I felt slightly sick with shock. How easy it would be for my two worlds to collide and shatter.

WHEN I GOT home, a piece of paper was lying on the doormat. "Where are you, what are you doing and why aren't you answering my calls? RING ME NOW! Gwenxxxx."

I pushed the message out of my way, took the new phone out of its box and plugged it in to charge. Then I opened my Hotmail account and copied out the new email address. "This is my phone number," I wrote, and keyed it in. I took a deep breath and pressed send. There, it was gone. Now all I had to do was wait.

I couldn't put off listening to my phone messages any longer: Gwen, Joe, Gwen, Gwen, my bank manager, Joe, Mary, my mother twice, Mary again, Gwen and Gwen and Gwen, my sister, Fergus twice, a woman calling about a chest of drawers that needed stripping, my bank manager again, a wrong number, Gwen, who sounded frantic with anxiety now. I felt a pinch of guilt. I would call her soon. Tomorrow. After I'd sorted this latest thing out. I couldn't talk to anybody until then. It wasn't possible.

But even as I was thinking this there was an insistent knocking at the door. I got up to answer it, then sat down again. No:

it would be Gwen or Mary or Joe or Fergus and I wasn't in the mood. If I didn't open the door, they'd go away. The knocking continued. Did they know somehow I was in there? Then it stopped.

I breathed out with relief and stood up. What now? I opened the fridge door and stared dispiritedly into the white space. A lonely knob of hard cheese, a past-its-sell-by-date packet of butter and a shrink-wrapped stub of chorizo sat on the otherwise empty shelves. As I stood there, I had a creepy feeling that I wasn't alone. I heard a rustle behind me, coming from the garden and, very slowly, I turned. Someone was staring in at me through the window. Gwen. Her sweet-natured face was transformed by a huge scowl. Another face appeared beside her and the two glared in at me. Then Mary raised her fist and rapped sharply on the glass. "Let us in!" she yelled.

I opened the back door and stood aside so that they could enter.

"What are you playing at?" hissed Gwen, dumping a large shopping bag on the table.

"What are you wearing?" said Mary.

"Didn't you get my messages? My note? Do you know how worried we've all been?"

"I—I was busy," I mumbled.

"Busy? Well, I was busy too, as it happens. You can't just hide away, you know. Fuck. I pictured you lying in a ditch—or in a bath with your wrists cut or something. If you don't want to see us, fine, but at least tell us you're all right. We were going to ring the police if you hadn't been here this evening."

"I'm sorry. I didn't think."

"Well, you should have done! That's no excuse. You should have a bit of consideration."

Gwen started pulling items out of the bag. Ground coffee, milk, shortbread biscuits, wholemeal bread, salad, carrots, a bottle of wine, eggs. She thumped them down on the table angrily.

"Was that suit Greg's?" asked Mary.

"Yes," I said shortly.

"You look great." There was a hint of accusation in her voice. It would have been better if I'd been haggard and red-eyed with grief. "Doesn't she look great, Gwen?"

"Hmm. Where have you been?"

"Trying to sort things out."

Gwen snorted. "That's a feeble answer."

"It's true," I insisted, and after all, it was in its own way.

"Have you been getting back to your work?"

"Not exactly. A bit."

"A bit. Have you dealt with your financial stuff, been to the bank and your solicitor, visited his parents, like you said you would?"

"I will soon."

"So what have you been sorting out?"

"I—There's a lot of bits and pieces." It sounded so lame that I blushed to the roots of my hair.

"What are you up to, Ellie?" Gwen asked.

"I'm not up to anything." But I couldn't meet her gaze.

"This is us, remember," said Mary. She had sat down at the table and was now chewing absentmindedly at one of the carrots Gwen had brought.

The phone rang suddenly and I stiffened. But it was only my landline and we waited in silence as the answering machine picked up and Joe's voice came on: "Ellie. Ellie, honey? It's me. Come on." There was a pause, and then he said again, "Ellie?" before hanging up.

"See? Another anxious friend."

For a moment I considered telling them everything I had done. But to do that wouldn't I also have to give up my subterfuge, my lies, deceits and unhealthy obsessions? "I'm really, really sorry," I said. "Honestly I am. I know I'm behaving oddly, wrongly. I can't explain it properly. I've been all over the place." I twisted my hands together, my naked, ringless fingers. "I keep thinking things will get better."

"We're here to help you," said Gwen. "You know that. Don't shut us out."

"No," I said.

"Now we're here, shall I make us tea?" asked Mary. "Tea and biscuits and then we can go out. Eric's looking after Robin this evening so I'm free. What d'you say? Film and meal, just the three of us, like it used to be?"

What I wanted to say was that I felt tired and agitated and my heart was bouncing in my chest like a rubber ball and all I wanted to do was wait by the phone, but their two kind, familiar faces showed such concern that I said, "That would be very nice."

I GOT HOME just after midnight and ran to check the new phone. There were no messages but there was one missed call. I picked up the mobile. Resting in my hand, it felt like a bomb that might go off at any time. In bed, the phone on the table beside me, I could feel myself fizzing with excitement and dread, and when I finally slept, it was fitfully, to taunting dreams.

FRANCES KISSED ME on both cheeks. "I'm so glad you're here. I've got to dash out in an hour or so and I won't be back until midafternoon. It would be great if you could go through the new brochure for me. I've got to get it to the printers this afternoon and it's littered with errors."

"It's not that I mind, but what about Beth?"

"Oh, you can show it to her, but she's no use. She studied events management at university, which means she can barely read or write."

"Fine. I'll do my best."

"Let's have coffee first, though."

"Shall I get it?"

"No, no. Let me."

There was a hectic air about her: she couldn't seem to sit still; she kept taking her glasses off and putting them on again, running her hand through her hair.

"Are you all right?" I asked.

"Me? Fine. Why do you ask?"

"You seem a bit restless."

"Maybe I am. Strange times."

"I'm sure."

"I'm really glad you're around, though, Gwen. I don't have many women friends I can talk to."

That she counted me a friend filled me with fresh shame. I buried my face in my coffee cup to hide my expression.

"It's funny, isn't it?" she continued. "Sometimes I think women are much more rivalrous and catty with each other than they ever are with men. Don't you agree?"

She was probably remembering Milena, but I thought of Gwen and Mary as they had been last night, their grumpy, un-flagging loyalty and love, and shook my head. "Not always," I said.

"Do you have close friends?"

"A few."

"Good." She sounded wistful. "I'm glad. We all need friends. Listen, there's something I need to talk about. Otherwise this feeling I have, of guilt and disgust with myself, will rot away inside me and poison me. I need to confess."

What could I say? I gave a small nod for her to continue.

"In your relationships," she asked, "have you always been faithful?"

"Yes," I said, because it was the truth.

"That must be a nice feeling." Her voice was so soft I could hardly catch her words. She stared into my eyes for a few seconds, then looked away. While she spoke, she gazed at a spot a few inches to one side of me.

"When I married," she said, "I made promises, but I didn't really think about what they meant, not properly. And David and I—Well, you've seen us together. It's not great. It hasn't been for some time. He was busy, I was busy, we had sepa-rate lives. Bit by bit we drifted apart without realizing it. And bit by bit I became lonely—but I didn't realize that either. It happened too gradually. And one day I knew I was unhappy. My life felt all wrong but I was stuck in it. And then . . ." She stopped and turned her gaze on me briefly. "It's such a fuck-ing cliché, isn't it? I met a man. A very special man. He made me feel good about myself. It was as if he recognized me, saw someone precious behind the façade I'd built up."

She rubbed her eyes wearily. "It was such a mess, though. Not just because I was married—for a bit that hardly bothered me. He'd had a thing with Milena first."

I managed to make a small sound. My heart felt large and painful.

"Just a fling, really, but you know what Milena was like. She didn't take it well that he preferred me. That was putting it mildly. She hated me, really hated me. I felt her hatred would literally scorch me when I walked into the room." Frances shuddered. "And then she died."

"So this man," I said, "she knew you were with him?"

"Oh, yes. Milena always knew everything."

"Was he married as well?" I barely recognized my own voice.

"What do you think, Gwen? Yes, he was married."

"Who was he?"

Her expression hardened. "That's not what it's about," she said, in a tone almost of distaste. "What does that matter?"

"I didn't mean . . ."

"It's over, that's all that matters." She gave a laugh that wasn't really a laugh at all, closer to a sob. "Something hap-pened. I still can't make sense of it, Gwen. It's tormenting me. That was why I had to tell someone—otherwise I'll go mad."

She leaned forward, and at that moment there was a ring at the front door. She straightened. "That'll be my cab." She gave me a rueful smile. "To be continued," she said, and with that she was gone, tossing her gorgeous coat over her shoulders, picking up her bag, throwing me a pleading smile, running up the stairs. I heard the front door slam.

After she had gone I stayed where I was. I was trying to breathe. I felt as though I had knives in my chest and each small inhalation hurt. It was several minutes before I felt able to get up, but even then I stood in the middle of the room, not sure what to do next. Thoughts hissed in my brain. Everything was murky and confused.

But I had come here to work and work I did: I went through the brochure very carefully and marked it up for the printers. When Beth arrived, I gave it to her to check. I had worried that she might be resentful, but Beth never resented anything that made her workload even lighter than it was already. While she leafed through it and talked on the phone and made tea, I filed the few remaining invoices and receipts; I answered calls when they came in; I even tidied the room a bit. And all the time the phone was in my pocket with its single missed call. The more I tried to put it out of my mind, the more it occupied it, so that by the middle of the day it was all I could think about. That, and Frances's secret, the one that had been rotting away inside her and was now out in the open.

I couldn't call the number because what would I say? Yet if I didn't call, what had been the point of going to all that effort? Maybe I should try and match the number with one in Milena's various address books. I started and quickly gave it up as impossible.

I went out to the deli down the road and bought lunch for the two of us: panini stuffed with roasted vegetables, green pesto and melted mozzarella. While we ate, Beth asked me about my life and quickly shifted the conversation back to hers. We were both more comfortable with that and she told me about the failings of her current boyfriend.

Afterward I shuffled pieces of paper. I put books back on shelves. I took the phone out of my pocket and laid it on the desk. I put it away again: out of sight, out of mind, I instructed myself sternly. I made more coffee, very strong this time, which I drank while it was still too hot so it burned my tongue and the roof of my mouth. I took the phone out once more, stared at it as if it could talk. I fed unwanted mail through the shredder and watered the plants on the windowsill. When Beth left for the day, I couldn't stop myself. I took my phone, pulled up the missed-call window and pressed call, then canceled it immediately.

I pressed the number again and this time I held my nerve. I could hear it ringing now and closed my eyes, swallowing hard, trying to breathe normally in spite of the rushing in my head and the pounding in my ears.

"Hello?" said a male voice down the phone. And "Hello?" it said, outside the door.

"Who . . . ?" I began in confusion, before realization flooded through me. I jabbed end call and slammed the phone on the desk. It skittered along the shiny surface and clattered to the floor.

"Hello?" said the voice outside the door again, irritable now. "Are you there? Hello? Hello?"

I was trembling so much I could barely sit upright. The door swung open.

"Hi, Gwen," said David, pushing his mobile back into his pocket.

I pretended I was so hard at work that I hadn't heard him properly. I stared at some figures and underlined a few. My hands shook and the pen made incomprehensible scrawls across the page. David, I thought. So it was David.

"Gwen?"

I felt unable to speak coherently. I could barely manage to breathe. But I made myself say something, as if I were a normal human being. "David," I said, "how are you doing?"

Although he had spoken to me, he didn't seem to hear my reply. He just wandered restlessly around the office. I stared at the paper, and tried to make sense of what I had just learned. There was so much of it that I could only process it in fragments. David was one of Milena's lovers. Those tender, effusive emails had been from him—he was usually so ironic and amused. Milena had sat in this office reading his messages, writing to him, while Frances had been in the same room just a few feet away. How could he have done it? With her friend and colleague? Right under her nose? How could she have done it? Or was I reading it the wrong way? Was that part of the excitement? They say that there's no point in gambling for small amounts of money. It has to hurt when you lose. Maybe it's the same with infidelity. Anyone can have a one-night stand on a business trip, at a conference in another country. The real thrill is doing it like an illusionist, risking discovery at every moment, witnessing your victim's lack of knowledge.

When I thought of Milena's messages, the chill of them, the manipulation, I wondered if she was more interested in the power than in the sex. Was sex for her just a demonstration that she could have any man she wanted? That she could triumph over any woman, in any circumstances? Was it likely that Greg could have held out against that? Was he so different from the others?

I tried to remember what David had said to me about Milena and Frances. In all those conversations when I had been lying to him, he had been lying to me, as he had also been lying— had he?—to Johnny and Frances. Well, if he had, he wasn't the only liar. There was Frances, with her own infidelity. They had been betraying each other.

"Is Frances around?"

I felt like someone very, very drunk trying to imitate someone sober and not knowing whether the act was convincing or ludicrous. "I don't know," I said, enunciating each word carefully. "She's seeing the printers sometime this afternoon."

"Don't worry," said David. "I can phone her."

I couldn't stand this any longer. I stood up and reached for my jacket. David gave me the appraising look I always found so hard to read.

"I'm not driving you away, am I?"

"I've got a meeting," I said. "I have to go."

"At your school?" he asked.

"No," I said, and stopped myself elaborating. I didn't want

to risk any lies I might trap myself inside. "Could you tell Frances I'll give her a ring?"

I walked to the door. Just as I was opening it, I heard David call my name. What was it? Had I made a mistake?

"Sorry, Gwen, I forgot."

"What?"

"Do you want to come out to lunch with us tomorrow?"

"Sure."

"Hugo Livingstone's coming. We thought it would be good if you could join us. What with Milena, Hugo's in a bad way. It would do him good to meet a friend."

"That would be great," I said, hearing my voice tremble. "Look forward to it."

All the way home I felt as though I was stained with something. I had turned over a stone and found horrible slimy things, but in the end what did it amount to? What had it really told me? Yet still I felt contaminated by it. When I got home I had a long shower, trying to wash off all the Gwen-ness, all the deceptions and entanglements. I stood there until the tank began to empty and the water turned lukewarm. Afterward I pulled on a torn pair of jeans and a scraggly old sweater. I went outside into the garden and stood for a while, feeling the cold darkness on my face.

I thought of calling Gwen and asking her to come over, but I knew she was with Daniel tonight. Mary? She was looking after Robin, and I couldn't abide the thought of talking to her while she held his little body to her chest and cooed into his downy hair. Fergus? He was with Jemma, waiting for the labor pains to begin. Joe? I could call Joe and he'd be over like a shot, with a bottle of whisky and his gruff brand of tenderness, calling me "sweetheart" and making me cry. I almost picked up the phone, but then I had a vision of myself as they must see me: poor Ellie, sucking misery into a room, needy and sad and not moving on, battening on to the lives of others.

So I went back into the kitchen, and first of all I made a phone call to Party Animals, knowing Frances would not be there so all I had to do was leave a message saying I wasn't coming back and wishing her luck with the future. That done, I opened the small drawer in the table, where I pushed miscellaneous leaflets, flyers, bills, and took out the list that had been given to me all those weeks ago by the policewoman, the leaflet with helpful phone numbers for victims, for the stricken, the harmed, the bereaved, the helpless.

Chapter Twenty-Two

Judy Cummings was a short, stocky woman in early middle age. She had abundant coarse dark-brown hair with occasional strands of gray, thick brows over bright brown eyes, and was wrapped in a long, bulky cardigan. Her handshake was firm and brief. I had been dreading the kind of handshake that a grief counselor might give, which goes on for too long and tries to turn into a condolence, a fake intimacy that would have had me running for the door. But she was almost businesslike. "Take a seat, Ellie," she said.

The room was small and warm, empty except for three low chairs and a low table on which, I noticed, there was a discreet box of tissues.

"Thanks." I felt awkward, tongue-tied. "I don't know why I'm here," I said. "I've no idea what to say."

"Why don't you start at the beginning," she said, "and see where that takes you?"

So I began with the knock at the door, on that Monday evening in October. I didn't look at Judy as I spoke but bent over in my chair and put my hand across my eyes. I didn't tell her about my amateur-detective work, or about my disbelief that Greg had had an affair. I just talked about losing him: that seemed to take up all the time.

"I feel so bleak and empty," I said at last. "I wish I could cry."

"I'm sure you will in time." Her voice was softer and lower now; the room felt darker, as if the light had faded while I was there and we were in some twilit world. "There are so many things going on, aren't there?" she continued. "Grief, anger, shame, loneliness, fear of the future."

"Yes."

"And having to see the past differently."

"My happiness. I thought I was happy."

"Indeed. Even that must seem unreliable. But by coming here you have taken an important step in your journey."

I took my hand away from my eyes and met her brown gaze.

"It hurts so badly," I said. "The journey."

We arranged to meet the following week, and I went from her to the shops. I had made myself a promise that I would start looking after myself. No more empty cupboards and midnight snacks, eaten standing up, of cheese and handfuls of dry cereal. Regular meals; regular work; *honest* work. I put pasta, green pesto, rice, Parmesan, olive oil, six eggs, tins of tuna and sardines, lettuce, cucumber and an avocado into my trolley. Muesli. Chicken breasts, salmon fillets—it's hard to buy for one; everything comes in couple sizes. "For sharing," it said, on the flat bread I added to the rest. Tonight, I thought, I would make myself a simple supper. I would sit at the table and eat it, with a glass of wine. Followed by—I tested it with my thumb for ripeness and put it in the trolley—a mango. I would read a book and go to bed at eleven, turn out the light.

IT DIDN'T HAPPEN quite like that, although I started well. I listened to my answering machine, called Greg's parents and arranged to see them the following weekend. I checked my mobile and saw that there were three messages and two texts from Frances. Basically, they all said the same thing. I need you. Beth's away. I'm alone. Please come back. I turned on my new pay-as-you-go mobile and saw that there were three missed calls from the person I now knew to be David. I put on a CD of jazz music, washed the dishes lying in the sink, then marinated one of the chicken breasts in coriander and lemon and put the other in the freezer with the salmon fillets. I got as far as opening the bottle of wine, laying a plate, a knife and a fork on the table, and setting a pan on the hob to heat the oil. But I was interrupted by a knock, so I took the pan off and went to answer.

As the door swung open and I saw who was standing there, I considered slamming it, putting on the chain, running upstairs and pulling the duvet over my head, jamming my fingers in my ears, blocking out the world and all its mess. But even as I thought it, there we stood, face to face, and there was nothing I could do except fix an inane smile in place and hope he couldn't see the panic behind it.

"Gwen?"

"Johnny!"

"Don't look so surprised—you didn't think I was just going to let you disappear, did you? You can't get away as easily as that."

"But how did you know where I lived?"

"Is it a problem?"

"No—it's just I don't remember telling you."

"I heard you give your address to the taxi driver that night. Aren't you going to invite me in?"

"Everything's a mess. Maybe we should go out for a drink instead," I said wildly.

"You've seen how I live. Now I'm going to see how you live," he said, and stepped over the threshold. "It doesn't look that messy."

"I was about to go out."

"It looks to me," he said, entering the kitchen as if he owned it, "as if you were about to make a nice little supper for one. Shall I pour us some wine?"

"No," I said. "Or yes—yes. Why not? Just half a glass."

"So, you like jazz, do you?"

There were envelopes lying on the table with my name on them and I clutched them, crumpling them in my fist. And, oh, God, there was a photograph of me and Greg attached to the fridge by a magnet. I lurched across the room and stood in front of it. Or maybe it didn't matter if Johnny saw it—did it? I couldn't think. My brain fizzed and sweat prickled on my forehead. "Jazz?" I said stupidly. "Yes."

My eyes flicked nervously around. There were so many things in this room that could give me away. For instance, lying on the windowsill, and pushed into the frame, were several postcards bearing my name, or even my name and Greg's. Lying on the floor, just beyond Johnny's left foot, there was the bit of paper that had been pushed through my door: "Where are you, what are you doing and why aren't you answering my calls? RING ME NOW! Gwenxxxx."

And then, suddenly, there was the sound of the telephone ringing—and if the answering machine picked it up someone would be saying loudly and insistently, "Ellie, Ellie? Pick up, Ellie."

"Just a minute," I croaked, and dashed into the hall to pick up the phone.

"Yes?" I said. From where I stood, I could see Johnny examining the photo of me and Greg on the fridge.

"Ellie, it's me, Gwen."

"Gwen," I said idiotically. Then, to cover up, I said it again, neutrally, as if I was explaining my identity to the caller: "Gwen here."

"What? This is Gwen."

"Yes, I know."

"Can I come over?"

"What? Now?"

"The thing is, it's Daniel, and I wasn't going to confide in you because of, you know, everything, but then I thought it wasn't fair on you or me, because after all—"

"Hang on. Sorry. Listen. You have to come over, of course you do, but give me half an hour."

"If it's a problem . . ."

"It's not." Fuck, was he going to look at the postcards now? "Half an hour, my dearest friend. Got to go. 'Bye."

I slammed down the phone, but picked it up again and left it off the hook so nobody else could call. Then I tore back to the kitchen.

"I can't be long," I said to Johnny, putting my hand on his

shoulder so he turned away from the postcards on the window-sill. "Come and sit in the living room to finish your wine."

"Who's the guy you were with in that photo?" he asked, as we sat down—he on the sofa and me in the chair, and oh, no, no, no, the chart on the table just beyond him. Couldn't he see? Even from here, Milena's name, in capitals and neatly underlined, throbbed in my field of vision.

"Someone I used to know."

"He looks familiar. Could I have met him?"

"No."

"Is he why you're so evasive?"

No point in beating around the bush. "Yes. I'm sorry, Johnny. The thing is—and I should have said this before—I'm not ready for another relationship."

"So that's it?"

"Yes," I said.

"You think you can behave like that and get away with it?"

"I didn't mean to hurt you."

"You're all the same," he said, standing up. Now he was even nearer the chart. I willed him to look my way and he did, resentment burning in his eyes.

"I'm not coming back to work," I said. "It was all a mistake. So you won't have to see me again."

"I felt sorry for you. You seemed so sad."

"Johnny . . ."

"I thought you liked me."

"I do."

"Women are so good at pretending. Like her. Milena."

"I don't think I'm like Milena in any way," I said. "We're opposites."

"That's what I thought, too, when I met you," he said. "Maybe that's why I liked you—you seemed calm and kind. But I was wrong. You're both actresses. You take on roles." I stared at him, panic flowing through my veins. "I've seen the way you are with Frances—Ms. Capable. You led her on and made her depend on you; she thinks you're her friend. Milena could do that too, be all things to all people. Everything was a mask. You thought you'd got a glimpse of the real Milena and all of a sudden you understood it was just another mask. I've never forgotten one time when she was talking to a very nice Muslim man about Ramadan, which had begun that very evening, and he was explaining how he couldn't eat after sunrise or before sunset. She was so sympathetic and intelligent about it that I thought I was seeing a new side to her. Then an hour or so later, when we were together at my flat, she went on this extraordinary rant against Islam and its believers. She was so witheringly contemptuous of the man she'd been so sweet to. It was like a window into her soul."

"Johnny . . ."

"I said to myself then that I should kick her out, that she would only bring me grief. Of course I didn't, though: she stayed all evening and all night and I made her eggs Benedict for brunch." He laughed bitterly. "Never believe women. Especially when they're being nice to you."

"That's not fair," I began. But I didn't have time to argue with him. Gwen was on her way, the real Gwen. "You should go," I said.

"I haven't finished my wine."

"I really think you should go."

"Let me cook that meal for you."

"No."

"You're lonely and I'm lonely and at least we can give each other—"

"*No*," I said. "I haven't been fair. We can't give each other anything."

"Dumping me, dumping Frances, moving on. That it?"

"Stop it," I said. "We weren't married. We slept with each other twice. It was a mistake. I apologize. Now you have to go."

He put his glass down on top of the chart. "Right," he said. "Right." He stared at me. "You're not how I thought you'd be."

THREE MINUTES AFTER Johnny had left, Gwen arrived. She burst into tears on the doorstep and I pulled her into the house, shut the door and hugged her until her sobs subsided. "I'm such an idiot," she said.

"What's he done?"

"Nothing." And she gave a long, disconsolate sniff.

"Come and tell me about this nothing. I'll make us supper, unless you've eaten already. Wine? I've got an open bottle."

"Thanks."

"Tell me, then."

"He was with this woman for ages and she went off with one of his mates. It took him ages to get over it. You've met him—he's such a big softie. Anyway, she got in touch with him because that relationship's over. He's with her now, 'comforting' her. I think she wants him back."

"He told you all this?"

"Not the last bit."

"Does he want to go back to her?"

"He swears it's me he wants. But I don't know whether to believe him. You know my luck with men. Can I have a tissue?"

"Help yourself. Here's your wine."

"Am I being an idiot?"

"Who am I to say? All I'm sure of is that he'd be an idiot to leave you—and by the sound of it he's being totally straightforward with you. Plus he seems pretty devoted to you."

"Do you think so?"

"All I know is what he looked like to me: kind, honorable, besotted."

"Yes. Sorry. I don't know what came over me. I was sitting alone in my flat and suddenly I couldn't bear it."

"I understand."

"It's been so nice, being in a couple."

Gwen gave me a hug. We chinked glasses. I cooked the chicken and divided it between us with a bag of salad leaves. It was rather a tiny meal for two emotionally drained and ravenous women, but we finished off with the mango and lots of chocolate bourbons, then sat on the sofa together with my duvet over us and watched a DVD before I called a cab to take her home.

I WOKE WITH a start and looked at the clock beside me. It was just past three. I must have been dreaming about Greg, because I had an image of him throwing grapes into the air and trying to catch them in his mouth but they spun everywhere.

Perhaps what Johnny had said about fasting at Ramadan had prompted it. It had been a comic dream, but happy. I lay in the dark and tried to hold the picture in my mind.

I WOKE AGAIN at five. Something was bothering me, a wisp of a thought I couldn't get a hold of. Something I had seen? Something someone had said? And just as I stopped trying to remember, and sleep was pulling me down again, it came to me.

I got out of bed and pulled on my dressing gown. It was very cold in the house. I went to the computer and turned it on, and when it came to life, I Googled "Ramadan". I knew it always took place during the ninth month of the year; this year it had begun on September 12.

How long did I sit there, staring at the date? I don't know, perhaps not so long. Time seemed to slow right down. At last I went into the living room and stood in front of my chart. Johnny's empty wineglass was still on top of it. I took it off and looked very carefully at all the grids. My breath sounded loud in the silent room. I went to the drawer of my desk and pulled out the menu card Fergus had given me, stared at the date at the top and at the scrawled message: "Darling G, you were wonderful this evening. Next time stay the night and I can show you more new tricks!"

The evening of September 12 was the one and only time that I knew for sure Greg had been with Milena. But now I also knew he hadn't, because she had been with Johnny.

Chapter Twenty-Three

I was tempted to cancel my next appointment with the counselor. I didn't, but when I arrived I felt I was there under false pretenses, which was how I felt almost everywhere I went and whatever I did. She sat me down and then sat opposite me, but not in an inquisitorial way. "So, how has your week been, Ellie?" she asked.

I considered saying, "Fine," and leaving it at that. But then I decided that there, in that protected space, I would make an attempt at telling the truth, although nothing like the whole truth. "You talked about me being on a sort of journey," I said. "I think I've gone backwards a bit. In fact, quite a lot."

She looked puzzled. "How do you mean?"

"Last week you asked me if I accepted that my husband, Greg, had been unfaithful. I said I did. That was an incredibly hard step for me to take. Now I've taken another hard step, which is to go back from that. I'm not sure anymore. In fact, I think it's possible that he wasn't."

Judy didn't look cross. I continued before she had a chance to speak, because I knew that there was worse to admit to and that I'd better get it all out of the way. As I spoke, she watched me.

"I've come straight from the police station," I said. "I phoned them up and made an appointment to see a detective. Before, I'd mainly seen this female police officer. I suspect she was assigned to me to hold my hand and calm me down as a sort of amateur therapist. This time I made sure I had a proper meeting with someone who had the authority to make decisions.

"I'm going to be honest with you, even if it makes me seem crazier than you already think I am." I paused and waited for Judy to interrupt and say she didn't really think I was crazy, but she didn't, so I continued. "It would have been much easier to prove Greg had had an affair with this woman, and in fact I did find that proof, or at least I thought I did. Are you going to ask what the proof was?"

Judy seemed confused. "I'm not sure it's really my function," she said.

"It was a note written on a menu, a menu for a particular date, referring to that date. It looked like evidence that there really had been an affair and that somehow he'd managed to conceal it from me. It should have been a relief, and maybe it was. But I've since found out . . ." I felt a rush of horror, as if an abyss had opened at my feet, at the idea of telling Judy the details of how I had found out. "I won't go into the details, but suffice to say that I now know, without any doubt, that on that day Milena couldn't have been sleeping with my husband because she was sleeping with someone else. And discovering that left me with a problem—two problems, actually. The first was that I just couldn't give this up and get on with my life. The second was that once I trusted Greg again, the proof got much harder and more complicated."

I wanted to be as honest as I could, so I told Judy about

how I had constructed the charts, how I had cross-referenced them and how, this morning, I had wrapped them up in a giant folder and lugged them into the police station. I had been taken into an interview room and then I had unwrapped them in front of the startled gaze of the young detective. I had taken him through the most important details while he had consulted his own pretty skimpy file.

"I knew I wasn't going to convince them," I told Judy finally. "What was it that someone said? In order to understand me, you have to agree with me. For the police, the most important aspect of the case is that it's closed and a line has been drawn under it. They don't care about truth; it's a matter of statistics. If they reopened the case and solved it, their statistics would look the same as they do now, except that they would have done a great deal more work."

Judy looked at her watch.

"I'm sorry," I said. "Am I boring you?"

"I was going to say that our time is up," she said. "I make it a rule to be very strict about that. I find it's helpful if the participants know that the time is limited. But just this once I'm going to continue for a few minutes. What did the detective say?"

"He said lots of things, all negative. He looked carefully at my charts and then he called for another detective to come and look at them as well, but I think that wasn't because he found them interesting or convincing. It's more likely that he thought it was all so bizarre that someone else needed to witness it so they wouldn't think he was making it up when he told them about it in the pub later. What he said was the sort of thing that people have been saying all along. Namely, that I haven't proved

Greg and Milena weren't having an affair. I've just proved they weren't on those particular days. And then he said that maybe they weren't having an affair, and if they weren't he hoped that would be of some comfort to me.

"We had a bit of an animated discussion about that. I said I hadn't even found evidence that they knew each other. He said if it came to that, they didn't even have to have known each other. They might have met for the first time that day. He might have given her a lift for no reason at all. I tried to point out that there was a problem with that: there was a note from Milena to Greg, which I had found in Greg's possession, about a sexual encounter on a day when they couldn't—absolutely couldn't—have had one. Didn't he think that was a problem?"

"What was his response?" asked Judy.

"You're a psychologist," I said.

"Actually I'm a psychiatrist."

"It's the same thing."

"Well . . ."

"You must know that when people have adopted a position in a controversy, if they encounter evidence that contradicts it, that just entrenches them more strongly in the view they already hold. He had no answer to that. Well, no *real* answer. He just said every case had aspects to it that didn't fit together and it was never possible to dot every *i* and cross every *t*. He saw no reason to reopen the case and he might even have said something about my needing to get a life or some cliché like that. He made it painfully clear that he didn't want to see any more of me or my theory. So I gathered up my charts and left, and now I'm here telling you about it and I don't expect you to be any more sympathetic than Detective Inspector Carter was."

"There's one thing I don't understand," said Judy.

"What's that?"

"How did you compile the chart about Milena?" said Judy. "I can understand how you could reconstruct the movements of your husband, but how could you do it for someone you didn't know?"

I cursed myself silently. Lying was so much harder than telling the truth because the truth fitted together automatically. "It wasn't exactly a chart," I said in desperation. "I had bits of information from here and there."

Judy leaned toward me and her face took on a shrewd expression. "Ellie, are there things you're not telling me?"

"Not relevant things," I said, with an uneasy sense that, as I spoke, my nose ought to have been growing like Pinocchio's.

There was a silence during which Judy looked at her watch again.

"I should probably go," I said.

"What would you say if you were sitting where I'm sitting listening to you?"

"I'd probably think I was mad," I said. "But, then, when I've heard a tape of myself speaking I've always hated my voice. It sounds different from the inside. In the end, I don't really care about convincing other people. I knew the police wouldn't be interested, but I felt I had a responsibility as a citizen to tell them what I'd discovered. I need to know the truth. It's as simple as that. As long as I know, I don't care what else happens."

"Ellie, I once had a patient, a woman, and her child was ill with cancer and after a time she died. There was a suggestion that the early signs of the disease might have been missed by the doctors. The father became obsessed with this while his child was still alive. He started a campaign and took legal action, and he fought the case for years. I think it may still be going through the courts even. He took early retirement from his job. The case *became* his job, really. I was never quite sure of the rights and wrongs of it but the result was that the time he should have spent with his child, when time was precious, and later mourning after her death, was spent going to meetings, filing files and writing letters. He kept telling his wife he wanted something good to come out of their child's experience, but to the wife it just felt as if he was avoiding facing up to what had happened and living through it. He kept busy so he wouldn't have to stop and think and feel."

"His efforts might have changed procedures so that other children were saved," I said. "And you wanted him to give it up just so that he and his wife could feel better. Anyway, I'm not like that man. I don't have a dying child to nurse. I don't have a partner I might be neglecting. The only way I could neglect my husband now would be to allow people to have the wrong idea about him when he's dead and can't speak for himself."

"If you believe that, why are you here?" asked Judy. "You know I'm not a policeman. I'm not someone who can evaluate evidence or discuss the legalities. I'm a person who helps people heal. So they don't have to go out into the world and do things, they don't have to set things right or revenge themselves on their enemies. They simply give themselves permission to be normal."

"That's why I came," I said. "It's like a reminder. You're a reminder to me that there's another way of living. It's like someone who's incredibly depressed trying to remind themselves that there will be a time in the future when things don't look as they do now. There'll come a time when I'll buy shoes and meet people for drinks and flirt and be a good friend again . . ."

"You make being normal sound frivolous."

"I don't mean to. What I mean is that coming here is like looking through a window at a garden I'd love to go into and that maybe I will someday. But for the moment I'm not giving myself permission to be normal, quite the opposite. I'm giving myself permission to be abnormal. I'm going to stick with my charts and my conspiracy theories and I'm not going to play the part of the grieving widow who's accepting and passive and basically invisible."

Judy shook her head. "It doesn't work like that," she said. "These aren't just roles you can choose between. You can't put off healing as if it were a foreign holiday."

I thought for the moment. "Maybe I'm on holiday now," I said. "A holiday from being normal and nice and what everybody wants me to be."

"It's called grief," said Judy.

"No, it isn't," I said. "The grief comes later, when I know what I'm grieving for."

Chapter Twenty-Four

There were some things, however, that I couldn't put off, no matter how much I wanted to. "I'm dreading it," I said to Gwen on the phone, just before I left. "Why am I dreading it quite so much? It's almost like a phobia."

"Then don't go. Say you're ill."

"I might as well get it over with."

I'd seen Greg's mother and father at the funeral, and spoken to them briefly twice since then, I'd erased several of their messages from my answering machine, along with some from his brothers and his sister Kate. I had tried not to think about them because I knew that, whatever I was going through, it was probably worse for them. No parent should ever bury a child. Greg was their firstborn. However they had treated him when he was alive—his father had patronized him, bullied him and lost his temper with him, while his mother had compared him unfavorably to his more conservative and prosperous siblings—they had loved him in their fashion. And presumably it made it still more painful to have lost him before they had had a chance to become reconciled. Their last words (Paul had accused Greg of being part of the selfish generation who hadn't even given his parents grandchildren yet) had been bitter and heated.

They were waiting for me at Bristol Temple Meads station, and I climbed into the back of the car before leaning forward to kiss their cheeks and hand over the flowers I'd bought.

"You're a bit late," said Paul, starting the car and fiddling with his rearview mirror, so that for an instant I found myself gazing straight into his slightly bloodshot eyes.

"The train was delayed."

"You'd have done better to drive."

"I don't have a car," I said. The fact hung in the air between us. I didn't have a car because Greg had died in it. With someone else.

"You're looking well," said Kitty, unenthusiastically, as the car drew away from the curb and joined the queue nosing out on to the main road.

"Thanks." I knew I wasn't. "You too, Kitty. How have you been?"

She turned in her seat and gave me her plaintive smile. "I've got a bit of a sniffle this morning. I think I'm coming down with a cold."

"I'm sorry to hear that. But I meant since Greg's death."

"Oh," she said, flummoxed. Paul coughed. Clearly Greg's death was a taboo subject.

"It's been hard," said Kitty. "Very hard. Especially with—" She stopped dead. Her eyes filled with tears and she started fiddling nervously with her hair.

"With him dying with another woman?" I suggested.

Paul coughed again, then said, "Here we are. Our humble abode."

The house was scrupulously tidy and filled with objects Paul and Kitty had collected over the years: the teddy bears on the sofa, the thimbles in the glass cabinet, the snow domes ranged along the mantel, the glass cats on top of the piano that nobody had played since Greg had left home at eighteen. There were photos on the windowsill, and while Kitty went off to get lunch for us, I examined them. "Where have all the photos of Greg gone?" I asked Paul.

He gave his short cough. "We thought you might like them. I've put them in a bag for you to take, with things like his school reports."

"But don't you want them? I mean, now more than ever, I would have thought—"

"This has been painful for his mother," he interrupted me. "The photographs upset her."

Kitty called from the kitchen, announcing lunch. As we sat down to eat, I made myself say what I had come to say. It came out sounding too much like a prepared speech. "One of the reasons I'm here is that I wanted to give you some things of Greg's as keepsakes, Ian, Simon and Kate as well as you two. Just books, mostly ones I thought you might like. There are photos too. But if you don't want them . . ."

"Well," said Paul. He blinked at me. "We can have a look at least."

"I brought you his one and only tie."

"Paul's very particular about his ties," said Kitty. "Nothing fancy."

"I just thought it would be a memento."

We were sitting on three sides of the small table, with a curried egg salad in the middle, and the fourth—where Greg should have been, his complicit smile meant just for me— empty. Kitty divided the salad neatly into three and put my portion on the plate in front of me. I could feel her eyes on me. She and Paul had never taken to me: my job was too odd, not a proper job at all, really; my clothes were strange; they didn't approve of my opinions, which was strange because I'd never thought of myself as someone who had them. Yet now here I was, the publicly wronged and tragically widowed daughter-in-law.

"Aren't you hungry, Ellie?" said Kitty.

"This is lovely." I took a determined bite of my egg and swallowed it with an effort. "I just wanted to say that it seems strange to me that we've never talked about what happened."

Paul looked grim and embarrassed and didn't speak.

"I didn't like to ask Greg about things," said Kitty, placidly. "If he had come to me and said he wasn't happy I would have listened. I'm his mother after all. I suppose he must have had his reasons for doing what he did."

"Our marriage was very happy," I said, pushing the plate away.

The two of them exchanged a glance.

"It must be hard for you to bear," said Kitty.

"I don't need to bear it," I said. "That's another reason why I'm here today. I wanted to tell you that Greg was a good man. He was the most loving husband." I looked at the clock on the wall: I had only been there for twenty-five minutes. When

could I decently leave? "I trusted him." Then I corrected myself: "I trust him."

"It was awful," I said to Joe, who had insisted on taking time
off work to pick me up from the station and drive me home,
even though it would have been much quicker to catch the
Underground, and even though I didn't want to go home. It
was warm and luxurious inside the BMW and I sank grate-
fully back into the seat.

He grinned and put a hand on my knee. I pretended it wasn't
there and eventually he moved it to change gear.

"I'll bet it was," he said. "I've met them, remember? How
Greg came from a family like that I'll never know. At least
you've done your duty."

"I took them books they didn't want, photos they gave
back, and memories they were trying to erase. We all hated
every minute of it."

"What are you doing later?"

"This and that."

"Are you working?"

"A little," I said evasively.

"Good. You need to get back to things, Ellie."

"You're probably right."

"You look a bit tired. Have you been okay?"

"Some days are better than others."

"If you ever want someone to talk to . . ."

"I've talked enough. I just go over and over the same things.
There's nothing left to say that I haven't said already."

"Are you all right for money?"

"What?"

"Money," he repeated. "Are you all right?"

"Fine, I think. As far as I know. I haven't gone through everything. I've let things slide. Greg and I weren't big savers, but we didn't spend much either."

"I can give you some. Lend," he corrected himself hastily. "If there's a cash-flow problem."

"That's good of you. But I'll be all right."

The car pulled up outside my house. I went to kiss his cheek but he turned his face and, before I had a chance to pull away, kissed me on the lips. I pushed him away. "What do you think you're doing?"

"I'm kissing you."

"Don't be ridiculous. You're my friend. And you were Greg's friend. And you're married to Alison. Who knows what you get up to behind her back? But not with me."

"Sorry, sorry, sorry," he said, with a groan that was also a half-laugh. "I don't know what came over me. You're a lovely woman."

"Do you pounce on every lovely woman?"

He held up his hands in mock-surrender, trying to make it into a joke. "Just the ones I can't resist."

"Poor Alison," I said, and saw a flash of anger cross his face.

"Alison's fine. We have a good marriage."

"I'm going to forget it happened," I said. "Don't ever do that again."

"I won't. Sorry, sweetheart."

I looked at him as if he were a strange, exotic specimen I'd observed. "Is it easy?"

"What?"

"To have an affair and then go home at night."

"You make it sound as if I do it all the time."

"Do you?"

"Of course not! You know me."

"What about at the moment? Is there anyone?"

"No!" But something in his voice, in his expression, told me he was lying.

"Come on, Joe—who?"

"No one."

"I know there is. Is she married?"

"You've got a one-track mind. Ever since Greg died, you've been on the lookout for adultery and deception."

"Someone from work? Someone I know? It is, isn't it?"

"Ellie." He was half laughing, as if this was a great joke.

"Oh, God, I know who it is."

"This is ridiculous. I don't know what you're on about."

"It's Tania, isn't it?"

"No!"

"Joe?"

"It's nothing, I promise. But she's so young and eager."

"Oh God, Joe," I said. I felt anger well inside me as I gazed at his handsome, rugged face, his smiling mouth. "She's half your age."

"Maybe that's the point, Ellie," he said. "And maybe you should stop judging everyone."

"I don't."

"You do, and I understand why."

"I don't mean to. I just can't bear to think of Alison getting hurt."

"She won't, I promise. And that—just now"—he gestured around the car as if the kiss was still floating in the air—"That was wrong of me. Greg's death has left me feeling at a loss. Forgive me."

AFTER HE HAD driven away I entered my house, but only to dump the shopping bag of Greg's effects I'd brought back from his parents. Then I walked to the Underground station, eyes watering in the easterly wind. In spite of everything I made up my mind to go back to Party Animals, and I couldn't bear to wait, even though I wasn't sure what I would do there, except more snooping.

The first train was thirteen minutes away, and I wanted to weep with impatience. I paced up and down the platform. I had three new pieces to add to Life's Most Difficult Jigsaw Puzzle: Milena had been having an affair with Frances's husband; Johnny had been with Milena on the one night when I had evidence to show that she was with Greg; the menu card with Milena's note written to Greg and finally discovered by Fergus tucked inside a book was therefore . . .

I stopped, my brain hurting with the effort of holding together all the information that wanted to fly in different directions. Therefore what? Therefore a typo, a tease, a slip of the pen, a red herring, a mistake, a contradiction, a fraud, a mystery—something manufactured to drive me mad.

I rang the bell, and when Frances didn't answer the door,

let myself in with the key I still had. I called from the top of
the stairs. The basement light was on. I knew Beth was away
on holiday, so I thought that Frances was probably about, but
there was no answer. I went down, wriggling out of my coat
as I did so, pulling off my scarf, tossing them both over the
easy chair as I came into the room.

Frances had obviously been there earlier and was expecting
to return. The radiator was warm, the Anglepoise lamp over
her desk was turned on, although the rest of the room was in
shadow, and there was a mug beside her computer, as well as
her glasses and several glossy holiday brochures with exotic
destinations.

I prowled restlessly around the office, pulling random
books off the shelves. I opened the drawers of Frances's desk
and peered inside: a drawer for receipts, one for stationery,
another for an assortment of old menus, leaflets and empty
bottles. I felt more than usually uneasy now that I knew David had had an affair with Milena, and Frances had had an
affair with—with who? The ghastly suspicions I had were
eating away at me, although I knew I was probably being ridiculous. Frances, with a husband who cheated on her under
her nose with her business partner, and a woman she thought
of as a friend who had snuck in under false pretenses, gained
her confidence, and now spent her time digging out her most
intimate secrets.

Eventually I sat down at Milena's large desk, switched on the
side lamp, and turned on her computer, drumming my fingers
on the keyboard as I waited for it to boot up. It was very quiet.
I could hear the radiators hum and the wind blow against the

glass. Every so often, a car passed or a door slammed, far off. It was quite dark outside now, and the room was dim apart from the two pools of light cast by the lamps. I had a sudden overwhelming urge to be back in my down-at-heel little house—not on my own, though; not in the lonely here and now. I wanted to be there with Greg, blinds drawn, the kettle boiling, him singing loudly and tunelessly and asking what we should eat for supper, reading out crossword clues that neither of us ever got, putting his arms around me from behind and resting his chin on the top of my head. My world of safety, no matter how scary it was outside.

I shivered and concentrated on the screen, typing in Milena's password, accessing once more her hectic private life. I heard footsteps on the pavement drawing nearer, then receding. A dog barked. I clicked once more on the messages from David and stared at them, as if some secret was hidden between the lines.

"Oh, God, Greg," I said out loud, and leaned forward, rolling the chair a bit closer to the desk and resting my head on my arms. My foot touched something solid. I sat up and pushed the chair back again. I bent down, just a little, to see what was there.

A boot, lying lengthways, but a boot wasn't heavy, was it? Two boots, black with elegant pointed toes and small, sharp heels. The room shifted around me; the walls seemed to close in. There was a sour taste in my mouth. I bent down further. I heard a gasp, and it had come from me but it didn't sound like me. I stood up, the floor tipping beneath me, sweat prickling on my forehead, and held on to the desk to steady myself. Then I saw. Her body lay bundled under the desk, but her head stuck out, and her eyes were looking up at me. I staggered back, my hand over my mouth. I closed my eyes, but when I opened them again, she was still there: how could I have missed seeing her until now?

I don't know how long I stood there, almost gagging, staring into the sightless eyes. But gradually thought returned. First, I had to make sure she was dead. I knew she was—you don't have to be familiar with death to recognize it—but I had to check. I crouched and dragged the body clear of the desk. It was heavy and awkward. I put my ear against her mouth and felt no breathing; I put my thumb where the pulse should have been and felt nothing. There were bruises on her throat and her lips were faintly blue. The sight struck fresh horror into me, even though I had known from the moment I'd seen the body bundled under the desk that this was no accidental death. I gave a few feeble presses on her chest, all the time certain that it was useless. And yet she was warm. Not so many minutes ago she must have been alive. I held her head in my hands and gazed at her thin, intelligent face, her blind, open eyes. Frances stared up at me. Her beautiful linen skirt had risen up above her knees. I saw that her legs were the legs of an aging woman, and her face had lines and creases I hadn't noticed before. There were tiny strands of gray in her highlighted hair. Her wrists were thin. A thought spiked through me: perhaps the killer was still there. Fear turned me cold and shivery; my legs shook and when I stood up they would barely hold me. I listened. I heard the radiators still humming, the far-off noise of the main road.

As quietly and calmly as I could, I put on my coat and scarf. I walked across the room, eased the front door open, closed it softly behind me and went out into the street without looking back. I wasn't sure if there were other people around. I wasn't aware of them but there was nothing about me that would make them remember.

My first impulse was to escape, to return home, to pretend I hadn't been there. But I thought of Frances. Had I made sure she was really dead? It felt as if it had happened years before and to someone who wasn't quite me. I had felt her pulse. She had looked dead. Could I be sure? Weren't there people who had been revived long after they were apparently dead? As I turned out of Tulser Road onto the bustling main street I saw a phone box that hadn't been vandalized. I could dial 999 without having to put money in. Some strange bit at the back of my mind remembered that 999 calls were recorded, so I tried to make my voice different from normal, a bit muffled. I asked for an ambulance and said that someone was badly hurt, maybe dead, then I gave the address. When the woman asked for my name I said I couldn't hear, it was a bad line and hung up. Before I reached the Underground station, I heard the siren of an ambulance, though I didn't see it. I didn't know if it was the one I had summoned. In London, you hear so many.

When I reached the station, my hand was suddenly trembling so much that I couldn't extract the Oyster card from my purse, and when I managed it I dropped it and bent down to fumble for it. A young man stopped to help me and looked at me worriedly. When he asked me if I was all right, I couldn't speak properly. He must have thought I was on some strong medication. It took a supreme effort to do the simple things, to catch the train in the right direction, to get off at my stop. All the time a thought was repeating in my head, like a tic, like a dripping tap, like a rattling window: Frances is dead, Frances is dead.

When I arrived home I went straight upstairs and pulled off my clothes, just letting them fall, and got into a bath. I lay there for more than an hour, letting water out as it cooled and refilling it with hot, only my face protruding. If I had had the choice, I would have lain there for the rest of my life, warm and wet and safe. I scrubbed my face. I washed my hair and then I cut my toe-and fingernails as if I was purifying myself. Finally, reluctantly, I got out and put on what had become my normal domestic outfit of old jeans, baggy sweatshirt and slippers.

Then I started to clean the house. From cupboards and shelves I retrieved every bottle of bleach and disinfectant and polish in the house. With cloths and brushes and sprays, I scoured and scraped every surface. I filled two large bin bags with rubbish and things that weren't quite rubbish and things that weren't really rubbish at all but that I thought I'd be better off without or that I could do without. I thought of one of my grandmothers—my father's mother—who had seemingly spent her entire adult life cleaning. Even the thought of her conjured up a smell of pine-scented air freshener. For her, cleanliness was a form of display, a recurrent demonstration that she had the cleanest lavatory of all of her friends. For me it was about purifying, cutting away, eliminating.

I checked the time. It was just after seven. When I had got rid of ten items of clothing, I could have a drink. It was easy. I instantly disposed of clothes I'd kept out of sentiment, because I'd worn them as a teenager or at college, or I'd been given them by a boyfriend or bought them in a particular place, that time in Queensland or Seville. As I crammed them into another bin bag, I saw that I had put in far more than ten. Twenty at least. I deserved an extra-large drink as a reward for that. And if I drank a whole bottle of wine, I could throw away the bottle.

There were eight in the little rack in the kitchen. I found the oldest wine I had. We'd bought it in France a couple of years earlier for what had seemed a lot of money at the time, ten or twenty euros. It had been for a special occasion that had never come. I opened it and poured myself a glass. I sipped. It tasted bitter. Was it corked? I'd never quite known what that meant. It would do, though. Perhaps it needed to be drunk with food. I didn't have anything that seemed suitable so I toasted some bread and spread butter on it. I munched the toast and finished the glass of wine. Then I looked in the cupboard and found a tin of olives I'd forgotten. I opened the tin and cut my finger on the lid. I wrapped a tissue around it and poured myself another glass of wine. I ate an olive. Everything I ate, everything I drank, was emptying the house just a little more.

When the doorbell rang, I hadn't quite finished the second glass of wine, but I still felt lightheaded. I opened the door. It was Johnny.

"You'd better come in," I said wearily.

He walked inside, and although he'd been there before he

was looking around him as if he was seeing it for the first time. I picked up my glass. "I'm drinking," I said. "You want some?"

"All right."

I poured him some wine and handed it to him. He took a gulp and pulled an approving face. He picked up the bottle and studied it. Then he raised his eyes and looked me squarely in the face. "Have you heard about Frances?" he said.

"What? Tell me."

"She's dead. She was murdered." There was a pause. "You don't look shocked."

"I knew."

"How?"

"I found the body," I said. "I called the ambulance."

Johnny was visibly startled. He stepped back as if I'd struck him. "You did? Then why weren't you there when they arrived? Why didn't you talk to the police?"

"I came straight home."

"Why?"

"I wasn't ready to talk about it."

"I don't think it works like that," he said. "When you find a body, you're meant to stick around, you know, talk to the police, that sort of thing."

"There's too much to explain."

"Is there now?" He raised his eyebrows and a shiver of apprehension ran through me. "David rang me. One of the things he said was that the police want to talk to everybody involved. Apparently they're having trouble tracking you down. For someone who's been working in the office for several weeks, you haven't left much trace."

"I wasn't on the books," I said.

"No address. No phone number."

"You've got my address," I said. "Why didn't you tell them?"

I had a sudden sense of alarm. Had I miscalculated? Did anybody know that Johnny knew me? Did David?

"Is there any reason why I shouldn't?"

"I don't know," I said. "I've been thinking about it."

Johnny frowned at me. "I don't understand this and neither do I like it. Not one bit. You found the body. What's the problem with talking to the police about it? Don't you want to help them? And why are you so difficult to track down? Is there anything you want to tell me?"

It may have been the memory of Frances's body in my arms or the wine or the sheer tiredness, but I couldn't spin any more lies, not just then. But I took a deep breath before I spoke, because I felt I was stepping out into a different sort of world and I was scared. My skin was cold with fear.

"I'm not Gwen," I said.

"I don't understand. What does that mean, you're not Gwen?"

"It means that my name isn't Gwen. There is a Gwen Abbott. She's a friend of mine. I borrowed her name. Stole it."

"I . . ." He stopped, his mouth hanging open as he stared at me.

"My real name is Eleanor. Eleanor Falkner."

"You mean you were lying?" he said. "All the time?"

"Yes."

"So when we were in bed together and I called you Gwen and you just . . . I don't know what to say."

"I'm sorry," I said. "It got out of hand."

Johnny gave a horrible laugh. "Got out of hand?"

"I didn't mean it like that."

He sat down heavily and some of his wine splashed on to the sofa. He took a handkerchief from his pocket and dabbed at it. "I'm sorry," he said. "You'll want to put salt on that."

"It's a crappy old sofa."

"So, Eleanor." Johnny said my name as if it was one he'd never heard before, from a different language, hard to pronounce. "Why did you do this? Or should I just call the police?"

I thought for a moment and then I went and sat beside him on the sofa. I told him he could call the police if he wanted, but first . . . And then I told him everything I could, not like a proper story but in a mess of fragments, all out of order, with additions and little explanations. I told him about Greg. I even fetched the picture of the two of us together. Johnny had seen me naked, slept with me, but now I felt even more naked, even more exposed to him. I told him about my connection to Milena. At first he asked questions, but as I continued he became quieter, his expression darker. When I finished he was silent for a long time.

"I don't even know where to start," he said. "How could you do such a thing? How could you lie to so many people?"

"I didn't plan it," I said. "Really I just wanted to see where Milena worked. I got invited in and it developed a momentum of its own."

"Just to take one example, almost entirely at random, you used me to get the password so that you could read Milena's secret mail, things she wanted nobody to see."

"I didn't plan things. I didn't plan us. But she died with my husband. I needed to know everything I could."

"So I was just a step on that road," said Johnny. "Something a bit like Milena's password."

"No," I said. "It wasn't like that at all. I wasn't using you. It was something that happened and I didn't stop it happening—I still don't know why."

He looked at me with a sharper expression. "So it meant something to you?" he said. "It wasn't just to find out about Milena."

"No! But it was wrong all the same. I was so hurt and so confused and I should never have slept with you. It wasn't fair."

"But you did. And now someone has been killed."

"Yes."

"Perhaps because you came and stirred things up."

"I've thought of that."

Johnny put the glass down and then put his hands on my face, ran them down to my neck. I willed myself to stay entirely still, although my skin was crawling with dread. "So who do you think killed her?" he said at last.

"I don't know."

"What if it was me?"

"Was it?" I asked.

He raised his right hand from my neck and slapped me across the face so hard that tears came to my eyes. I didn't speak.

"That's for lying to me," he said. He got up.

"Wait," I said, as he turned to go. "I need to show you something."

"What?"

I went over to the little chest, opened the drawer and drew out the menu card. Without saying anything I passed it to him and he stared at it.

"I don't understand," he said eventually. "Why the fuck have you got this?"

"It was found among Greg's possessions. It was what made me believe he was having an affair with Milena. It even has the date on it. But then you said something that made me realize you were with her on the twelfth of September."

"But this is mine."

"What do you mean, yours?"

"She sent it to me."

"She can't have done."

"You think I wouldn't remember?"

"But it's to " 'Darling G.' "

He examined it for a few seconds. "No. That's just a continuation of the J—you can even see the join if you look closely."

"How come it was in Greg's stuff," I asked weakly, "if she sent it to you?"

"I sent it back. I sent everything that had ever belonged to her back when she finished it—marched around to her house and dumped it in her lap."

"So it was in *her* possession, not yours."

"I thought she'd just burn it or something."

I rubbed my face, trying to concentrate. "How did it get from her house to here?"

Johnny shrugged. "I don't know and I don't care."

"Maybe it was Frances all the time," I said drearily.

"What the fuck are you on about now?"

"Frances was having an affair too," I said. "I thought maybe—"

"I don't want to hear what you thought about Frances," he said angrily. "She's dead. Killed by some maniac. Let her alone, do you hear me? You've done enough. She was a good woman. Now leave her in peace."

"Are you going to call the police?" I said.

"I think that's for you to do, don't you?" he said. "At the moment they're curious. Soon they'll be suspicious. Don't leave it too long. Or I'll make up your mind for you."

As soon as he was gone, I rang Gwen. I didn't even say hello. "Have the police been in touch with you?" I asked.

"Ellie? Yes, some policeman rang me. How on earth did you know?"

"I need to talk to you."

Chapter Twenty-Five

You're kidding me." Gwen was staring at me across the kitchen table. She'd been running her fingers through her hair as I talked so now it stood up in small blonde tufts. She looked bewildered and accusing all at once. Her eyes were owlishly round.

"No, I'm not."

"I think I'd better have that drink, after all."

"Red or white?"

"Whisky?"

"Whisky it is."

"So all this time . . ."

"Yes."

"And you said you were—"

"You. Yes." I poured her a large whisky, neat and ice-less. She took a deep gulp; her eyes watered. I poured another for myself and let it burn a trail down my throat.

"And you got away with it?"

"Yes. Until now."

"And now, this woman, Frances . . ."

"Has been murdered."

"Fuck."

"Yes."

"Fuck fuck fuck."

"Is that all you've got to say?"

"I don't know. What should I be saying?"

"You could scream at me. Don't you feel angry?"

"Angry?" She considered, swilling her whisky in the glass, then taking another vast swallow so that I could see her throat jumping. The drink was nearly gone already.

"Because I pretended to be you, because I lied to you about what I was up to, because I didn't confide in you, because I've been so stupid, because—"

"OK, OK, I get it. Here, give me another of these." She held out her glass. "Angry's not the right word, Ellie. I can't get my head around it. You've been using my name, infiltrating this poor woman's business, breaking into computers, like some sort of spy, to find out—what?"

"Something. Anything. I thought I'd go mad otherwise. And, in fact, I did find out something. I found out that Frances's husband was having an affair with Milena, and that there was another man who was with her the night I'd thought she was with Greg. And then I found out that the menu card with the love note on—it was a forgery."

"What?"

"It wasn't to Greg at all."

"This is all too much to take in. You say this woman—Frances—was murdered."

I nodded, trying not to let the image of Frances's open, staring eyes flood through me again. "She was."

"And are you assuming that this has anything to do with Greg?"

"I've no idea. It must have something to do with Milena. Though she was having an affair too—that's probably irrelevant. I can't think straight. Everywhere I look I see these betrayals."

"Are you in danger?"

"Me?"

"Or me?" said Gwen.

"No, I don't think so, but I'm going to the police. I'll clear up the confusion."

"Who else knows?"

I could feel the flush rising up my neck and covering my face. "There's this guy. He's called Johnny."

"Who is he?"

"Kind of a chef."

"And?"

"He was Milena's lover—one of many."

"How did he find out you weren't me?"

"He tracked me down here after he'd heard about Frances. I probably should say that I missed something out. It's not particularly relevant, but we had a kind of thing. I slept with him. Twice."

"Oh."

"What does that mean—oh?"

"All these secrets."

I sloshed more whisky into her glass and my own. "It's a great relief that you know," I said, after a pause.

Gwen opened her mouth to speak, but at that moment there was a loud knocking at the door. My head was swimming as I made my way down the hall and opened it.

Joe stood there, wrapped in his thick coat, a huge grin on his face, which was rosy with the cold.

"I've brought you a rowing machine," he said. "I could hardly get it into the car."

"Why?"

"I thought it would be good for you, keep you fit through these winter months. And I didn't actually go out and buy it, a client gave it to me."

I didn't want a rowing-machine. And after our last encounter I didn't much want to see Joe.

"And I wanted to say sorry for—you know—what happened. Aren't you going to invite me in?"

"Gwen's here."

He stepped past me and walked toward the kitchen, calling greetings to Gwen.

"Hi there, Joe," she said.

"You've been drinking," he said cheerfully.

"So would you have been in my position."

"What position is that?" He took off his coat and slung it over the back of a chair.

Gwen might not have been angry, but Joe was. He was furious, shocked and hurt. His blue eyes blazed and his lips turned white. He banged his glass down on the table so that the whisky splashed everywhere and told me I'd been very, very stupid and why the fuck hadn't I told him what I was doing? Didn't I understand that he and Alison wanted to look after me? Greg had been like a son to him and I was like a daughter.

"What the fuck were you up to?" he said. "What the fuck were you playing at?"

"I don't know. But I don't have to explain it to you."

"You're upset that your husband dies so what do you do? Weep and mourn? No. Get your life together? No. Talk things through with friends? No. See a counselor? No."

"I have actually seen a—"

"You pretend to be your own best friend and dabble in half-baked conspiracy theories—oh, Jesus. It defies belief. And where did it get you? Greg's still dead. He still died in the car with a woman who liked having affairs with married men. Have you unearthed some deep plot?"

"No," I said.

"And now somebody's died. What are you doing about that?" He put his head into his hands, breathing deeply.

"I don't need help. I'm going to the police."

"You haven't been to the police yet?"

"No."

"I can drive you there now." Gwen stood up, placing both hands flat on the table to steady herself.

"For Christ's sake, you can't drive anywhere," said Joe. "Why on earth haven't you been to the police, Ellie?"

"I was scared and stunned. I know I should. It's all so complicated."

He leaned back in his chair. He seemed so shocked that the fight had gone out of him.

"I don't know what it all means," I said. "Greg and Milena, and then Frances."

"Why does it have to mean anything except an unholy mess?"

"I'm so tired, Joe." Having him there being so angry and fatherly made me feel younger and more foolish. Tears came to my eyes. "Maybe that's the reason I haven't been yet—I'm so very tired of thinking about all of it."

"Oh, Ell." Joe got up and crouched beside me, taking both my hands in his. "Of course you're tired. I tell you what, leave it for tonight. Go tomorrow. I'll take you myself, if you want."

"Will you?"

"Yes."

Then the phone rang again and at first I let the answering-machine take the call, but when I heard Fergus's voice, I ran to pick it up.

"Fergus? Has labor started?"

"It's nothing like that, Ellie. I've just seen some news on-line. It's the weirdest thing. You know that woman in the car with Greg? Well, her partner—"

"Fergus," I cut him short, "there's something you should know . . ."

LATER, WHEN I'D finished talking to a stunned and stuttering Fergus, and Joe had gone home, leaving an enormous rowing machine in the middle of the living room, Gwen said, "So why didn't you feel able to confide in me?"

She was sitting on the sofa, her legs curled up under her, floppily relaxed and moving in a slightly uncoordinated way. Daniel was coming to take her home; she could collect her car the next day, when the whisky had worn off.

I hesitated. "I don't know exactly. I think I didn't want anyone to tell me that what I was doing was wrong. I knew it was wrong, and stupid, and maybe even a bit unhinged, or a lot unhinged, but I didn't intend to stop. I'm sorry, though."

"And now?"

"Now I've honestly got no idea what I think about a single thing. She was nice, though."

"The woman who was killed?"

"Frances, yes. She came from an entirely different world and I would never have met her in the ordinary run of things—she was rich and stylish and ironic, and had that well-bred, well-groomed English reticence. But in spite of that I liked her. She was good to me. And I don't understand why she's dead. And I don't understand why someone wanted me to think Greg was having an affair with Milena. I don't understand at all."

Chapter Twenty-Six

I wasn't sure which police station to go to, but I knew it would be bad either way, and it was. I went to see WPC Darby because I hoped she might be sympathetic to me, knowing me as a grieving widow. When she greeted me, I noticed the wary expression people adopt when they open their door to someone trying to give them a pamphlet about a fringe religion. But she sat me down and gave me some tea. I started to explain why I was there and her expression changed from wariness to puzzlement, then from puzzlement to what looked like alarm. She hushed me and almost rushed out of the room.

She returned five minutes later and asked if I could follow her. She led me through a door and into a room that was bare, except for a table and three orange plastic chairs. She sat me down and stood awkwardly by the door. I told her she didn't need to stay but she said it was all right. It looked as if she had been told to stay with me and also not to say anything more. So I sat and she stood and we spent ten awful minutes avoiding each other's eyes until the door opened and a detective came in. I recognized him as Detective Inspector Carter, the one I had talked to before. He didn't even sit down.

"WPC Darby tells me that you found the body of Mrs. Frances Shaw."

"That's right," I said.

"And you called it in?"

"Yes."

"Anonymously."

"Yes."

"Any particular reason for that?"

"Kind of," I said.

He held up his hand to stop me. "It's not our patch," he said. "I need to phone the Stockwell lads. You'll have to wait here for a bit, if that's all right."

He was just being polite. I don't think I had a choice. WPC Darby brought me a newspaper and another cup of tea, and I flicked through the pages without taking anything in. It was almost an hour before two more detectives, a man and a woman, came in and sat opposite me. WPC Darby left but DI Carter stood to one side, leaning against the wall. The man introduced himself as Detective Chief Inspector Stuart Ramsay and his colleague as Detective Inspector Bosworth. She opened her bag and took out a bulky machine, which she placed on the table between us. She loaded it with two cassette tapes and switched it on. She said the date and time and identified everybody present, then sat back.

"The reason we're being so formal," said Ramsay, "is that you have already made admissions that lay you open to being charged with a criminal offense. And that's just to be getting on with. So, it's important that, before you say anything else, we make clear that you're entitled to legal representation. If you don't have a lawyer, we can obtain one for you."

"I'm not bothered," I said.

"Does that mean you don't want a lawyer?"

"I don't care," I said. "No."

"And you need to understand that anything you say in this and later interviews can be used as evidence and introduced in court."

"Fine," I said. "So how can I help you?"

The two looked at each other as if they didn't know quite what to make of me.

"For a start," said Ramsay, "you can tell us what the hell you were playing at, leaving a crime scene, interfering with a police inquiry?"

"It's a complicated story," I said.

"Then you'd better start telling it," said Ramsay.

I had promised myself I would leave nothing out, make no attempt to justify myself or explain things away. I'm not used to telling stories and I started from the murder and worked backward, and in other directions as well, when necessary, or when I remembered something that seemed relevant. When I first said I'd been working for Frances under an assumed name DI Bosworth's jaw dropped, like that of a character expressing surprise in a silent movie.

"I'm sorry," said Ramsay. "I didn't quite get that. What did you say?"

"It's probably easiest if I tell you everything and then you ask questions about what you don't understand."

Ramsay started to say something, then stopped and gestured to me to go on. As I meandered through the story, I felt as if I was talking about the misadventures of someone I didn't really know—a distant cousin or a friend of a friend—whom I didn't much care for and certainly didn't understand. When I got on to the subject of Milena dying in the car accident with Greg and how I'd read her emails and how she had also had an affair with Frances's husband, David, Ramsay's head sank slowly into his hands. I then told him that Frances had confided in me that she, too, had had an affair.

"I thought, or wondered, if the man she had had her affair with was Greg," I added.

"What?" He raised his head and stared at me; there was a glazed expression in his eyes.

"You see, she said this man, I never got to know his name, had also had a fling with Milena, then turned to her. It doesn't sound like the Greg I knew, but by that stage I was so confused I didn't know what to think about anything."

"I know the feeling," he growled.

The one detail I deliberately withheld was my sexual relationship, such as it was, with Johnny. I don't think it was out of any concern that it would make me look bad. It was far too late for that. I just felt it wasn't an important detail and that at least I could spare Johnny the attention it might bring him.

Anyway, there was hardly a shortage of damaging revelations. When I talked about my attempts to find out about the relationship between Milena and Greg, DI Carter interrupted me. "She compiled charts," he said.

"What?" asked Ramsay, in a weak tone.

"Like they do with school timetables on big pieces of cardboard. It established the whereabouts of her late husband and of the woman."

"Charts," said Ramsay, looking at me.

"I had to know," I said. "I needed to prove to myself, and to the world maybe, that they really did know each other, or that they really didn't."

"You've been told it's hard to prove a negative," said Ramsay. "Kind of a police motto."

"People keep telling me," I said. "Not that it's a police motto, that it's hard."

There was a pause. I leaned over the tape machine to see if the little spools were turning.

"Is that all?" asked Ramsay.

"I think so," I said. "I'm not sure if I told it in the right order. I may have left things out."

"It's difficult to know where to start," said Ramsay. "For example, as someone who was working for Frances Shaw under an assumed name, you are an obvious suspect in her murder. If you had stayed on the scene, forensic examination might have exonerated you."

"It might not have," I said. "I pulled her out from where she was lying to see if she was still alive. I examined her. I wasn't sure if there was something I ought to do to help."

"So you moved the body!" said Ramsay. "And then you didn't tell anybody. Our investigation to date has been based on a complete misunderstanding of the crime scene."

"I'm sorry," I said. "That's why I decided I had to get in touch with you."

"How kind," he said. "I still don't understand. Why did you leave the scene?"

"I was scared and confused. I thought the person who killed

her might still be there. And maybe a part of me was wondering whether I was responsible for her death."

"How?" asked Ramsay.

"Perhaps I'd been stirring things up. I'm the one person who didn't believe that Milena and Greg's death was an accident."

"What on earth has that got to do with it?" said Ramsay.

"It's obvious, isn't it?"

"Maybe we're not clever enough to understand," said Ramsay. "Could you explain why it's so obvious?"

"My husband and Milena died in a car crash in circumstances that haven't been explained."

"That's not true," said DI Carter.

"And then Milena's work partner is murdered. There must be a connection."

"Oh, for fuck's sake," said Ramsay. "I started off saying you ought to talk to a lawyer, but you really need a psychiatrist."

"I'm seeing one, as a sort of grief counseling."

"I'm surprised he lets you walk the streets."

"She."

"I don't fucking care."

"I haven't told her the details of all of this."

Ramsay threw his hands up in exasperation. "What's the point of a psychiatrist if you're not telling her the truth? And, furthermore, if you're lying to your own doctor, why the hell should I believe you're not lying to us now?"

"It wouldn't be much of a lie, would it?" I said. "I don't come out of it very well."

"I'm not so sure about that," said Ramsay. "Quite a few coppers would be happy enough to charge you immediately but

you'd get off with an insanity plea—deranged widow runs
amok."

"You forget," I said. "I don't care."

"Your not caring is a big part of the problem."

"What I mean is that I don't care what happens to *me*."

Ramsay leaned forward and switched off the machine. "I
can honestly tell you there's a bit of me that would like to toss
you into a cell right now for fucking us around the way you
have. I can tell you that judges do not like people who get in
the way of inquiries. If we charged you now, you'd be facing
six months inside, a year if you pulled the wrong judge—and
that's just for not coming forward sooner. I don't need to tell
you there are more serious considerations at stake here. Murder, Ms. Falkner. Murder."

At that moment I thought suddenly that it would be an immense relief to be arrested and charged, convicted and sent to
prison. It would halt my endless, hopeless, undirected need to
do something. Clearly I had done the wrong thing. I had lied
to so many people. Above all—*below* all—I had lied to Frances. I had betrayed her trust and now she was dead. If I had
stayed at home and grieved, as everybody had told me to, and
in the end gone back to my work, this probably wouldn't have
happened and maybe, just maybe, Frances would still be alive.
I cared about the crimes I had committed. It was possible that
my lies and cowardice had stopped Frances's murder being
solved quickly. Maybe I had destroyed an essential clue. But
what seemed even more painful was that Frances had thought
of me as her friend, as someone she could trust, and everything she had thought she knew about me was a lie.

"You're right," I said. "I deserve to be punished. I'm not going to defend myself."

"You bet you fucking deserve it," said Ramsay. "And don't pull that pathetic act with us because it won't work. Maybe we will charge you, and not just for behaving like an idiot either. I'll need to talk to some people about that. We're going to think about it. In the meantime, you're going to supply any physical evidence you have. The clothes you were wearing would be a help."

"I've probably washed them."

"Why was I expecting you to say that?" said Ramsay.

"Were you wearing a jacket or a coat?" said DI Bosworth, speaking for the first time.

"A jacket," I said. "I haven't washed that."

"And shoes?" she continued.

"Yes, and I haven't washed them."

"When you return home," said Ramsay, "an officer will accompany you in order to collect any items that may be relevant to the investigation."

"So I'm going home?" I said.

"Until we decide differently," said Ramsay. "But before that, you're going to give us the mother of all statements."

"Isn't that what I've done?"

Ramsay shook his head. "You've only just started," he said.

I sighed. "It's a relief, really," I said, "that someone apart from me is doing the investigating."

Ramsay looked at me, then at DI Carter, then back at me. "That was an investigation? For fuck's sake."

Chapter Twenty-Seven

The first Christmas I had spent with Greg, we had escaped our families and gone walking in the Lake District. I knew I was in love with him—no, I knew I *loved* him—when he took a miniature Christmas pudding out of his backpack on the top of Great Gable and insisted we eat it. I can remember it vividly: the cool gray blustery day, the rock we perched on looking out over the empty landscape, the way the wind blew his hair into his eyes and turned his cheeks ruddy, the rich crumbs in my mouth, his warm hand in my cold one, a grateful sense of belonging—of being at home, even though we were up in the hills and far from anywhere. Despite all that had happened, the memory remained intact and robust.

The next Christmas we had spent with Fergus and Jemma, and Fergus and I had cooked a goose; Greg had insisted on making his version of champagne cocktails, singing loudly, filling their house with his tipsy cheerfulness. Last year, we had been in this house; we had planted the small Christmas tree at the end of the garden, planning to retrieve it. I used to dread Christmas; then, with Greg, I had learned to love it. Now I dreaded it again. In ten days' time I would wake up on my own in this house, which seemed to be on its own downward slide (the faulty heating system, which meant that most of the radiators were lifeless and at best the water was tepid, the freezer kept icing up so that little lumps of ice lay across the kitchen floor, a window was cracked and I hadn't got around to mending it, a cupboard door was coming drunkenly off its hinges). I'm usually good at mending things—of the two of us, I'd always been the efficient, practical one—but for weeks I'd been unable to summon the energy for domestic maintenance and all of my organizing skills had been used up on Frances and Party Animals.

But now I was going to put my life in order. I'd said that before, but this time I meant it. After weeks of claustrophobic murk and madness, I had to make a fresh start. I had to look ahead, not back—because what lay behind and all around me was so scary and inexplicable. So, I threw myself into clearing up the physical mess of my life. I started each day at six in the morning, when it was still pitch-black outside. I bled the radiators and felt them returning to life; I called in a heating engineer to replace the fan on the boiler; I mended the cupboard door and defrosted the freezer, hacking out months of ice; I measured the broken window and bought a new pane of glass, which I fitted with a glow of competence. I painted the walls of the kitchen white and my bedroom pale gray. I bought new bath mats.

I threw out every jar and tin that was past its sell-by date. I stocked the fridge with healthy food, and every day I made myself proper meals (for breakfast, yogurt, toast and marmalade or porridge made with half water, half milk; for lunch a bowl of pasta with olive oil and Parmesan or a salad; for supper, fish or chicken with one glass of wine). I went to the pool every morning, and swam fifty lengths. I bought myself a new pair of jeans and a gray cardigan.

I met Gwen and Daniel at the cinema. I went through my ledger and billed clients for outstanding payments. I made a list of the work I needed to do and wrote myself a timetable that I pinned on the notice board in the kitchen. I put a storage heater in my shed and spent at least eight hours of every day in there, trying to meet deadlines and make up for the broken promises of the past months. I replaced the legs on a Queen Anne sideboard, sanded and revarnished a rosewood table, put a new top on a scratched school desk that clearly had sentimental value to its owner. I even put a notice in the local paper advertising my services, and called at the nearby shops with business cards. I went late-night shopping and bought a beret and miniature dungarees for my soon-to-be godchild, and two beautiful scarves for Gwen and Mary's Christmas presents. I rang my parents to tell them I would not be with them for the day itself, but would it be all right if I came on Boxing Day instead? I bought my mother a glass vase and my father a book on houseplants. I drew the line at sending Christmas cards, and the ones that arrived for me I put in a pile on the kitchen windowsill so that I didn't have to read the dozens of sympathetic messages behind pictures of robins, virgins and comic turkeys.

And I did not look at the newspaper, so that I would not have to read any stories about Frances. I did not turn on the television for the same reason.

I did not respond to the message Johnny had left on my answering machine, or reply to the long, angry letter he pushed through the door.

I did not investigate the missed calls on my mobile, though I suspected they might have been from David.

I did not go back to the counselor, even though she had made it clear she thought it would be useful, not to say necessary.

I did not take up Gwen or Mary or Fergus or Joe on their offer to talk about what had happened, or describe in detail how the police had behaved toward me, particularly during the second interview I had had in Stockwell—their mixture of mounting incredulity and moral disgust. I was attempting to look ahead, move ahead, and the only way I knew how to do that was to blinker myself, choosing not to see what lay at all sides and behind me.

I did not let myself think of Frances, spread out under the desk with her sightless eyes staring up at me.

I did not insist to anyone who crossed my path that Greg had never known Milena. I understood at last that the past was gone and beyond my comprehension.

I did not cry.

I rolled up my two charts very tightly, bent them in the middle and stuffed them into the bin, along with carrot peelings and tea bags. I gave the menu card with Milena's scrawl on it to the police, who didn't seem very interested even when I pointed out how the "J" had been changed to a "G."

Each night, I went to bed so exhausted by my frantic activity and by all my desperate evasions that I fell asleep as if I'd been hit on the head with a brick. If I dreamed, I didn't remember of what. I wasn't exactly ecstatic, but I was purposeful, like a soldier going into a battle or running away from one.

IN THE MIDDLE of one Thursday morning, just as I was about to go out to my shed, the phone rang. I decided to leave it, but after the ringing stopped, my mobile immediately started up. I looked at the caller's ID before answering, in case it was someone I was trying to blank out of my consciousness.

"Fergus?"

He was gabbling something. I couldn't make out many words, but I got the sense. I was a godmother. Once I'd disconnected, I went and sat for a while in the kitchen. Outside, the sky had turned a dull white, as if it might snow. The house was quiet; the day ahead felt long and empty. I looked down at my hands, plaited together on the table, and told myself to stand up at once, go to my shed, get on with the work I'd planned for the day. My legs were heavy. It took an enormous effort to heave myself out of the chair.

The phone rang again. It was Detective Chief Inspector Stuart Ramsay—he said his whole name again, as if I might have forgotten him—and he wanted to know if I would come to the station.

"Why?" I asked. "What's changed? What's happened?" There was a deep breath at the other end, but before he could answer I interrupted him. "No, it's all right. I'll come. When?"

"Now? Do you want me to send a car to collect you?"

"No. I'll make my own way. I can be there in about half an hour. Is that all right?"

RAMSAY HAD MY statement in front of him and looked tired. He did not offer me tea, barely glanced up. At last he said, "Is there anything you didn't tell us in your statement?"

I thought back to the long interviews, one in Kentish Town and the other in Stockwell. I had rambled, repeated myself, repeated the repetitions, gone round in circles and off at tangents, included irrelevant information. Had I left anything out?

"I don't think so," I said eventually.

"Take your time."

"I don't need time," I said. "I think I told you everything."

He shuffled the papers, frowning. "Tell me, please, did you ever visit the site of your husband's accident?"

"I don't think it was an accident."

"I'm asking you a question. It's quite simple. Were you ever there?"

"How did you know?"

He looked up sharply. "Was I meant not to know?"

"Why are you asking me now?"

"Answer the question."

"Yes, I went there."

"And you didn't see fit to tell us?"

"I didn't think it was relevant."

"Is this yours?"

He took a transparent bag out of his drawer and held it up: my scarf.

"Yes."

"It has blood on it. Whose blood would that be?"

"Mine!"

"Yours?"

"Yes. I cut myself, that's all. Look, I went because I wanted to see where Greg had died. It was purely personal."

"When?"

"When did I go?"

"That's right."

"I don't know exactly. It was a long time ago. No, I do know. It was the day before Greg's funeral and that was on the twenty-fourth of October so it must have been the twenty-third."

He wrote the date down and looked at it thoughtfully. "You're quite sure?"

"Yes."

"And were you alone?"

"Yes."

"Did you tell anyone you were going?"

"No. It was something I had to do on my own."

"And afterward did you tell anyone you'd been there?"

"I don't think so. No, I didn't."

"Why not?"

"Like I said, it was personal."

"But you have close friends—friends in whom you confide?"

"Yes."

"And it must have been an emotional experience."

"It was cold and wet," I said, remembering slithering down the bank.

"So isn't it a bit odd that you didn't tell anyone something like that?"

"It's not odd. The next day was the funeral, and I had lots of other things to think about."

"I see. So there's no one to verify your story?"

"It's not a story, it's the truth. And no, there's no one to *verify* it, though I don't see why it needs verifying. Why is it so important?"

But even as I said the words, I realized why he thought it was so important. My mouth opened, but no words came out. I stared at him and he looked back at me implacably.

"It's just funny you never mentioned it," he said.

Chapter Twenty-Eight

A re you serious?" said Gwen. "What are they playing at?"
I tried to hush her but she wouldn't be hushed. I had
arrived at what Fergus had called the baby-boasting party
with a miniature pair of dungarees and a beret. When I'd
bought them, they had seemed impossibly small, like doll's
clothes, but when I peered into the cot I realized they were
much too big.

"She'll grow into them," I said. "Eventually."

"She's called Ruby," said Jemma.

"Oh, great," I said. "That's a lovely name."

"Admittedly Ruby sounds like someone who should be
dancing on a New Orleans riverboat," said Fergus.

"Don't be ridiculous," said Jemma, picking Ruby up and
telling her she wasn't going to let that horrible man say such
horrible things about her. She was talking in a tone I'd never
heard used by an adult. It was clearly something I'd have to
get used to over the coming years. Jemma insisted that I hold
Ruby. She told Ruby I was her godmother and that we ought to
get to know each other straightaway. Sensibly enough, Ruby
was fast asleep as Jemma showed me her miniature fingernails and her equally miniature toenails. Then she woke up
and Jemma retrieved her, coaxed her and contentedly fed her.

I went into the kitchen, where Gwen was making tea. Mary had brought a cake and was getting out plates and cups, keeping a watchful eye on Robin, who was fast asleep in his car seat in the corner. He used to look tiny, but now, compared to Ruby, he was big, on a different scale. I was still feeling a bit awkward with Gwen, having stolen her identity and everything, but I made an effort to tell her about things, the way I always used to. That was when she erupted in disbelief, and just as she did so, Joe came through and joined us. It was like the meeting of a secret society.

"I'm just escaping from Babyland," he said. "Not that she isn't beautiful. She's very sweet, isn't she?"

We all agreed that she was.

"Obviously every parent is convinced that their own baby is the most beautiful in the world," said Joe. "I can remember saying something of the kind when Becky was born." He picked up a slice of cake before Mary could stop him. He took a bite as he continued talking, crumbs spilling from his mouth. "The difference is that when I said it I was right."

"Hmm," said Mary, and I could see she was about to launch into a Robin-is-best speech.

"To return to what we were saying," interrupted Gwen, hastily, "Ellie has to do something to stop the police messing her about."

"What are they up to now?" asked Joe, raising his eyebrows at me and grinning. I could tell he was trying to make me feel better about the mess I'd caused, turning it into a kind of joke that we could laugh at.

So, of course, Gwen had to explain to all and sundry about

my latest encounter with the police. I was a bit ashamed to be the center of attention again. They'd had to be sympathetic to me as a widow, listen to my rants about Greg and his innocence, then deal with my activities as some kind of fraudster. And always it had been me, me, me at the center of things, with everyone else in a supporting role, their concerns pushed aside.

"You should have asked us to come with you," said Mary. "I can't bear to think you went on your own. It must have been grim."

"You'd done enough already, all of you. Besides, it was something I needed to do alone."

"What's outrageous," said Joe, "is that visiting the scene of your husband's death is something they should find suspicious. Of course you had to go. It would be stranger if you hadn't."

"Do you think they were really suspicious?" asked Gwen. "Of what, for God's sake?"

"I get the impression that they're extremely irritated by me," I said, and then cast a glance at Gwen. "As you probably are. Or, at least, you should be."

There was a joint, rustling murmur that of course they weren't and how none of it mattered.

"On the other hand," said Gwen, "have you thought that you may need some advice? I mean, legal advice."

"Legal advice?" Fergus had come into the room with a plate of biscuits. "What do you mean?"

"Well," said Gwen, slowly and carefully, "if they were talking to Ellie about when she went to the scene, and asking if anybody was with her to corroborate what she was saying . . ."

She turned to me. "It feels awful even to say it but you're the one, after all, who's been claiming that Greg's death was not what they assumed, was inexplicable. So it looks as if they might be thinking that . . ." But she stopped, unable to say it out loud.

"That I had something to do with it," I finished for her. "Yes. That I was taking revenge on my husband and his presumed lover . . . So, are you going to ask if I've got an alibi?"

"No, of course not," said Mary, in a shocked tone.

"Of course it'll never come to that," I said. "But I sort of do." I tried to recall the day in accurate detail. The terrible news had been such a blow that it was as if it had eliminated everything that went before. But I could remember. "I'd had a good day, funny as it may seem. I'd been working on a rather beautiful Georgian chair. It had taken longer than I'd expected so in the end I had to jump in a cab and take it down to the company who had hired me to do it for them. It was a solicitors' office just off Lincoln's Inn Fields. I remember the time because I was in a rush to get there before they closed. It must have been just a couple of minutes before six. When I handed it over, I had to sign a receipt for them, showing I'd delivered it. I wrote the date and the time on it. So I couldn't have been in East London tampering with my husband's car, if that's what was required. There we are. Too much information."

There was another awkward silence.

"But why are they even looking at the scene of the crash?" said Joe.

"Yes," said Mary. "It was an accident. We were at the inquest."

"God knows," I said. "I've caused so much trouble with my blundering around that the police don't know what they think anymore. It doesn't bother me. I'm finished with it all. I'm going to do what I should have done a long time ago, which is get myself sorted out, be good, do some useful work."

And so I did. Or, at least, I made a start. I helped carry the cake back into the midst of the baby celebrations. I picked up Ruby, who looked drunk after her feed, like a spaced-out old woman with blurry eyes and a milk blister on her lower lip, and held her in my arms, terrified I would drop her. I offered her my little finger to grip in her fist, and pressed my face to her neck; she smelled of sawdust and mustard. Then I handed her over for someone else to coo at and left.

The previous day, a man had dropped off six dining chairs at the house. They had been in his shed for years and he had forgotten about them. Could I do anything with them? Yes, I could. I could strip off the surfaces with wire wool and white spirit. I could replace broken slats and balance the legs so that they sat flush. I could arrange for the seats to be re-covered, and then I could smooth and polish the surfaces. I had given a quote that would have paid for a reasonable second-hand car and the man had seemed happy enough. I was happy too. The chairs would give me days of tricky, fiddly, messy, scrapy, lonely, lovely, satisfying work. It gave me a possibility of happiness. Well, maybe not happiness, but something to lose myself in, somewhere to escape, or so I thought.

IF I HAD known who it was, I would never have answered. I had just come in from the shed to make myself a cup of tea and was caught off guard. I picked up the phone automatically, without thinking it might be someone I wanted to avoid, and when I heard his voice I was so shocked that I slopped scalding tea over my wrist, then dropped the mug, which shattered on the floor. I stared at the receiver, thinking I might simply put it back in its holster and shut myself up in the shed, where no one could get at me.

"Hello." The voice was cool and uninflected; even now, he wasn't going to show his emotions. I imagined him at the other end: his graying dark hair, his impeccable clothes and manicured hands, his languid air of slightly contemptuous amusement; above all, his watchfulness.

"David," I said at last, trying to match my voice to his. "What do you want?"

"Straight to the point." He gave a small laugh that held no mirth. "I want to see you."

"Why?"

"I'm surprised you need to ask. There are certain things that need to be made clear."

"I've got nothing to say to you that I haven't already told the police."

"I, on the other hand, have things to say to you. And I'd prefer not to do it over the phone."

"I don't want to come to your house."

"I imagine not." At last I heard the current of anger in his voice. "Shall I come to yours?"

"No, I don't want that either."

"I have a cast-iron alibi, you know, Eleanor." He gave a light emphasis to my name, to remind me that I had been an impostor. "If you're imagining that I might be a murderer, you needn't trouble yourself."

"I wasn't," I said, although of course I had thought about David murdering Frances, and had found it very easy to picture: he was a cold, clever, ruthless man, rather than a messy creature of conscience. However, the reason for keeping him out of my house was not fear but an instinctive, deeply felt revulsion at the idea of him setting his well-polished brogues in my own shabby, Greg-haunted world.

"We could meet in my club, if you want. There are private rooms."

"No. Somewhere outside, public."

"All right, Blackfriars Bridge. North side. In one hour."

"It's raining," I said stupidly.

"Indeed. I'll bring my umbrella."

I hung up and ran my wrist under cold water for several minutes until it went numb. I considered changing out of my work clothes but in the end I didn't. After all, I no longer needed to pretend to be anyone other than myself. I searched in the cupboard under the stairs for an umbrella, but only found one with a broken spoke, which flopped uselessly when opened. I would just have to get wet.

I ARRIVED WET and cold, smelling of glue and dressed in paint-spattered canvas trousers under a streaming waterproof. David was as dry as a bone under his large black umbrella.

I stopped a few feet from where he stood on the deserted pavement, and gave him a stiff nod. His beautiful camel-hair coat was familiar, as were the brown shoes that shone like new conkers. I couldn't have pointed to any particular change in his appearance, yet I was struck by a difference in him. His skin seemed to be drawn tighter over his bones than the last time we'd met, giving him a pinched, sharp expression.

"This won't take long," he said.

I waited. He had asked to see me and I wasn't going to be the first to speak.

"My wife trusted you," he said. I didn't respond. There didn't seem to be anything I could say. "She liked you," he went on. "For once she showed bad judgment. Catastrophically bad judgment."

"I didn't kill her."

David gave a shrug. "That's for the police to decide," he said indifferently.

"Did she trust you as well?"

"You mean, because I was unfaithful to her? I know, of course, what you told the police."

"I told the police what was true—that you had an affair with Milena."

I had also, I thought, told them that Frances had had a lover. Did David know that? I stared at him, his unreadable face. Had he discovered that, and was that why Frances was dead?

"You disapprove of me," David said. "Of course you do. After all—and let's put the whole thing with Johnny to one side, just for the moment, shall we?—you think you're living in a romantic novel where husband and wife marry and live happily ever after, where first love doesn't fade, where your precious husband couldn't possibly have deceived you because he loved you so much. What makes you think Frances didn't know?"

"Did she?"

That dismissive shrug again.

"I've no idea. If she did, she would have had the good sense not to muddy the waters. She was sensible. We understood each other. We suited each other."

"You mean you turned a blind eye?"

"That's one way of putting it. Another is to say that we didn't snoop, pry and poke around in each other's worlds, thinking we had a right to know everything about each other. We treated each other like grown-ups. There are worse ways of being married."

"Are you saying she would have understood about you and Milena?"

"You've no right even to ask that. You were an outsider who came blundering into our house, putting your nose into business that didn't concern you."

"Did you love her?"

Real anger flared in his face and suddenly he stepped out of the circle of his umbrella so that large drops of water splashed on to his coat. "You want to know what I felt?" he said, his face a few inches from mine. "You still want to find things out? Frances was a good woman and Milena was a bitch. A hard-core, monstrous bitch. Bitches always win. She played with people. She played with me, lured me, hooked me, pulled me in, and when she was done with me she threw me back into the water. She never loved me. She was only interested in me because she could use me to get back at Frances. Yes, yes. I know there was another man in Frances's life. Milena told me when she dumped me that I had been her revenge on my wife, who'd stolen someone from her."

As I watched him, he seemed to crumble. His mouth trembled, and for a moment I thought he was going to cry or hit me.

"If you want to know who he was, I can't tell you. I never asked. I didn't want to know. I'm not like you. Some things are best kept hidden. We depend on that; we'd go mad if we knew everything. So if this had anything to do with your precious husband, I can't tell you. Nobody can now. Everyone's dead."

He snapped his mouth shut and stepped back under his umbrella. We stared at each other.

"I liked her a lot," I said at last. "I felt very guilty that I deceived her."

"Her, me, Johnny, everyone."

I walked all the way home in the rain, barely noticing the Christmas lights, the festive shops billowing out warmth through their open doors, the brass band on Camden High Street playing carols and collecting for the blind. Cars and vans thundered past, spraying water from puddles all over me. David must have arranged to see me because he wanted to prod me, taunt me, play with me, scare me. Had it just been sadistic revenge or something else?

I SAT IN the living room and stared at the empty grate. Greg used to love making fires. He was very good at it, very methodical. He would never use fire-lighters, saying they were a cheat, but started instead with twisted pieces of paper, then kindling. I remembered how he would kneel and blow on the embers, coaxing them into flames. I hadn't lit the fire since he died and I thought about doing so now, but it seemed too much effort.

Out of the blue a thought occurred to me that was both trivial and irritating. I tried to brush it away, because I was done with my botched attempts at amateur sleuthing, but it clung like a cobweb in my mind: why hadn't Greg written down his appointment with Mrs. Sutton, the old lady I had met on the day of his funeral? I was sure she had told me she'd arranged to see him on the day after his death, but it hadn't been in his diary.

I told myself it didn't matter, it was meaningless. I made myself a cup of tea and drank it slowly, sip by sip, then rang the office.

"Can I speak to Joe?" I asked.

"I'm afraid Mr. Foreman isn't here."

"Tania, then?"

"Putting you through."

After a few seconds, Tania was on the line.

"Tania? It's me, Ellie."

"Ellie," she said. "How are you?"

"Fine. Listen, Tania, can you do me a favor?"

"Of course!"

"I need the number of one of Greg's clients."

"Oh," she said doubtfully.

"I met her at the funeral. A Mrs. Sutton, I think—I don't know her first name. She was very nice about Greg and there was something I wanted to ask her."

"All right." There was a pause and then her voice again: "It's

Marjorie Sutton and she lives in Hertfordshire. Have you got
a pen handy?"

"Hello?" Her voice was crisp and clear.

"Is that Marjorie Sutton?"

"It is. Who am I speaking to?"

"This is Ellie Falkner, Greg Manning's widow."

"Of course. How can I help?"

"I know this sounds peculiar, but I was tying up loose ends
and there was something I wanted to ask you."

"Yes?"

"You told me you were going to see Greg the day after he
died."

"That's right."

"You're quite sure about that? Because there's no record of
an appointment in his diary."

"He'd only arranged it the day before. It must have been
just before the accident. He was very insistent that he should
come and see me."

"Do you know what it was about?"

"I'm afraid not. Is there a problem?"

"No problem," I said. "Thank you very much."

I put the phone back in its holster and returned to my chair
by the empty grate.

Chapter Twenty-Nine

I saw a nature documentary once that showed a baby seal lying in a little hole in the Arctic ice sheet. Above, in the outside world, it was about fifty below but in the hole it was warm, at least by baby seal standards. It must have felt safe as well. But it wasn't. Miles away, a mother bear, desperate to feed its cub, had caught the scent of the subterranean baby seal and smashed her way through the snow and ice to get at it.

That was more or less how I felt when DCI Stuart Ramsay came to see me in my work shed. It felt wrong. The whole point of me being there was to pretend that people like him didn't exist.

"I was working," I said.

"That's fine," he replied. "Don't mind me."

"All right." I continued with my sanding while he wandered around the room, picking up tools, occasionally glancing at me with a look of puzzlement, as if I was doing something unimaginably exotic.

"What are you working on?"

"It's a storage chest Greg and I found in a skip months ago. I said I'd repair it and they could have it in the office. It's really quite nice—look at the carvings on the top. I thought, after

Greg died, I wouldn't bother with it, but now I've decided I'm going to do it for them anyway. Joe will like it."

Ramsay picked up a plastic squeezy bottle and sniffed at the nozzle. He pulled a face. "What's this?" he said.

"It's a laminate," I said. "It's the sort of thing teenagers sniff and then go to hospital."

He put the bottle down. "My gran used to hate old furniture," he said. "She said she hated the idea of sitting in a chair that a dead person had sat in."

"It's a point of view," I said.

"When people got married, they were supposed to buy themselves nice new furniture. That was the tradition then." He knelt over one of the chairs I had dismantled. "This is the sort of thing that would have been put on a bonfire in the old days."

"I guess you haven't come to hire me," I said, "so why are you here?"

"I'm on your side, Ms. Falkner," he said. "You may not think so, but I am."

"I wasn't thinking about it."

"It's just that you make it difficult for someone to be on your side."

"You're a policeman," I said. "You're not meant to be on anybody's side. You're meant to investigate and find out the truth."

He looked dubiously at my workbench, then leaned back on it, half sitting. "I'm not really here," he said. He consulted his watch. "I finished work half an hour ago. I'm on my way home."

"Do you want a cup of tea?" I said. "Or a drink?"

"My wife's waiting at home for me," he said, "with a drink. Cold white wine, probably."

"Sounds nice," I said. "But if you're not on duty . . ."

"I just wanted to tip you off that things might get a bit messy."

"Why do you want to tip me off?" I said. "And why should they get messy?"

"Obviously it's all rubbish. You—Well, it sounds stupid even to say the words, but I'm going to anyway. You obviously couldn't have been involved with the death of your husband, could you?"

I'd been carrying on intermittently with my piece of sandpaper, but now I stopped and stood up. "Are you waiting for me to say no?" I said.

"You've been going around making yourself look suspicious but it still doesn't work."

"It doesn't work because it isn't true," I said.

"We don't work on truth. We work on evidence. Even so. The death of your husband was recorded as an accident. You were the one who was going around screaming that it wasn't. I've tried to think about it as a double bluff, or a triple bluff, but I can't make it work. And then not only did you claim you didn't know about your husband's infidelity, you actually made a bloody . . . . Well, you kept claiming it was all a mistake, that they weren't even having an affair. Even when you found evidence that they were."

"But the evidence doesn't work."

"Evidence is always messy."

"Not messy," I said. "Impossible."

He was rocking himself back and forth on the bench. "You really didn't know about the affair?" he said. "I mean before your husband's death."

"I don't believe he was having an affair."

"Did you have an argument on the day of your husband's death?"

"No."

Ramsay stood up and walked across the room to look out of the window. "Do you need planning permission for a shed like this?" he asked.

"No," I said.

"Interesting," he said.

"Is that relevant?"

"I've been thinking of buying one," he said. "Somewhere to go that's out of the house. To get back to what I was saying, you'll notice I'm asking you these questions informally, not taking an official statement. If I had been, it might have seemed I was trying to catch you out."

"How?"

"We've been talking to various people." He took a notebook from his pocket and flicked through several pages. "Including people in your husband's office. Mr. Kelly, for instance, who was in the office that day doing a software update. He said that early on the afternoon of the day your husband died, he heard one end of an argument on the phone between your husband and someone Mr. Kelly assumed was you. Perhaps it wasn't you."

"Fergus said that?"

"Yes."

"He's right. It was me."

"You said you hadn't had an argument."

"It wasn't an important argument."

"What was it about?"

"Something completely trivial." Ramsay didn't reply. He was clearly wanting to hear more. "It was about him coming home late."

"You had an argument about that?"

"All our arguments were about trivial things. Oh, for God's sake, I've still got the text he sent me afterward." I picked up my mobile phone and scrolled down to one of the messages I hadn't been able to delete. I handed the phone to Ramsay. He extracted some reading glasses laboriously from his top pocket and put them on.

"'Sorry sorry sorry sorry sorry. Im a stupid fool.' That's a lot of sorries. Do you mind if I take this?"

"It's my phone. I need it."

"It'll be returned to you. Pay-as-you-go phones are available in the meantime."

"What do you want it for?"

Ramsay put the phone in his pocket. "A cynical person would say that your husband doesn't say what he's sorry about. He could be sorry that he's been unfaithful."

"He wasn't unfaithful."

"I'm sure you're right."

"Your wine will be getting warm."

"I'm not cynical," he said. "I'm on your side. I know you've worked hard to incriminate yourself, but you haven't done a good enough job. That crash, with your husband and Milena Livingstone. You couldn't have done that on your own."

"Why do you say on my own?"

"No reason. Besides, who would you do it with? I've talked to her husband as well. Her widower. We don't really say 'widower,' do we? I've always wondered why. He didn't seem like someone to arrange a murder. He seemed more like the tolerant type. If you see what I mean."

"If you mean do I agree that he didn't kill his wife, I do."

"And your husband."

"Well, of course."

"And then there's Frances Shaw."

"I didn't kill Frances!"

"I'm just playing devil's advocate here, trying to construct the sort of theory that a hostile person might. It might be seen as an unfortunate coincidence that you worked for the company run by your husband's lover."

"It wasn't a coincidence," I said. "And she wasn't his lover. I was working there to prove that. Or to find the truth."

"I mean, how would you really do it?"

"What?"

"Kill two people and make it look like an accident."

"I thought you were talking about Frances Shaw."

"We'll come to Frances Shaw. I was thinking about the car. How would you do something like that? Tamper with the brakes, the way they do in films?"

"How do you tamper with brakes?" I said. "Anyway, what

would that do, driving in London? You don't kill two people driving along at thirty or forty miles an hour. At least, not reliably."

"Sounds right," said Ramsay. "So what do you do?"

I broke the promise I had made and made myself think about the event once more as I had hundreds of times before.

"They would have to be already dead. And you drive them to somewhere quiet . . ."

"Like Porton Way," said Ramsay.

"That would be a perfect choice," I said. "Where you can steer the car over the edge, set fire to it and then get away."

"Making sure you don't leave any traces," said Ramsay. "Or drop anything."

"Do you think I'd have left my scarf behind if I'd committed the murder?"

"You wouldn't believe what people leave at murder scenes. False teeth. Wooden legs. I'm sure it'll never come to this, Ms. Falkner, but if you're ever called upon to construct a defense, I wouldn't stress the point that leaving evidence at the scene is an argument that you weren't there."

"I was there. I went later."

"Obviously the case with Frances Shaw is very different. Traces of your presence were found everywhere at the scene, including on the body."

"I worked there," I said, "and I pulled the body clear. I wasn't sure she was dead."

"That's what the emergency services are for," said Ramsay. "They can revive people who might seem completely dead to civilians like you and me."

"She was dead."

"I believe this argument has been had before. My point was that there's no doubt you were there, even though you fled the scene. But while there's obvious motive for you to kill your husband and his lover, even though you couldn't have done it, there's no motive at all for you to kill Frances Shaw, is there?"

There was a pause because I didn't know what to say. I wondered if he knew something and was waiting to catch me out once more. If there was damning evidence—*more* damning evidence—it was better coming from me. And now was the time to give it. There was a moment when I thought, Why not? I had this feeling that somehow everything was closing in on me, everything was turning out bad. Why not go along with it? What if I was blamed for it, convicted and imprisoned? How did that matter, really? But I just couldn't do it. I couldn't think of the words with which to say it.

"We got on well," I said. "She thought of me as a friend. I felt bad about deceiving her. I meant to tell her but . . ."

"So you're sticking to your story that you didn't know about your husband's affair and you had no problem with Frances Shaw . . ."

"I didn't say no problem."

"Nothing that would be a motive for violence, I mean."

"Of course not."

"Although you accuse her husband of having an affair with your husband's lover."

"He *did* have an affair with her—and she wasn't Greg's lover. And his wife was also having an affair, don't forget."

"Hmm." He scratched the side of his nose. "You can see why

we're so confused, can't you? The problem is that it's all these negatives, proving that someone didn't know something, that they didn't have a motive. I'm not clever enough for that. A knife with blood and fingerprints. Preferably caught on CCTV. That's what I like."

He looked around. "Do you ever make new furniture?" he said.

"I have, as a sort of hobby. It's more expensive than old furniture."

Ramsay seemed disappointed. "I can't afford either on my salary. I'll stick with IKEA." He paused and appeared to remember something. "You're not playing any more of your games, are you?"

"Like what?"

"Pretending to be someone else."

"No."

"It wasn't even funny the first time."

"I've got an alibi."

"Ah, yes. It seems we're going to have to look into that."

I told him about the delivery on the day of Greg's death. I even went into the house, found the name of the solicitors' office, then wrote out the address and the phone number for him. "You can check yourself."

"I will," he said.

Chapter Thirty

When Detective Chief Inspector Ramsay came to see me on the Monday morning it wasn't anything at all like his previous visit. Even his ring at the door sounded different, more insistent and uncompromising. A younger colleague had come with him, awkward in his shiny new suit, as if Ramsay needed someone to protect him from any hint of flirtatiousness, of informality, of special treatment. There was no jovial suggestion of watching me work. He insisted on going through to the living room, where I felt out of place in my smelly, dusty work clothes. Worst of all was his expression, closed off, almost glassy-eyed, as if we hadn't met before, as if he was only going by a first impression and it wasn't good. When I offered them tea, he began speaking as if he hadn't heard.

"I thought you might be interested to know. We sent an officer around to Pike and Woodhead to check your alibi. Unfortunately they didn't have the receipt."

He stopped and looked at me, his expression still and unyielding, as if waiting for some justification.

"I'm sorry about the waste of time," I said. "I remember signing for it but they must have thrown it away."

"No, they didn't," said Ramsay. "But someone had collected it and taken it away before we got there."

"Who?"

"You."

For a moment, my vision went dark, dark with little golden speckles, like it does when you've looked at the sun by mistake. I had to sit down. I couldn't speak. When I did, it took an immense effort. "Why do you say it was me?"

"Are you serious?" said Ramsay. He took out his notebook. "Our officer talked to an office manager at the firm. A Mr. Hatch. He checked the file, found the piece of paper was missing, but there was a note saying it had been taken by a Ms. Falkner. By you."

For a vertiginous moment I let myself wonder whether it was possible that I really had gone over to the office, collected the docket and suppressed the memory of it. Perhaps this was what being mad was like. It might explain everything. Part of my mind had known about Greg's infidelity, had been responsible for other terrible things and had hidden them behind a mental wall. Hadn't I heard about that? About people who had suffered traumas and buried them so they wouldn't have to confront the implications? People who had committed crimes, forgotten them and truly believed they were innocent? It would almost have been a relief to yield to that, but I didn't.

"Where is it?" said Ramsay.

"I don't have it," I said. "It wasn't me."

"Stop," said Ramsay. He held up his right hand, the tips of his first finger and thumb almost touching, as if he was holding an invisible match. "I'm this close—this close—to arresting you now. Ms. Falkner, I don't think you realize the trouble you're in. Perverting the course of justice is not like crossing the road when the little red man is showing. Judges don't like it. They see it as a kind of treason and they send people to prison for a surprisingly long time. Do you understand?"

"It wasn't me," I said.

"Of course it was you."

"It doesn't make sense in any possible way," I said. "If it was me, why would I tell you about the company, give you the address and then take away the evidence before you got there?"

"Because it didn't say what you said it said."

I stopped for a moment, confused. "But getting rid of the evidence doesn't help. It just makes it worse. Why would I do that? And give my name while I was at it?"

Ramsay gave a snort that was almost a laugh but then his expression turned serious and when he spoke it was quietly and deliberately. "If a jury was informed of everything else you've been up to, I don't think they'd have difficulty swallowing one extra piece of insanity."

There was more before the two of them left and none of it was very pleasant. Ramsay said that in the near future I would be interviewed under caution, which meant there was the possibility of an imminent criminal charge, and that I ought to have a lawyer present. He also muttered about having a psychological evaluation and that it might be my best hope. As they were about to leave he regarded me with a mixture of bafflement and pity. "I felt sorry for you," he said, "but you don't make it easy. I don't understand what you're up to. But we're on your case. Don't piss us around."

As soon as they were gone, as soon as the car had pulled away, I changed into more businesslike clothes. Half an hour later I was at the office of Pike and Woodhead, whose entrance was in a small road, almost an alley, just off Lincoln's Inn Fields. A middle-aged woman was sitting at a desk just inside the door. I asked her if a Mr. Hatch was in.

"Darren? Yes, he's around somewhere."

I asked if I could see him and a few minutes later he appeared, not, as I had expected, in a pin-striped suit but in jeans and a Fred Perry T-shirt. I hadn't met him when I had delivered the chair. I had left it at Reception, signed a piece of paper, taken a copy and left.

"You deal with deliveries?" I said.

"You got one?"

"Not today. My name's Eleanor Falkner. I delivered a chair here a few weeks ago."

His face became suspicious. "A policeman was here about that this morning."

"I wanted to check up on it."

"What for?"

"When I delivered the chair, I signed a receipt. They said I collected it from you. But I didn't."

He walked over to a filing cabinet against the wall and pulled open the top drawer. He took out a file and flicked through it. "We have a slip for everything that's collected or delivered. Here we are. It's just a note saying, 'Docket retrieved for Ms. Falkner'."

"When?"

"That would be yesterday."

"I don't understand. Who wrote it?"

He examined it more closely. "Looks like my writing."

"So was it me who collected the docket?"

"That's what it says here."

"But can't you remember the woman who collected it?"

"What I mainly do is sort out deliveries. Twenty, thirty, forty a day. That's why I need the pieces of paper."

"But why did you let someone take a piece of paper away just like that?"

"Because it wasn't important. The receipts for documents go upstairs and we keep those. This is just office stuff, you know, pens, photocopying fluid. Every couple of months we chuck it out."

"So anyone could have walked in off the street, asked for the docket and you would have given it to them?"

He looked back down at the file. "It says Ms. Falkner here."

"Yes, but . . ." I stopped. I'd realized the futility of pushing it any further.

EIGHT HOURS LATER, or thereabouts, I was drunk. In the afternoon I had phoned Gwen and Mary, left messages and assumed they were busy, out of town or understandably sick of hearing from me. Of hearing about me. Of even knowing I existed. But later in the afternoon, Gwen rang and said that the two of them were taking me out. I had that infallible sixth sense when you know that people have been talking about you and making arrangements for you without your knowledge. I told her it was very kind of her but it was a Monday night and they had lives to lead. Gwen said that was nonsense. I had to put a dress on and they would pick me up at eight.

They took me to a new Spanish bar in Camden Town where we ate tapas with little glasses of dry sherry, then had more tapas and more sherry, and then we got into a discussion about what our favorite drink was. Someone said a dry martini and Mary said it should be served with a twist of lemon peel and Gwen said it should be with an olive. So we had one with the lemon followed by one with the olive. I was given the casting vote as to which was the winner, so I chose the lemon peel and we had to have another of those to celebrate.

It was at that point, as I was taking a delicate sip of my third dry martini, that Gwen asked how I was. Even in my alcoholic stupor, I realized that this was what the whole evening had been leading up to. My messages on their mobiles must have sounded terrifyingly abject and they had clearly decided something needed to be done.

"I'm all right," I said.

"No," said Mary. "This is us."

I thought for a moment and I—or perhaps it was the gin on my behalf—saw things with a new clarity.

"I am, really," I said. "In a way. There was something wrong with me, but now it's different. It's the things around me. I know you're getting tired of Widow Falkner and her endless tales of woe, so I'll give you the short version."

Well, fairly short. I told them the events of the previous days in as compressed a way as I could manage. At the end of it, Mary and Gwen exchanged an alarmed, confused glance. I drained my glass. "I mean, what would be the point of giving the police an alibi that I knew wasn't true, then removing the evidence before they could check it? I mean, what's the point of that? How would you explain it?"

There was a pause.

"There must have been a mix-up of some kind," said Gwen.

I was now having to concentrate very hard to speak, let alone think. "I keep trying to think of logical explanations," I said, "but all I come up with are illogical ones. For example, I thought that maybe one of you went down there to check whether the alibi was right, found it wasn't and took it away to protect me. But you wouldn't do that, would you?"

"Of course not," said Mary.

"We should have had margaritas," said Gwen. "Martinis are too dangerous."

"You can't have margaritas here," I said. "Margaritas are Mexican. They'd be offended."

"But martinis are even foreigner," said Mary. "More foreign."

We came out of the bar as it was closing and the cold air seemed to clear my head immediately. I hugged my friends and thanked them.

"You don't think the police will arrest you, do you?" Gwen said. "They can't. Not really."

I pulled my coat tightly around me to protect me from the wind whistling up Camden High Street. Suddenly things came into focus.

"I don't know," I said. "I'm not sure if it all fits together. If suddenly I was found dead and it looked as if I'd killed myself, it would be good enough. A grief-stricken widow, a guilty murderer who felt the net closing over her and couldn't take the pressure anymore. They would be able to close the files on three cases at the same time. If the pieces didn't quite fit, if it didn't make complete sense, well, life's messy, isn't it? But it would be good enough for the police."

"Ellie," said Gwen, horrified, "you mustn't say that."

I saw a taxi and raised my arm to hail it. "But if anything happens to me," I said, "you'll remember I said it, won't you?"

I WENT TO bed exhausted, but my nerves were jangling, my mind racing and I knew that sleep was impossible. I tried every trick I could think of to make my brain forget about trying to go to sleep so that it could just go to sleep. I relaxed, I concentrated, I mimicked a supposedly sleep-like regular breathing, eyes closed. I opened them, stared into the darkness and said to myself, That's what blind people see. I tried to think of something boring, I tried to think of something interesting. I began to wonder how I had ever managed to fall asleep in the past. How can you manage an action that isn't an action, but instead just a letting-go? I became obsessed with the idea that you can never observe yourself going to sleep, in the same way—I supposed—that you can never experience yourself dying. So I began to think that there must be an earlier falling-asleep you do before you fall asleep, like the premed before an operation, so that you don't observe yourself falling asleep. But you're not conscious of that either, so that must be preceded by another, and another, so that actually it's impossible ever to fall asleep.

As a deranged way of trying to tire myself out and force my-self into unconsciousness, I went for a journey in my head, as if thinking about something was as tiring as doing it. I walked out of the house, turned left, then left again and went down to the canal, past Camden Lock through Primrose Hill, then out into Regent's Park, along Euston Road and back through Somers Town, Camden Town and toward home. It was like a feverish dream, except that I was awake and in control of it.

At first I tried to imagine it as a simple walk through the city but then I had the impression I was being chased, but I couldn't see who was behind me, couldn't tell whether I was being pur-sued by one person or many, or even whether it was a person or a thing. I just had the feeling that people were out there and that they were hostile to me. Suddenly, overwhelmingly, I knew that on my imaginary trek I wasn't being hunted. I was looking for something, following something and I realized it was you. I wasn't just looking for you but I started talking to you and I wondered whether it made any sense for me to talk to you, whether you existed outside my mind and the minds of people who knew you. Was some remnant of you somewhere in some darker dark than the dark in which I was lying? If I didn't believe you were out there somewhere—and I didn't, not really—it didn't make sense for me here, in the dark, to talk to you, and you were "him" again, Greg, a thing, something past and gone.

Suddenly the temptation to yield not only to sleep but to death felt irresistible, leaving the harsh noises and bright lights, the jabs, pains and torments of life for the absence, for the nothingness, to join you, to be with you, or at least to share nothingness with you. For a time, as I lay there, listening to sounds from outside, watching the beams of headlights crossing the ceiling, I felt that anyone who killed me would be doing me a favor.

I lay in bed, peacefully, stolidly awake, for what must have been hours, waiting for the curtain edges to grow light, and then I realized that the shortest day of the year had only just passed and that daylight was still far away. I fumbled for my watch on the bedside table, knocking a lamp over. It was just after five. I got out of the bed, pulled on jeans, a shirt, a sweater, a thicker sweater on top of that, walking boots, then a bulky jacket of the kind you might wear on a trawler and a woolly hat. I left the house and started to walk, not as I had in my waking dream but northward.

Remember in the summer when we walked out on Hampstead Heath late at night? It was so warm that we had been in T-shirts and it was never entirely dark. From the top of Kite Hill we watched the glow in the sky over in the far east of London, and the office blocks of the City and Canary Wharf glowed wastefully even after midnight. We saw shadows and silhouettes around us, but we didn't feel threatened by them. They were out walking like us, or even, some of them, sleeping under the stars, by choice or necessity.

As I walked up Kentish Town Road I saw a few other pedestrians, stragglers from last night or early birds heading for work. There were taxis and delivery vans and cars, because the traffic never stops, barely even slackens. But once I turned on to the Heath, I felt as safe as we had felt in the summer. It was too dark and cold even for criminals or mad people, except mad people like me who were just looking for one of the few places in London where you could escape. I walked up the hill so that I could look over the lights of London, distant and abstract and glittering, as if I was flying above it. I went further up the hill and to the right, and walked deeper into the Heath on paths lit only by the moon, finding my way by memory on routes I had taken dozens of times before. The early-morning air felt fierce and good on my cheeks.

Finally I found myself surrounded by the dim skeleton shapes of oak trees. I stopped and listened. There wasn't even the hum of traffic that you hear everywhere else in the city. I was in the center of London and yet I was in an ancient forest as old as England. I looked up at the branches. Were they standing out more clearly as the sky turned from black to gray? Was the dawn coming? Sometimes on these winter mornings you couldn't tell.

I started to talk to you, not because I thought you were somehow present, not in the wind that was shifting the branches, but because it was a place we had been together and that had somehow become a part of us. I told you the story of my life since you had gone away. I told you about my strange behavior, my madness, my distrust of you and then my belief in you. How it had been so hard, such an effort, how I had wanted to give up.

There was a sudden breath of wind that shifted the branches above me and I wondered what you would have said if you had been there, whether you would have teased me or got cross or said something encouraging, or just put your arms around me and said nothing. Then I told you about the strange things that had happened, the disappearing evidence. I know what you would have said about that. You always wanted to know how things worked. When you didn't know, you found out. Even once when we had been to the Hampstead fair, you had got into conversation with a sinister tattooed man who ran one of the merry-go-rounds and he had shown you the gears and the machinery underneath. And as I told you all that I realized I had to know, even if I died at the moment I knew. It didn't matter, as long as I knew, as long as I could tell you.

I looked up at the branches. Yes, they really were standing out more sharply against the graying sky.

Chapter Thirty-One

I sat on the sofa in Fergus's living room. Jemma had left the house for the first time since Ruby's birth to go a few hundred yards down the road for a cup of coffee with a friend, but leaving enough instructions for a week's absence, and I had come around with croissants and freshly squeezed orange juice for Fergus. There were Babygros over the radiators, congratulation cards and flowers on every surface, and a buggy in the corner. Ruby's Moses basket lay at my feet, with its downy snuggle of crocheted blankets, but I held Ruby on my lap, her soft head on the crook of my arm, her little bag of body slumped against me. Her eyes were closed and her lips puffed slightly with each sleeping breath she took. I needed to look at her puckered old-woman's face, smell her musky breath, feel how her hand gripped my middle finger firmly, as if she knew she could trust me.

We had talked about broken nights, miniature nails, eye color, stork marks, the shape of her nose, the shell of her ear and upturn of her nose.

"Who does she look like?" asked Fergus.

"Not you," I said, staring at her features. "But she's got Jemma's nose and mouth."

"Everyone says that."

"Maybe your chin," I said doubtfully, because he seemed to want me to spot a resemblance.

"No. She's got Jemma's father's chin," he said.

I smiled at him: dear Fergus, Greg's best friend, father of my goddaughter. "This was what I needed," I said.

"Are you all right, Ellie? You seem—I don't know—very thoughtful. A bit subdued."

"I don't mean to. I'm fine, Fergus. Weary. I didn't sleep very well. Actually, I came around to tell you that I think I'm going away for a while. I've been a bit mad, haven't I? I feel more peaceful now."

"Do you?"

"I think so. The stages of grief."

"If there's anything I can do . . ."

"You already have."

"What a ghastly time this has been for you."

I smiled at him and looked down at the baby in my arms. "There's been one light in all the darkness. A new life among the deaths."

IT WOULD SOON be dark again. So much darkness and so little light. I went to Gwen's house and she let me in. Daniel was there, too, wearing Gwen's stripy apron and covered in flour. "He's decided to make pasta," said Gwen, proudly.

He led the way into the kitchen. There was flour on the floor, the work surfaces and the table. Bowls sticky with dough were piled in the sink and clothes hangers draped with long strips of gunk hung from the backs of chairs. Two large pans of water were boiling on the hob, filling the room with steam.

"Do you want to eat it with us?" Gwen asked.

"I don't think so. I'm sure it'll be delicious."

"Have a cup of tea at least."

"One cup and then I must go."

"Busy?"

"Busy in my head."

Daniel picked up one sagging strip of pasta dough and dropped it into the boiling water.

"Are you using your car at the moment, Gwen?"

"Not that I know of. I never use it if I can help it. It stands there from one week to the next. I'm thinking of selling it."

"If she does need it, she can use mine instead," said Daniel, hurling another strip into the pan and jumping back as water splashed over the rim. "This isn't looking quite the way I imagined it would. They're disintegrating."

"Can I borrow it? I'm insured to drive any car. I was thinking of going away."

"Where to?"

"I don't know. Just for a few days."

"But it's Christmas."

"Exactly."

"Don't go away on your own. Come and stay here, Ellie." Gwen seemed close to tears.

"That's really lovely of you but I need to go right away. Not for long. I'm sure you understand."

"As long as you know that there's always . . ."

"I do know. I've always known."

"Of course you can take the car. Take it now."

"Really?"

"No problem."

"I'll be very careful of it."

I DROVE GWEN'S car home and parked it outside the gate, then let myself into the house. It was so empty, so silent, so cheerless. I wandered from room to room, picking up objects and putting them down again, running my finger along shelves to collect dust. Perhaps I would move. After I came back from wherever I was going, I would put the house on the market.

I came to a halt in the chilly living room where I closed the curtains. I decided I'd light a fire to brighten it up. The basket already contained pieces of kindling and some tightly screwed up pieces of paper. We'd got into the habit of doing it with used envelopes, letters we didn't need, scraps of paper. Greg used to talk about identity theft and that it was better than buying a shredder.

I collected a bag of coal from my work shed, then set to work, although I'd rarely lit a fire before—that had always been Greg's task. I made meals, he made fires. I laid several of the homemade fire-lighters in the grate, then arranged kindling in a wigwam over the top before striking a match and holding the flame against one of the twists of paper. It caught quickly on the dry kindling and I immediately felt the comforting warmth on my face. I sat cross-legged in front of the fire and began to toss the little screwed-up pieces into the flames and watched as they were consumed. Some I unrolled and read. Articles in six-month-old newspapers seem more interesting when you're about to throw them on the fire. Mostly there were useless old envelopes and letters offering to lend us money or telling us we'd won some in a competition. It struck me that these were the last traces of Greg's ordinary daily life that were left in the house, the rubbish that surrounds all of us. I was about to toss another into the flames when something caught my eye.

It was just a fragment of handwriting scrawled on the edge of the paper but it looked familiar and I couldn't think why. I untwisted the paper and smoothed it out.

It had the office letterhead—Foreman and Manning Accountants—but above that, in her flamboyant calligraphy, was written: "I'll ring you about this—Milena Livingstone." And underneath the letterhead, in a different ink, a name was written over and over again. Marjorie Sutton, Marjorie Sutton, Marjorie Sutton . . . About twenty signatures running down the page.

I sat on the floor and held the paper in both hands, staring at it. What did it mean? The message was in Milena's handwriting. There was no doubt about that. After my days in the office, I knew it as well as my own. And it was on a piece of paper from Greg's office with Milena's name on it. It was the thing I had been looking for all this time, the connection. And I was more confused than ever. Why was Marjorie Sutton's name written on it over and over again? And what was it doing here?

I tried to remember. I thought so hard it hurt. I looked at one of the newspapers. It was from the day that Greg had died. Yes, that was it. These were the scraps from the tidying I had done that day, just before the knock on the door, before my life changed. The connection between Greg and Milena had been in my hands on the day he had died, before I knew, perhaps while he was still alive. Before I had heard of Marjorie Sutton, before I had heard of Milena, or had known her handwriting. I looked down at the crumpled sheet of paper. Suddenly it seemed fragile, as if it might crumble away and the connection would be lost forever.

I found her number and dialed it. She seemed confused to hear from me again. She said she had told me everything she remembered.

"Did you know a woman called Milena Livingstone?"

"No," she said firmly.

"Are you sure?" I said. "You might have forgotten."

"It's a funny, foreign sort of name," she said. "I would have remembered it."

I described the piece of paper I'd found. "Were they your signatures?"

"I don't see the importance of this," she said, with a touch of impatience. I felt as if I was talking to a small child whose attention was wavering.

"I think it's very important," I said. "I'm going to take the paper to the police. They may want to ask you about it."

"I certainly didn't sign any piece of paper in that way."

"What exactly do Greg's company . . . I mean Foreman and Manning, what do they do for you?"

"I'm not sure that's your concern," she said.

"I suppose they do your accounts."

"Since my husband died . . ." she began.

"Oh, I'm sorry."

"It was twelve years ago, thirteen almost. They handle the

money side of things for me, the things my husband used to look after. I couldn't do it myself."

"But there's something about that piece of paper," I said. "It must have been connected with why Greg wanted to see you."

"I don't know what you mean," she said.

"But have you had any trouble with the firm? Have they behaved strangely in some way? Were you having problems with them? Had you complained?"

"No, I hadn't. Really, Ms. Falkner, I don't know what you're talking about."

"But there must be something," I said, in desperation. "I've found this piece of paper, Greg wanted to see you urgently, just at the time he died. You must try to think."

"I'm sorry," she said. "I can't help you anymore."

"But don't you see—" I realized the line was dead. I couldn't believe it. She'd actually hung up on me.

Almost in a dream, I walked through to the kitchen. I laid the paper on the table. I boiled the kettle, made coffee and stared at it as if it was a mathematical problem that would yield an answer if I thought about it hard enough. Those signatures. I was sure I'd seen something like it before, but I couldn't think where. It was like a fragment of a story and I tried to piece it together. I'll ring you about this. Milena Livingstone. You? Greg? Milena calls Greg? Greg calls Marjorie Sutton? Had he seen something in the note that I couldn't? Had Milena told him something?

I looked at the coffee mug. It was empty. I refilled it. It didn't matter now. I would take it to Ramsay. Finally it was the connection I'd been looking for. The professionals could deal with it. I found an old envelope and slipped the piece of paper inside. I put the envelope into my shoulder bag. As I was pulling on my jacket, the doorbell rang. It was Joe. I must have looked almost comically puzzled. He smiled.

"What are you doing here?"

"I was worried about you," he said.

"Everybody's worried about me. I'm fine."

"One of our clients phoned the office. She's in a state. She said a woman had been ringing her and asking her strange questions."

"Marjorie Sutton. But you don't need to concern yourself about me," I said, pulling the door shut behind me and walking toward Gwen's car. "I was on my way out."

"The way that woman was talking, I thought you might be having some sort of breakdown. You can't go disturbing old ladies like that."

"There are things I need to know."

"What things?"

I unlocked the car door. "I can't talk," I said. "I've got to go. One of my regular visits to the police."

"Do you want me to come with you?"

"No, I don't," I said, and then stopped myself. "No, thank you."

"Could you at least drop me at a station? I let my cab go."

"Sure," I said. "So long as you behave yourself."

As I drove off, I half expected to feel Joe's hand on my knee.

"What are you seeing them about?"

I told him about the piece of paper and where I'd found it.

"Isn't that just a scrap of paper?" he said.

"It's a scrap of paper from Greg's work with Milena Living-stone's handwriting on it."

"What does that mean?"

"I don't know," I said. "But it feels like the thing I've been looking for."

We drove for a couple of minutes in silence and then I thought, He'll suggest going somewhere else. We continued in silence for several minutes.

"I could drop you over there."

"It's probably nothing, but why not come back to the office? We could look through Mrs. Sutton's file and see if your piece of paper refers to anything."

"All right."

"It's not too far out of your way," he said.

"No."

"At least you'd know," he said.

"That's all I want."

I felt, almost for the first time, in the midst of all the fog and all the darkness, that I was seeing with clarity. The office was no good to him. If he suggested something else, I'd know. We stopped at some traffic lights.

"There's a shortcut ahead," he said. "I'll direct you."

"All right."

"Turn left along there."

I started the car, and as it moved forward, it jerked and stalled.

"Sorry," I said. "I haven't done that since I was seventeen."

"I could drive for you," he said.

"I'm fine."

I drove as if hypnotized, as if someone else was doing the driving and I was just getting a ride and looking around in curiosity. I saw people walking on the pavement and it seemed to me that they were different from me, as if I was a visitor from another world, shortly to depart. I glanced at Joe, who was also glancing around. He rubbed his face. He looked tired. In fact, he looked worn out. Why hadn't I seen that before? I had been so busy looking in the wrong direction. I wasn't afraid. I felt a sense of peace. I wanted to know and after that nothing mattered.

"You just turn left ahead. The second on the left."

It's funny. Wherever you are in London, however busy it is, you're just a minute or two from somewhere desolate and abandoned. One day it'll all be turned into bijou apartments, but not yet. A left and a right and we were among some abandoned office buildings. I saw a sign, almost eradicated by graffiti, for a carpet factory. There was another warehouse building at the end. And there were no cars in sight, and no pedestrians.

"Bloody hell," Joe said. "It's a cul-de-sac. I got it wrong. You'll need to turn around. You'd better pull in here."

"Some shortcut," I said, as I stopped the car.

This was it. This was where it had all been heading. All roads meet here. All stories end here. Now I felt Joe's hand on the nape of my neck, soft, caressing. "This reminds me of Porton Way," I said.

"What's that?"

"You know. Where Greg was killed."

"I don't."

And now I remembered where I'd seen those signatures.

"I used to play a game when I was little," I said. "My friend and me, writing each other's names, copying each other's signature. You could do a lot with Marjorie Sutton's signature. I guess she's not someone who checks her accounts very thoroughly. It was you, wasn't it?"

Joe looked at me stonily. I could feel his hand, hardly more than his fingertips, brushing the back of my neck.

"The thing about Milena," I said, "is she had a nose for weakness, for something she could use. She saw it, picked it up, and when you dropped her for Frances, she used it. No wonder you wanted to clear out my house for me. You needed to find it. You must have been frantic. And when Frances guessed—as she must have done, or why would you have killed her?—was it easier the third time?"

Joe stared at me, but didn't speak.

"I just wanted to know," I said.

"So now you do," he said quietly.

"So this is what it's going to be?" I said. "Poor Ellie. Couldn't take it. Couldn't live without her husband. There's just one thing."

"What's that?" said Joe.

"I don't care," I said, and I pushed the accelerator to the floor so that the rubber on the tires screamed and the car leaped forward. No stalling this time. I heard a shout but I couldn't make out what he was saying. I was in a dream anyway, in the car with this man whom Greg had trusted and loved until he hadn't trusted him anymore. Forty miles an hour. Then fifty. Then sixty. We were running out of road.

I heard a scream and I didn't know whether it was Joe's scream of terror or something inside my head or the tires against the rough road, and I had a moment to remember that this was Gwen's car I was destroying, and then it wasn't fast and loud and violent, but slow, silent, peaceful. And it was no longer winter, a day pinched by darkness and ice; it was warm. A summer afternoon, fresh, soft and clean, the kind that's like a blessing, full of blossom and birdsong. There he was at last—oh, I had waited so long—walking toward me over the grass and such a smile on his face, his dear, familiar face. The smile he gave only to me. How I've missed you, I said, I wanted to say. How badly I've missed you. And I wanted to say, Have I done well? Do I make you proud? And I love you, how I love you. I will never stop loving you.

He held me in his arms at last, wrapped me in his solid warmth. And at last I could close my eyes and rest because I had reached the end and come home.

Chapter Thirty-Two

It didn't feel good to be dead, not the way it should have done. There were bits of me that hurt and bits of me that felt sticky and bits that were bent in different directions and there was something over my face and there was an insistent electric noise that went on and on and wouldn't stop. Everything was dim and far away and becoming dimmer. I felt something from outside and there were presences close to me and hands on me, voices. I was being roughly handled. Didn't they know I was fragile? That I was broken inside? I tried to protest that I wanted to be left alone so I could sleep, but something was forced into my mouth and I couldn't speak. I felt cold air on my skin and then I was inside once more and I felt jostling. Something was shouted in my ear that I couldn't recognize, and then I did recognize it. It was my name. How did they know? And then I sank without fear or regret into darkness. Not sleep but a state of nonbeing with no dreams, no thoughts.

I didn't wake up from that nothingness. I gradually found myself in an existence of feverish semi-sleep in which I sometimes saw faces around me, flickering and unsteady, like candle flames. Some were familiar: Mary, Fergus, Gwen. I tried to say sorry about her car but my mouth was full and the words wouldn't come. Once my eyes opened to see a police-man looming over me. It took an effort to put a name to the face. Ramsay. At first I wasn't sure if he was real. I mumbled things to him and when he had gone I couldn't remember what I had said.

The sign of my gradual return to life, to reality, was that I started to hurt in almost every part of my body. In that period when I could still barely tell night from day, sleep from wake-fulness, a doctor came and sat by my bed and talked to me slowly and patiently. He talked about fractures and rib dam-age and a punctured spleen and operations and about gradual recovery and patience and determination. When he had fin-ished he paused as if he was waiting for me to ask some ques-tion. It took an enormous effort.

"Joe," I said.

"What?" said the doctor.

"In the car," I said.

His expression changed to one of professional sadness. He started talking about how they had tried to revive him and how, unfortunately, they hadn't succeeded and how they had been waiting until I was strong enough to bear the shock.

One morning I felt for the first time that I was really waking up and that I wasn't stuck somewhere on the brink of uncon-sciousness. Over by the window a man was standing, looking out. I could only see his silhouette against the brightness of the sky. When he turned and I saw that it was Silvio, I was so surprised it made me feel dizzy and tired.

"It's an amazing view."

"What are you doing here?" I said.

He walked over to the bed. "I brought you flowers but they didn't let me bring them in. They think they're some kind of risk. I don't know whether it's because they spread disease or the nurses don't want them around. Or maybe they just want to take them home themselves."

"Thanks for the thought."

"I gave them away and then I went around the corner and bought some blueberries and strawberries. I don't know if you like that sort of thing."

"I do."

"I'll put them on something." He lifted the cover off a plate on the table by my bed. "What's this?"

"I think it's my lunch."

"Gray sludge."

"There's some fish under it."

I felt the weight of him on the bed as he sat on the edge and offered me the blueberries. I took a couple, put them into my mouth and chewed, feeling them burst against my tongue. "Lovely," I said.

"Healthy," said Silvio. "Someone told me that if you have a handful of them every day, you'll never get cancer. Or anything else."

"Can you give me some water?" I said. "There's a jug over there."

He poured it into a plastic cup. I took a couple of sips. It was warm and tasted stale. I drank it all anyway and handed the cup back to Silvio.

"Do you know everything?" said Silvio.

"I don't know anything."

"But you know about the guy in the car with you?"

"He died."

"The police said you were lucky to survive. It was in the papers. I saw a photo of the car. I don't know how you walked out of that one."

"I didn't walk out of it. How did you find out where I was?"

"I just did what you've been doing," said Silvio. "Detective work."

"I didn't do any detective work," I said. "Mainly I found out things by mistake."

"You're like one of those women scientists."

"I've no idea what you're talking about."

"I've been studying history of science at school. There are these women scientists, they do all the research and the important experiments and at the end the guys come in and make the final discovery and get all the credit."

"What discovery?"

"You've been going around stirring everything up, causing trouble."

"You could say that. What about you?"

"Me?"

"Are you all right?"

He looked embarrassed; he flushed and turned to stare at the view again. "Yeah. I guess."

"I'm sorry about everything."

"Thanks," he muttered.

"Have a blueberry."

He popped several into his mouth. One split on his lip, leaving a dark stain. He looked about ten, angry, ashamed and full of confusion. Milena had certainly left her mark on the world she'd left behind.

DETECTIVE CHIEF INSPECTOR Ramsay came to see me one more time. "You were lucky to survive that crash," he said.

"So I've heard."

"You were wearing a seat belt," he said, "but Mr. Foreman wasn't. I suppose there's a moral there."

"I'm glad there's one somewhere. So, is the inquiry over?"

"More or less."

I forced myself to think. My mind felt so slow. "He must have had help," I said. "Who collected the docket from the firm of solicitors? The woman who said she was me. It was Tania, wasn't it?"

"We've interviewed Miss Lucas."

"Did she confess?"

"Confess?" said Ramsay. "She admitted carrying out certain tasks on his behalf."

"Criminal tasks."

"She claims she had no suspicion of anything criminal."

"She was pretending to be me."

"She said that must have been a misunderstanding."

"Bollocks," I said. "They were sleeping together, you know."

Ramsay coughed. "I've no evidence of that," he said, "not that it would be relevant. Except possibly to show she was in thrall to him."

"In thrall?" I said. "You mean she's a weak woman? So she's not to be charged with being an accomplice to murder, interfering with the course of justice?"

"We've got a file but we're not sure there's a reasonable chance of a conviction."

"What about the company?"

"It's currently in administration, pending investigation of certain irregularities."

"You mean Joe was stealing from his clients. That he was up to his neck in it."

"That has been suggested," said Ramsay.

"And presumably Tania knew nothing about that either."

Ramsay shrugged instead of replying. That *was* his reply.

"I suppose at least you accept that Joe killed Frances."

"Yes, we do. We're assuming that Mrs. Shaw knew, or at least suspected, what he had done and was going to expose him."

"That makes sense," I said, remembering Frances's agitation, the sense of guilt, how close she had come to confessing to me. If she had, she wouldn't have been dead now. "She was clearly troubled."

For a minute Ramsay stared at me gloomily, then turned to the window. A disheveled pigeon was sitting on the other side of the glass, its beady eyes glaring in.

"What about the deaths of Milena and Greg?" I asked. "Do you also accept Joe killed them?"

"We've reopened the file."

"You don't sound very grateful to me."

"Your role in the investigation has been mixed," said Ramsay, "but at an appropriate time . . ."

"Is that what you meant when you said the inquiry wasn't completely over?"

"Did I?"

"More or less, you said."

He paused, seeming shifty, ill at ease.

"When this accident happened, or shortly before," he said, "you had developed suspicions of Mr. Foreman's role in the case."

I suddenly felt under threat. "How do you mean?"

"What I'm trying to say, Ms. Falkner," said Ramsay, in a deliberate tone, as if he was speaking to a child, "is that I'm working under the assumption that you had suspicions of Mr. Foreman and then he realized you had these suspicions and that there was some sort of struggle while you were driving. Perhaps he tried to seize the wheel. And you crashed. Accidentally."

I thought for a moment. "I don't remember," I said. "I don't remember anything about the accident. It's a blank. Is that all right?"

"Yes," said DI Ramsay. "That'll do."

Chapter Thirty-Three

I walked to Fergus's house with the box in both hands. It was early, a soft dawn breaking over the rooftops. Even here, in the streets of London, birds were singing all around me. At that time of the morning the volume seemed to have been turned up. I could see the blackbird on the branch of a tree, its throat pulsing.

Fergus was waiting. He opened the door before I knocked and stepped out to join me, kissing me on both cheeks and giving me a small smile.

"Ready?" I asked.

"Ready."

We didn't talk. After twenty minutes or so we left the road and entered the Heath, making our way along the empty paths to the wilderness. We could no longer see the city glittering in the pale sunlight, or hear the noise of cars. I remembered that other dawn when I had walked there: then it had been winter, and I had come alone to talk to Greg. Standing under the boughs of an oak tree, I turned to Fergus.

"It began like this," I said. "The alarm went off and he woke and reached over to my side of the bed to turn it off, then he kissed me on the mouth and he said, 'Good morning, gorgeous, did you have nice dreams?' and I muttered something thickly in reply but he couldn't make out the words. He got out of bed and pulled on his dressing gown, leaving me still tangled up with sleep. He went downstairs and made us both a cup of tea, and he brought mine upstairs in my stripy mug—which was what he always did, every morning. He watched me struggle up to sitting, half laughing at me. Then he had a quick shower. He sang in the shower, loudly, humming where he couldn't remember the words. It was "The Long and Winding Road."

"Mornings were always a bit of a rush and that morning was no different. He put on his clothes, brushed his teeth, didn't bother shaving, then went downstairs, where I joined him, still not dressed. He didn't have time for a proper breakfast. He bustled around, making coffee, reading out snippets from the headlines, finding a folder he needed. Then the post arrived. We heard it clatter on to the floor and he went to get it. He opened it standing up, tossing junk mail on to the table. He opened the envelope containing Marjorie Sutton's signatures or, rather, Joe's practice versions of them. He read Milena Livingstone's scrawled message. He didn't understand what he was looking at but he was puzzled. He tossed the sheet of paper onto the table, along with the rest of the discarded post, because he was late and in a hurry. The last time I saw him, he had a piece of slightly burnt toast in his mouth and he was running out of the door, keys in one hand, briefcase in the other.

"He drove to work and got there by about nine. He made himself and Tania a pot of coffee, then went through his post and his emails, which he answered. Joe wasn't there—he'd left a message with Tania that he was going to see a client. Then you arrived, to help with the new software that was being installed. Greg sat on his desk, swinging his legs, and talked to you about the IVF treatment I was going to have. He said he was sure it would turn out all right in the end. He was always the optimist, wasn't he? Then he had a meeting with one of his clients, Angela Crewe, who wanted to set up a trust fund for her grandchild. After that, he made five phone calls, then another pot of coffee and ate two shortbread biscuits, which were his favorite. He kept them in the biscuit tin with the sunflowers on the lid.

"He went out to lunch with you at the little Italian place around the corner from the office, and he ate spaghetti with clams, which he didn't finish, and drank a glass of tap water, because he had just decided that bottled water was immoral. He probably told you that."

"Yes, he did," said Fergus.

"You also talked about running, compared times. You went back to work and he went into his office and shut the door. The phone rang and it was Milena. She asked if he had received the page of signatures in the post and he replied that he had. She said she was sure that an intelligent man like him must have grasped its implications and Greg responded sharply that he didn't deal in suspicions and implications and put down the phone."

"Is this all true?" asked Fergus.

It was starting to rain and the drops felt cold and good on my face.

"Most of it," I said. "Some of it's the sort of thing that must have happened. The rest of it is what I tell myself in the middle of the night.

"After he had put the phone down on Milena he sat for a while, pondering. Then he went into Joe's office to ask him about it, but Joe still wasn't there and he wasn't answering his mobile. So instead he called up Marjorie Sutton's files and went through them carefully. After he'd done that he rang her and made an appointment to see her the following day. He said it was urgent.

"He was going to go home after that. He'd promised me that we'd have a proper evening together. I was going to make risotto and he was going to buy a good bottle of red wine. We would make love and then have a meal together. But as he was preparing to leave the phone rang and it was Joe, saying something odd had just happened concerning Marjorie Sutton and they needed to talk. Greg was relieved to get the call: in spite of himself, he'd been worried about those signatures. He told Joe he'd been trying to reach him about the same subject, but perhaps they could do it the next day. He had a date with his wife. Joe insisted. He said it wouldn't take long, could Greg pick him up at King's Cross?

"Greg rang me. He said, 'Ellie, I know I said I'd be home early, but I'm going to be a bit delayed. I'm really sorry.'

"And I said, 'Fuck, Greg, you promised.'

"And he replied, 'I know, I know, but something's come up.'

"And I said, 'Something always comes up.'

"'I'll explain later,' he said. 'I can't talk now, Ell.'

"And I should have asked him if everything was all right,

and I should have told him to take care, and that it didn't matter if he was late, and I should have said I loved him very, very much. Or no, no, that's not it, that's not it at all. I should have told him to come home at once, to cancel whatever arrangement he had made. I should have shouted and insisted and said I was upset and I needed him. I could have done. I nearly did. A whole other story unwinds from that, the story that never happens and which I'll never get to tell, which is about a long life and happiness. Instead, I said goodbye rather coldly and slammed the phone down, and that was the last time I heard his voice, except on my answering machine. And sometimes I wake at night and think he's talking to me. He's saying, 'Good morning, gorgeous, did you have nice dreams?'

"You heard the argument, anyway, or at least his end, because you came into his office halfway through. He put down the phone and turned to you, saying I was a bit pissed off with him, and you told him you were sure it would blow over.

"When he was alone again, he sat back in his chair and put his hands behind his head. I don't know that, but I can see him doing it. I see exactly the way his head was tipped, the small muscle clenching and unclenching in his jaw. He closed his eyes and thought of me feeling downcast about not getting pregnant, and suddenly his irritation seeped away and he simply felt tender. So he sent me a text. 'Sorry sorry sorry sorry sorry. Im a stupid fool.'

"He stood up. He put on his jacket. He put his head around Tania's door and said he'd see her tomorrow. He waved at you as he went. He ran down the stairs two at a time, the way he always did. He got into the car and drove to King's Cross. Five minutes, and he'd drive home and barely be late.

"He pulled up and Joe opened the passenger door and climbed in, carrying a bag. He said there was something he needed to show Greg. Of course Greg knew he could trust Joe. He loved Joe, after all, looked up to him and often turned to him for advice. In many ways, Joe was the father figure Greg had never really had. So Greg innocently followed Joe's instructions and they drove east, toward Stratford, toward Porton Way. He would never have suspected anything was wrong. Why should he? How could he have done?

"Greg drove Joe to the disused wasteland. It was dark and cold and there was no one around. He kept asking Joe what this was all about, but he wasn't anxious, just a bit puzzled and slightly amused by the hush-hush air of it all. Joe, being Joe, would have come up with something plausible as they drove along, lots of details. It didn't matter. It would never be checked. Just so long as it kept Greg from becoming suspicious.

"Greg stopped the car when Joe told him to. He looked out of the window, to where Joe pointed. He didn't see . . . what was it? A spanner? Maybe one of the tools from the boot of the car? It's the sort of thing that's called a blunt object. It caught him just above his eyebrow, once and then again. He didn't know that Joe was his murderer—oh, Fergus, I hope he didn't know, and that the last few seconds of his life were not utter confusion and terror. No. He didn't. I know he didn't. Joe's aim was good and death came quickly.

"Joe drove to the spot where he had hidden Milena. He

lifted her body into the passenger seat. He undid Greg's seat belt. He pulled off the handbrake, and because the car was facing downhill, it didn't take much effort to push it a few feet until it picked up speed, careered off the bend and over the drop. He watched it hurtle to the bottom. Then Joe—who was crying by now, fat tears running down his face because he was always a great sentimentalist, Joe was, and he did love Greg, in his own fashion—Joe clambered down the hillside, slipping and sliding as he went, and he set fire to the car and then he stood back while the flames consumed his partner, his beloved partner and friend. He was probably still crying. No, he wasn't. He didn't have time to cry. He had to get away before the fire attracted attention. The plan worked perfectly. He left two corpses, total strangers lying together like lovers.

"The question is, did he walk away? That sounds a bit awkward to me. It would have been better to drive."

"What in?" said Fergus. "He'd set fire to the car."

"Someone must have picked him up."

"Who?"

"Tania, of course. But she says she doesn't know anything about it. And, anyway, she was in thrall to him. That's what the police think. Apparently that makes it all right."

I hadn't been looking at Fergus while I spoke, but now I turned to him. A single tear was running down his cheek. I reached up and, with the tip of my finger, wiped it away.

I pried the lid off the box and we crouched under the oak tree and, very slowly, I tipped the box until Greg's ashes flowed over the rim and on to the green grass. We didn't move, but Fergus held out his hand and I gripped it.

You were my best friend, you were my dear heart, my love. A small breeze stirred the pile. Soon it would be scattered by the wind and rain. It wouldn't take long.

FERGUS WANTED TO walk me home but I told him that today I preferred to be alone. Sometimes being alone is not so lonely as being with other people and, anyway, my heart was full of memories of happiness.

I walked back slowly through the beautiful blue morning, the sun on the nape of my neck, the air soft and warm. People flowed past me on their own journeys. When I unlocked my front door and stepped into the little hall, I almost called out that I was home. I went into the kitchen and stood in the silence that lay all around me. While I was waiting for the kettle to boil, I stepped into the sun-filled garden. I tipped my head back, closed my eyes and saw your face, the smile that was meant only for me. When I opened my eyes again, I noticed that a young blackbird was lying dead on the grass just a few feet away, beneath the old rosebush. I went into the house and collected an empty shoebox. Then I lifted the bird, with its damp body and yellow beak, into it and closed the lid.

I didn't want to throw it into the bin for the dustmen to collect, so I dug a hole in the soil and put in the miniature coffin, then scraped the earth over it until you wouldn't have known anything was there. But I knew, and although it was only a bird, I sank to my knees, put my head in my hands and cried bitterly, because it had sung so beautifully through the winter months and now it was gone. Then I stood up, wiped the earth from my hands, went back inside, and still you were not there.

Read on for an excerpt from
Nicci French's new electrifying thriller

HOUSE OF CORRECTION

Available now from William Morrow

One

The screaming started at three in the morning. Tabitha had never heard a human being howl in that way before. It was like the screeching of an animal caught in a trap and it was answered by shouts, distant, echoing. Tabitha couldn't tell whether they were cries of comfort or anger or mockery. The screams subsided into sobs but even these were amplified by the metal, the doors, the stairs and floors. Tabitha felt they were echoing inside her head.

She sensed a movement from the bunk above her. The other woman must be awake.

"Someone's in trouble."

There was silence. Tabitha wondered if the woman was ignoring her or really was asleep, but then a voice came out of the darkness. She was speaking slowly, as if she were talking to herself. Her voice was low and gravelly, a smoker's morning voice.

"Everyone's in trouble," she said. "That's why they're here. That's why they're crying, when they think about their children or what they did. Or what they did to their children. When there's real trouble, you don't hear any screams. You just hear the screws running along the corridors. When it's really bad you hear a helicopter landing out on the field. That's happened three times, four times, since I've been here."

"What's that for?" asked Tabitha.

"What do you think?"

Tabitha tried not to think about what a helicopter landing in the middle of the night meant. She tried not to think at all. But she failed. As she lay staring up at the bottom of the bunk above her, as she heard the sobs and the shouts and then another burst of crying from someone else, she had a sudden feeling of absolute clarity piercing the murk: this was real.

Up to now, it had all been so strange, so completely outside her experience, that it had felt like a lopsided fairy tale about someone else going to prison, someone she was reading about or watching in a film, even when she herself was experiencing it. When she was sitting in the tiny, windowless compartment in the van that brought her from the court; when she took her clothes off and squatted and was stared at and examined and heard a woman laugh about her small breasts and hairy armpits; when she stood in the shower afterward. She had been issued sheets and an itchy blue blanket and a thin towel and escorted through door after door. The doors really were made of heavy metal. They really did clang shut. The wardens really did carry huge bunches of keys attached on chains to their belts. The prison was so prison-like.

Yesterday afternoon, as she was escorted through the central hall, lined with cells on both sides and on the floor above, she felt stared at by women standing in groups. She wanted to say: "This isn't real. I'm not one of you. I don't belong here."

She lay there on her bunk trying not to think of that, trying not to replay it in her mind, over and over again. But even that was better than thinking of where she was, right now, this minute, in this space.

Tabitha had never liked lifts. What if they fell? What if they got stuck? She always took the stairs. When she went to London, she hated the Underground. Once she had been on a train during rush hour, standing up, crammed among the hot bodies, and the train had stopped between tunnels. There had been a muffled announcement, which she couldn't understand. It had stopped for five minutes, ten minutes. It was in the summer and the heat was stifling. Gradually Tabitha had thought of the solid clay and brick between her and the surface. And then she had thought of how she was in the middle of a train that was stuffed with people in carriage after carriage in front of her and carriage after carriage behind her. She had felt an impulse, which she could barely stifle, to scream and scream and fight her way out.

Now she was in a cell, four paces long, three paces wide. There was a tiny, barred window. It looked out on a yard, beyond that a wall topped with barbed wire, and beyond that, you could just make out the hills, hazy in the distance. Yesterday she had looked out of that window and she had thought that she saw a little shape moving on that hill. Someone walking. Someone outside. Someone free. But now it was dark and there was nothing but the spotlights illuminating the yard. The door of the cell would stay locked until the middle of the morning. When she thought about it, she felt like she was buried alive and wanted to yell for someone to come and rescue her. Perhaps that was what that woman had been howling about.

If Tabitha couldn't scream, then perhaps she could cry. But she knew that if she cried, she wouldn't be able to stop. And probably it wasn't good to be seen crying.

It was very cold, and the single blanket was inadequate. She drew her knees up almost to her chest and lay hugging herself in the darkness. She smelled different. Of prison soap and hair that needed washing, something slightly moldy. She closed her eyes and thought of the sea, waves swelling and cresting onto the rocky shore. Thoughts came in long dark curls and she tried to push them away. There was another scream, then someone banged on a door far away.

Although it felt impossible, she must have slept a little because she was woken by the woman sliding down from the top bunk. It seemed to take a long time. Her feet came first, long, with purple-painted toenails, a tattoo of a spider on the right ankle. Then her legs in gray jogging pants, on and on. Then a black tee shirt riding up to show a ring in the belly button. Finally, a smooth oval face, long thick dark hair with a fringe, circular hoops in her earlobes. She was very tall, maybe six feet, and looked strong; in her late twenties perhaps, although it was hard to judge. Tabitha hadn't seen her last night, not really. She'd just climbed into her bed and pulled the blanket over her head and lain there.

"Hi," she said now.

The woman didn't reply. She went across the cell and opened the little curtain.

That was another thing. The cell had been built for one person. Now it had bunk beds, two chairs, two narrow tables, two tiny chests, a sink and a toilet with a little curtain rigged up in front of it. The woman tugged her trousers down and sat on the bowl. Her face was quite expressionless; it was as if she were alone. Tabitha turned to the wall, wrapping herself in the blanket so that she couldn't hear.

The toilet flushed and taps were running. Tabitha waited till the woman was done, then climbed out of her bed and washed herself under her arms, splashed water on her face. Then she pulled on canvas trousers, a tee shirt and a sweatshirt. She slid out her sneakers from under the bed.

"I'm Tabitha," she said.

The woman was methodically brushing her hair. She looked down at her. *She must be almost a foot taller than me,* thought Tabitha.

"You told me that last night."

There was a pause.

"What's your name?" asked Tabitha.

"Michaela. I told you that as well."

There was a rattling sound at the door and it was unlocked and the door pushed inward. A stringy, colorless woman was standing next to a trolley with two stainless steel urns on it.

"Tea," said Michaela.

"Tea," repeated Tabitha.

The woman filled two mugs and handed them across.

Tabitha's breakfast pack was on the table. She opened it and laid it out: a plastic bowl, a plastic spoon, a miniature pack of Rice Krispies, a small carton of UHT milk, two slices of brown bread wrapped in polythene, foil-wrapped butter, a little tub of raspberry jam. There was no knife so she spread the butter and the jam on the bread with the handle of her spoon.

She couldn't remember when she had last had a meal and she ate the sandwiches in quick bites. The bread was dry but she helped it down with gulps of her tea. She tipped the cereal into the bowl and poured the milk over it. The milk was warm and had a sour under-taste. It almost made her gag, but she ate it all and when she was finished she tipped the bowl to drink the last of the milk. She still felt hungry.

She sat on the toilet behind the thin curtain. She felt like an animal. As she sat there, her trousers around her ankles, she felt as if lights were flashing and there was a ringing in her ears. She suddenly thought of smashing her face into the wall, over and over again, something that might bring relief, that might make all of this stop.

Instead, she wiped herself, pulled up her trousers, washed her hands and sat back on her bed against the wall. She didn't have anything to read and she didn't have anything to do. The day felt shapeless and vast. Anyway, if she had sat there reading, that would feel like this was now her life instead of a nightmarish mistake, a mistake that would be corrected when everyone realized that she didn't belong here and let her go.

Michaela was leaning over the sink, brushing her teeth. She was taking a long time over it. She spat into the sink, bent down and drank straight from the tap. She stood up, leaned her head back and gargled noisily. Tabitha felt like everything was turned up too high: the noises, the smells, the physical proximity of the other woman. Michaela pulled her hair back in a ponytail, then walked out of the cell. A few seconds later she walked back in. She leaned back on the table and looked down at Tabitha.

"Don't just sit there."

Tabitha didn't reply. It felt too much of an effort.

"It's worse if you do that. I know, I've been here for fourteen months."

"What did you do?"

Michaela stared at her, her face quite expressionless. "Did they give you the bit of paper with all the shit about exercise and showers and when the library's open?"

"I've got it somewhere," said Tabitha. "But I don't care about all that. It's just a mistake."

"Yeah? Well, don't think you can just hide in here and get through without anyone noticing. It's like a school playground. The little girl who stands in the corner wanting to be left alone, she's the one who gets picked on. You need to get up. You need to get up and get a shower."

"I don't feel like it. Not today."

Michaela reached under the little table that was reserved for Tabitha.

"Here." She tossed Tabitha the towel she'd been issued on her arrival. "You take the towel and the soap and you have a shower."

She went out of the cell, leaving the door open. Tabitha got to her feet. She was cold to her bones. She looked out of the little barred window again: the sky was white. *It might snow*, she thought. That would be something: feathery flakes falling thickly just a few inches from where she stood, covering everything in a blanket of unfamiliarity.

She took the towel and the soap from the side of the sink and walked into the central hall that was echoey with sounds: footfalls and doors and voices raised, laughter, coughs, the slap of a mop. A very thin woman with long white hair and her face a muddle of wrinkles hobbled toward her. She wore a thick brown dress to her shins and her hands were swollen with arthritis. She was holding a bundle of papers clutched to her chest.

"You're here too," she said, smiling.

"Yes, I'm here too," said Tabitha. She walked the length of the hall and into the little wing reserved for showers. The showers were in a row of stalls. Along the far wall was a wooden bench and hooks. Women were pulling clothes on and off. The tiled floor was wet and there was the smell of soap and sweat and bodies. She had a memory of school changing rooms that was so pungent that it hurt. She slowly took her clothes off, looking at the wall so she didn't catch anyone's eye. Before she took off her knickers, she wrapped herself in the thin worn towel, like a shy teenager on a beach, and then eased them down.

Inside a free stall she pulled the curtain across and hung the towel from a hook. She turned the tap and a tiny trickle of water emerged from the showerhead. She tried to twist the tap further but it wouldn't go.

"You need to bang it," said a voice. "Bang the pipe."

She tapped the pipe. Nothing happened.

"Harder," said the voice. "Really hard."

She made a fist and hit the pipe. There was a little sputtering, coughing sound and the trickle became a faint stream, just enough to wet herself all over. But there was nothing good about it, nothing to lose herself in, nothing to comfort her.

Two

This way." The warden was solid with a bored expression. When she walked, her feet slapped down, flat and hard.

"What?"

"Your brief's waiting."

"My brief?"

"Your lawyer. You were told about this yesterday."

Tabitha couldn't remember that. But then she couldn't remember much of yesterday, nor of the days preceding it. Everything was a jumble of faces, eyes staring, questions she couldn't answer, words she couldn't make sense of, people saying her name over and over again—her name and her address and her date of birth and then pieces of paper pushed toward her, machines clicked on to record what she was saying, long corridors and strip lighting, doors and keys and bars.

"In the visitors' room," the woman was saying. Keys jangled at her waist. "It's not a day for visiting."

The visitors' room was large and square and too brightly lit. There were small tables in rows with a chair on either side, two vending machines by the wall. The room was empty except for a middle-aged woman who was sitting at one of the tables with her laptop in front of her. She took off her glasses and rubbed her round face and then replaced them, frowning as she read. As Tabitha approached, she looked up and briefly smiled, then stood and held out her hand, which was strong and warm. She had peppery-gray hair and a steady gaze and Tabitha felt a surge of hope. This woman would sort everything out.

"I'm Mora Piozzi," she said. "I've been asked to represent you."

"What happened to the other one?" He'd been young and cheerful in a blustery, unreassuring way.

"He was the duty solicitor. He referred your case to me."

They both sat and faced each other, their chairs scratching across the linoleum.

"How are you?" asked Mora Piozzi.

"How am I?" Tabitha resisted the urge to shout at her. What kind of question was that? "I'm locked up in prison and I don't know what's happening."

"It's my job to bring clarity to this and to help you."

"Right."

"First things first. You need to tell me if you agree to me representing you."

"Yes."

"Good. I've got your prison number, in case you haven't been issued it yet."

"A prison number? But I'll be out of here soon. Why do I need a number?"

"Here."

She pushed a card across to Tabitha, who read it out loud: "AO3573." She looked up. "So I'm a number now."

"It's just bureaucracy. You'll need it for people who are going to visit."

"Visit?"

"As a remand prisoner you're entitled to have up to three visitors a week. Has nobody explained all this?"

"Everything's a bit of a blur."

Mora Piozzi nodded. "It's hard at first."

"I just want to leave here as quickly as possible."

"Of course. Which is why I am here. But, Tabitha, you do understand what the charge is?"

"I know what they say I did."

"Good. So this is what we're going to do today: I am going to lay out the summary of the case against you. And then you are going to tell me, in your own words, what happened on the twenty-first of December."

"Can I ask something first?"

"Of course."

"What day is it today?"

"Wednesday, the ninth of January."

"I see."

Christmas had gone by, and New Year's Eve, and now she was in another year and another world.

"So," said Mora Piozzi, looking down at her laptop. "In brief: you are charged with the murder of Stuart Robert Rees, on Friday the twenty-first of December, between the hours of ten-forty in the morning and three-thirty in the afternoon."

"Why?"

"I'm sorry?"

"Why those times?"

Piozzi flicked through her notes.

"There's a CCTV camera. It's attached to the village shop. His car drove past it." She looked down at her laptop. "At ten thirty-four. And as you know, his body was discovered at half past four that day."

"Yes," said Tabitha faintly. She paused. "But there's a spare hour then, between half past three and half past four."

"I understand the forensic pathologist is satisfied that Rees had been dead at least an hour when his body was discovered."

Piozzi continued speaking in a low, calm voice, as if it was all routine. "His body was found by Andrew Kane in a shed outside your back door, wrapped in plastic sheeting. You were in the house at the time of discovery. Stuart Rees's car was parked round the back of your house, out of sight of the road. He had been stabbed multiple times by a knife, but the cause of death was the slashing of his carotid artery." She looked up. "That's in his neck. His blood was all over you and all over the sofa where you were sitting."

"But that was from after he was dead," said Tabitha.

Piozzi tapped on the keyboard of her laptop. "The police have interviewed everyone who was in the village and—"

"Wait."

"Yes?"

"There must have been lots of people coming and going. They can't have interviewed everyone."

"Not on that day."

"What do you mean?"

"Don't you remember? The village was blocked off. There was a big storm and a giant chestnut tree that had blight was torn up by its roots and fell across the road. There was no way out and no way in. Apparently it took most of the day to clear it."

"I didn't know."

"But you were there, Tabitha, all day. You must have known."

"I didn't know," Tabitha repeated. She felt like the last fragments of memory were flowing away like water through her fingers. "I don't know if I knew."

"The police have a list of everyone who was in Okeham on the twenty-first of December. They also have your statement saying that you were in your house most of the day. They have statements from other witnesses, but I haven't seen them yet. All we have at the moment is a police summary. I'll get the rest later, well before the first court appearance."

"The trial, you mean?"

"No. On the seventh of February you will be officially charged. That's where you plead. You know, guilty or not guilty."

"Isn't there a chance they'll realize that this is all wrong and let me go?"

Mora Piozzi gave a smile that didn't look like a smile. "Let's not leap ahead. I want you to tell me what you remember about the twenty-first of December. Take your time."

Tabitha nodded. She closed her eyes and then opened them again. What did she remember? It was like looking into a night full of snow, a dizzying half darkness, when even up and down seemed reversed and the ground tilted beneath her feet.

"I woke up early," she began. "But I don't think I got up at once. It was cold outside, a horrible day. I remember it was half snowing and then it was sleety, with a hard wind blowing. I started to make myself breakfast, then I realized I'd run out of milk so I just put a jacket on over my pajamas and went to the village shop. I bought a paper, I think."

"What time was this?"

"I don't know. I wasn't looking at the time. Then I went home."

"Did you go out again?"

"I had a swim. I always have a swim."

"How?"

"What?"

"Where's the nearest swimming pool and how did you get there? Remember, the road was blocked after ten, so you would have to have gone and returned before then." She spoke with a warning tone.

"In the sea."

Piozzi's eyebrows shot up. "You went swimming in the sea, in the middle of winter, on a day you describe as horrible."

"I do it every day," said Tabitha. "It's a rule. My own rule. I have to."

"Rather you than me. You have a wetsuit, though."

"I like to feel the cold water on my skin. It almost hurts." She saw Mora Piozzi purse her lips slightly, as if Tabitha had said something she didn't like. "People in Okeham probably think I'm mad. Anyway, I swam that day." She thought she could remember the bitter splash of waves on her body and the sharp, icy stones under her feet, but perhaps she was making that up. She swam every day. How was she meant to tell one from another?

"What time?"

"I don't know. I can't remember. In the morning? I think it would have been the morning. That's when I normally go."

"Did you meet anyone?"

"I don't know. Maybe. I can't think. I go every day, so things blur together."

"And after your swim?"

"I went back home."

"Did you leave again?"

"I think I did, but I don't know for sure anymore. People have asked me so many questions that I can't tell things apart."

"What did you do in your house?"

"Not much. I can't really remember."

"Did you speak to anyone on the phone?"

"No."

"Or send any texts, or use your computer—you have a computer?"

Tabitha nodded. "I didn't do any of that."

"Did you send emails?"

"I don't think so. I might have done some work." She knew she hadn't worked. It had been one of those terrible days when she simply had to survive.

"So you have no clear memory of what you did during that day?"

"No."

"But you remember Andrew Kane coming round?"

"Andy, yes."

"Tell me about that. Be careful, take your time."

Tabitha wondered why she kept saying that: "Take your time." Anyway, it didn't matter. She had so much time.

"He knocked on the door. I was in the main room and I opened the door. Or maybe he opened it himself. It was already dark and very cold. I remember the icy wind rushing in. He was all wet. He was dripping onto the floor."

"Were you expecting him?"

"No. But he often just comes round." She saw the questioning look on Mora Piozzi's face. "He's helping me with the house. It was a wreck when I moved in, back in November, and we're doing it up together. I pay him by the hour and he fits me in between other jobs. We were going to lay some floorboards the next day and he just wanted to check on everything."

She stopped and took a deep breath. This was where her memory became clear, like a shaft of light in the gloom.

"He went outside to the shed where the planks were stacked and I heard him call out. I don't know what he said, maybe it wasn't even words. I went out to him, and he was sprawled on the ground inside the shed, on top of something." She swallowed hard. Her throat was tight. "I bent to help him and I felt something wet and sticky, it was everywhere, and I pulled him to his feet and he kept saying, 'Oh God, oh God,' over and over. I think he was crying."

Tabitha stopped but Piozzi didn't speak, just waited, her eyes narrowed.

"It was dark. We couldn't see anything really. Andy got his

mobile out of his pocket but dropped it on the ground and had to scrabble around to find it. Then he shone it downward and there was a body. Andy had blood all over him, even on his face. I looked down at my hands and saw I did too." As she spoke, she could see it all: the little beam of the mobile's torch picking out the stare of open eyes, the gaping wound in the neck, an unnatural twist of limbs.

"Did you see who it was?"

"I don't know what I thought. Andy said it was Stuart, I realized he was right."

"Just to be clear, you knew Stuart Rees?"

"Yes, he's my neighbor now." She stopped. "I suppose I should say he *was* my neighbor. And years ago, he was one of my teachers."

"So you knew him well?"

"What can I say? He was a teacher."

"Were you on good terms?"

"We weren't on bad terms. I didn't really see him much, though, just to say hello."

"What happened next?"

"We went back inside. Andy called nine-nine-nine. We waited. The ambulance arrived and the police and it all started. You know the rest."

Mora Piozzi closed her laptop.

"So you see, it makes no sense," Tabitha continued urgently. "Why would I have sent Andy outside to look at the planks if I'd just killed someone out there and left the body for him to trip over? Why would I kill Stuart anyway? It's just crazy. You see that, don't you?"

The solicitor glanced at her watch. "We've made a good start. I'll be back quite soon, by which time I hope to have a more detailed knowledge of the prosecution's case against you."

Tabitha nodded.

"In the next few days you'll have a medical assessment."

"Why? I'm not ill. I might be small but I'm strong. It's that swimming." Her voice jarred. She tried to smile. She was cold and shaky and she didn't want to go back to the central hall, where everyone watched her and shouts echoed, or to her cell, where she was trapped with herself. The day ahead seemed endless, but the day led to the night and that was even worse.

"It's just part of the process. And I want you to write down everything you can remember that you think might be useful."

"What kind of things?"

"Timings. People you saw or talked to. Give me a list of the people in the village you're friendly with."

"I only moved there a few weeks ago."

"You should tell me anything you think might be helpful to your case, or relevant. I would much rather hear things from you than from the prosecution."

Tabitha nodded.

"Make sure you arrange visitors. Family. Friends. Have you any of your things here?"

"No."

"Get someone to bring them. Keep yourself occupied. Keep healthy."

"And you'll get me out of here? Won't you?"

"That's my job," said Mora Piozzi. "I'll do it as best I can."

Tabitha watched her leave, the door opening and then shutting. She imagined her going through a series of doors, each one locked behind her, until at last she reached the exit and stepped out in the world, breathing in the fresh air, free.

About the Author

NICCI FRENCH is the pseudonym of English wife-and-husband team Nicci Gerrard and Sean French. Their acclaimed novels of psychological suspense have sold more than 8 million copies around the world.

MORE FROM NICCI FRENCH

HOUSE OF CORRECTION
In this heart-pounding stand-alone from the internationally bestselling author that *People* calls "razor sharp," a woman accused of murder attempts to solve her own case from the confines of prison—but as she unravels the truth, everything is called into question, including her own certainty that she is innocent.

THE LYING ROOM
In this thrilling stand-alone from the acclaimed author of the Frieda Klein series, a married woman's affair with her boss spirals into a dangerous game of chess with the police when she discovers him murdered and wipes the crime scene.

DAY OF THE DEAD
The final novel in the internationally bestselling series featuring London psychologist Frieda Klein—a gripping cat-and-mouse thriller that pits one of the most fascinating characters in contemporary fiction against an enemy like none other.

SUNDAY SILENCE
In this thrilling novel from the master of psychological suspense, Frieda Klein becomes a person of interest in a horrifying murder case, trapping her in a fatal tug-of-war between two killers: one who won't let her go, and another who can't let her live.

DARK SATURDAY
Enter the world of Nicci French with this electrifying, sophisticated psychological thriller about past crimes and present dangers, featuring an unforgettable protagonist.

THE OTHER SIDE OF THE DOOR
Everyone tells lies. But is anyone prepared to tell the truth to uncover a murderer? A sexy, intricate thriller about the temptation of secrets, the weight of lies, and the price of betrayal and suspicion.

UNTIL IT'S OVER
In this steamy and suspenseful stand-alone thriller from internationally bestselling author Nicci French, a group of housemates must determine who in their midst is a killer when a series of murders occur.

LOSING YOU
From the bestselling author of the Frieda Klein series, a suspenseful stand-alone novel in which a woman's frantic search for her missing daughter unveils a nefarious web of secrets and lies.